# The Starlight Prince

## THE THROVANI ETHRIONTH STAR SYSTEM SERIES BOOK ONE

CLARE DUGMORE

# Copyright

## Crimson Fox
### PUBLISHING

https://crimsonfoxpublishing.com/
First Edition
© 2025 Clare Dugmore
www.claredugmore.com

ISBN: 9798224949144 (eBook)
ISBN: 9781963870084 (paperback)

# Dedication

❝ *Reality is the lifeblood that makes a work pulse with energy! Reality itself is entertainment! You might think comics draw on imagination and fantasy, but that's wrong! To write something interesting, you have to write what you've seen, what you've done, what you've experienced!"* —JoJo's Bizarre Adventure: Part 4—Diamond is Unbreakable, by Hirohiko Araki

In conjunction with this quote, another popular phrase writers use to guide them is 'write what you know.'

I *know* what it's like to feel as though you don't belong—at school, at work, in your own family.

Being *different* is hard, and there are *too many* people out there who like to vilify the different. But it's our differences that make us special and unique.

This book is dedicated to all the people who are different—the ones who feel like they don't belong anywhere. I see you, I acknowledge you. I accept you. You belong!

# Blurb

*A love story written in the stars.*

Hunted for being a witch, Madelyne longs for somewhere to belong and performs a full moon spell to find her true love.

Across the galaxy, Kalas completes the aeons-old celestial ritual to show him the location of his fated mate.

Enchanted by Madelyne's beauty, Kalas flies to Earth to find her.

And, with nothing left for her on Earth, Madelyne agrees to accompany Kalas to his home planet.

But as Madelyne adjusts to her new life, old doubts linger, and she just cannot understand why someone like her would be worthy of the crown prince.

Madelyne has spent her entire life being told she doesn't belong, and now Kalas must convince her it's more than just 'fate' that makes him want to claim her as his own.

# Chapter One
# Prayers to the Moon Mother

The bell over the door jingled as I entered the shop, and a moment later, a familiar face framed with greying auburn hair appeared.

Janine smiled knowingly. "Ah, Maddie. I knew you'd be visiting me today," she said as though she didn't have the power to see glimpses of the future. "Your book has arrived."

It had taken me almost a year of searching the dark web to finally track down the ancient grimoire and then have it delivered to Janine's shop. Most people thought Janine was just some old kook who sold crystals and dried herbs. I knew the truth.

She was a real, bona fide witch. Just like I was.

With pale and wrinkled hands, Janine pulled the spell book out from under the counter and laid it on the table that separated us.

I'd only seen grainy pictures of the grimoire online, so I was a little startled by its appearance when Janine unwrapped it from the brown paper it had been packaged in.

"Is that skin?"

Janine chuckled dryly. "Yes. Most of the ancient grimoires were bound this way, and John Dee's was no different."

I reached out hesitantly, and my body hummed with magic as I turned the cover. I flicked through the vellum pages, looking for the spell I wanted.

"There's an ingredients list here," I said, and Janine moved from the counter to grab a basket. "It says I'll need an array of candles in shades of pink and red, three cinnamon sticks bound together with cord, dried rose petals, honey, two drops of musk essential oil, a handful of slivered almonds, five mint leaves, the peel of a red dessert apple, and a conker."

As I called out the different items, Janine loaded them into the basket and then brought them back to the counter with a shake of her head. "Casting a love spell is dangerous business, Maddie."

"I know, but this isn't just for love. I'm trying to find where I belong."

Janine nodded. We'd had this conversation many times over the years. "There was another raid last weekend. They closed the magic shop in the city. I know it won't be long until they come knocking at my door. I'm planning on moving back to the coast with my daughter and her family."

I was happy for Janine. She'd been estranged from her daughter for many years, but now it seemed they'd finally reconciled. I didn't hold my breath that the same would be true for my family.

"You're going to hang up your broom?" I asked. Janine had always been the one who'd encouraged me not to turn my back on my magic, so I was surprised to hear she was planning to do the same.

Janine sighed. "I'm old. Too old for this rubbish." She waved her hand vaguely around the magic shop. "And in case you hadn't noticed, you're my only customer."

That was another sad truth. Janine and I were the only witches in our small village. There had been more in the city, but the witch hunters had driven them away. The magical population was spread thinly across the world as it was, but now the witch hunters were cracking down on those who openly practised magic, witches had either gone underground or stopped using their abilities altogether. The alternative was being thrown into prison without a trial, or worse, burned at the stake.

I sighed too. "Which is why I'm sure you understand why I have to do this spell. Tonight's the new moon, which we both know represents new beginnings as we plant seeds for the future. It's a good time to set clear intentions for the month ahead, clarify goals, and start new projects. What better time is there to perform a spell to take me to the place where I truly belong and bring me to my true love?"

"I will pray to the Moon Mother that you find what you're looking for, Maddie," Janine said, placing the items I wanted into a canvas tote bag. I'd already paid for the grimoire when I'd ordered it online, so it was just the spell ingredients I owed Janine for. "That will be ten pounds, please."

I frowned. That was far too low for five candles, the dried ingredients, essential oil, and honey. But I also knew Janine wouldn't hear a word of protest.

I pulled a twenty-pound note from my purse and handed it over. "I'm sorry. I don't have anything smaller."

A lie. But it was also a lie when Janine replied, "Well, I don't have any change in the till."

We both knew she always kept the till fully stocked.

I waved her off. "Ah, well. I'll get the change from you the next time I visit."

We also both knew I wouldn't. I kind of hoped this was the last time I saw Janine. She'd be going back to the coast to be with her daughter soon, and if I was lucky, my spell would work and I'd finally find where I belonged.

BACK AT HOME, I FLOPPED down on the sofa for a well-deserved rest.

Unable to help myself, I pulled the battered spell book from the canvas tote bag. Part of me wanted to rush to the forest-crowned barrow that cast its shadow over my house that instant, but I knew the spell would be stronger if I waited until three a.m.—the witching hour.

Instead, I waited patiently. I made dinner and watched TV. I set my alarm for two a.m. and finally snuggled under the covers for the night.

When my alarm sounded hours later, it didn't take long for me to fully wake up. Excitement coursed through my body like a wildfire through dried-out grasslands. Nothing would keep me from what I intended to do.

I threw on the same comfortable clothes I'd been wearing during the day and grabbed the tote bag with the spell book and ingredients. To make sure I was both warm and well-hidden, I put on my black, hooded cloak and raced out of the house.

The streets were especially dark with no moon to illuminate the skies. I kept to the shadows, my hood drawn up to conceal my face as I tried to blend in with the usual gangs of teenagers on street corners or drunk partygoers returning from some bar or club. Witch hunters were everywhere and would pull over anyone they deemed even slightly suspicious. Thankfully, they focused much of their attention on the bigger towns and cities, leaving alone tiny villages like the one where I lived. That was exactly why I'd moved here when my parents had thrown me out of their home, threatening to call the witch hunters if I ever darkened their door again.

I shook the bitter memory from my mind. All that was in the past now. I hadn't seen my family for over five years. Their cruel words could no longer hurt me.

My heart pounded as I drew closer to the barrow. The hill wasn't too steep, about a half an hour's walk to the summit.

Sometime in the past, a forest of blackthorn trees had been planted at the top of the barrow, a clearing in the middle. Legend stated that if you walked around the forest anticlockwise seven times, you'd summon the devil. I didn't believe in the devil, but I wondered if the myth had some grounding in reality. Perhaps the clearing was a hotspot for magical energy, which was why I chose it as the location to perform my spell.

I weaved my way through the trees, their branches barren and bare at this time of year, reaching down to me like spindly fingers.

I suppressed a shudder and gazed up at the sky, wishing I had the moon's light to guide me.

Finally, I came to the clearing and sat down in the centre. Using the light from my phone, I took the ancient grimoire from the bag and opened it to the correct page. Then I started pulling out the ingredients I'd brought from Janine's shop, along with several things I'd brought from home.

First was the portable camp stove I'd bought especially, followed by an iron cooking pot I usually used for making stews and soup. I set the pot on the portable stove but didn't light it yet. Instead, I drew a circle with salt and then added lines to form a pentagram within the circle. With the cooking pot in the centre, I set the red and pink candles at the five points of the star.

Still holding the grimoire in one hand, I poured a bottle of pinot noir that I'd been keeping for an occasion like this into my makeshift cauldron.

Taking a lighter from the tote bag, I ignited the stove and lit the five candles. As the red wine started to simmer, I threw in the three cinnamon sticks and read from the grimoire:

"I call on the powers of North, East, South, and West."

I added the dried rose petals.

"In the name of the Moon Mother, take me to the place where I truly belong."

I poured about a tablespoon of honey and two drops of musk essential oil into the simmering potion.

"By the power of the moon and stars above, bring my one true love to me."

I threw the handful of slivered almonds and five mint leaves into the steadily bubbling concoction.

"By the power of three, I summon thee. As I desire, so shall it be," I cried to the night sky as I dropped the peel of a red dessert apple and a conker into the cauldron.

Despite not touching the camp stove or candles, the fire in all flared and the potion I'd created started bubbling rapidly.

Red smoke rose from the iron pot, shimmering with an otherworldly iridescence, and I felt my eyes grow heavier. I sank to my knees in front of the pentagram, and my vision darkened.

# At the same time, across the galaxy...

"Your Highness, the king and queen await you in the ritual chamber," the messenger told the young man sitting at a dressing table before him.

Kalas, Crown Prince of Kralis, turned from the mirror he'd been staring intently into, not looking at his reflection, but instead searching for something deeper, as though the glass might hold the answers he so desperately craved.

Today, he came of age and would not only take on the responsibilities of being the crown prince and heir of an entire planet, but he would also perform the ritual that would reveal his fated mate.

It was an aeons-old rite the Kralian people had partaken in since the beginning of their recorded history. Historians, scholars, and priests all agreed that the Kralian Elder Deity, Korvarith Thalun— also known as The Twilight Crow and regarded as the deity of the skies, moon, and stars, and of dreaming—spoke to Their people through the crystalline seeing pool that was housed within the sacred chamber of the palace.

His father, his grandfather, and his great-grandmother, all the way back to the first monarch of Kralis, had undertaken the ritual. It was how his father had found his mother, who had been a high lady on the eastern shores of the planet.

Kalas stood from the dressing table and picked up the onyx circlet that lay cushioned on a velvet pillow. He laid the circlet on his head, pushing back his long, dark hair and being careful that it didn't tangle with the three obsidian horns protruding from his hairline.

He was in full royal regalia, wearing a variety of jewels through his ears, nose, and lips, all made from the same precious gem that changed colour from turquoise to purple depending on how the light reflected off it. His chest was bare, but his shoulders were cloaked in a cape made from shimmering raven-like feathers—the feathers of his ancestors. Around his wrists were onyx bracers, again decorated with colour-shifting gemstones, and his modesty was preserved by a dark loincloth threaded with silver, turquoise, and purple.

If a human saw Kalas, they might have mistaken him for an ancient Aztec emperor. In fact, when the Kralians had visited Earth in large groups in the past, the natives had worshipped them as deities and styled themselves after these magnificent beings.

With the messenger leading the way, Kalas followed through the shimmering hallways of the royal palace to the ritual chamber, where his parents, the King and Queen of Kralis, along with many members of the royal court awaited him.

"My son," the king said, bowing and pressing his palms together in a gesture of respect as Kalas entered the room. The king was dressed in a similar way to his son, only with more finery. The circlet on the king's head was a crested diadem adorned with precious gems, and his raven-feathered cloak was even more impressive.

The queen too was dressed in courtly regalia, her breasts concealed by rows and rows of threaded beads and gemstones that resembled an Egyptian Usekh and reached down to her mid-stomach just above the belly button.

She smiled fondly at Kalas, pressing her hands together and bowing in the same way her husband did.

Just a few paces behind the royal couple stood the high priest. His cloak was the most magnificent of all, taking feathers not only from his ancestors but from the kings and queens of millennia past. It was a mark of his station as the sovereign pontiff of Korvarith Thalun.

Around the royal gathering were rows upon rows of stone benches, so the members of the royal court could witness this momentous occasion. Like the king, queen, prince, and high priest, the nobility also wore feathered capes and clothing adorned with precious metals and gemstones. A few factors unified all Kralians gathered. First was their intense height, with even the younger members of the race standing at almost six feet tall and mature adults a towering seven-foot. Additionally, all Kralians were well-muscled.

Many had dark hair like Kalas and his father, which shimmered and reflected the light in shades of turquoise and purple, while others had pure white hair that appeared threaded with starlight, like the queen.

Dotted throughout the gathered Kralians were other species, humans included, and beings from all over the galaxy. The Twilight Crow, in Their infinite wisdom, did not only choose fated mates from among the Kralians but from throughout the whole universe, knowing that the mixing of bloodlines and species was beneficial to all.

"Luminali solini, thalunoriani velithor," the high priest said, which translated to English meant, 'Welcome, children of starlight.'

His voice echoed through the chamber, carrying with it the mysteries of the cosmos and the secrets of the wind. Each syllable danced like a feather caught in a gentle breeze, and each word weaved a tapestry of starlight.

"Today, we are gathered, as Prince Kalas comes of age, to witness the time-honoured ritual that will reveal Korvarith Thalun's chosen mate for the crown prince," the high priest said in the Kralian language. "The chosen being will be bound in starlight, destined to be the lover and consort of his Highness. Regardless of race, species, or gender, we will welcome Korvarith Thalun's chosen mate for the crown prince. As the moonlit wings will it, so be it."

"Thalunori spirithar, luminali velithor. Aeloriani avethor," those in the ritual chamber repeated in the Kralian language.

As the chamber fell silent again, the high priest stepped aside, revealing a vast pool with water that acted like a mirror. Only, instead of reflecting the surrounding chamber, the liquid showed the expansive, shining cosmos. The surface of the pool shimmered like liquid mercury, undulating as if in possession of a life and consciousness of its own.

The king and queen nodded encouragingly, and Kalas stepped forward, closer to the high priest and the mirror-like pool.

From leather pouches on his robe, the high priest withdrew two items. An obsidian knife, its blade impossibly sharp, and a handful of the colour-shifting gems that adorned many of the Kralians' clothing.

"Do you know the words?" the priest asked, handing the blade and gemstones to Kalas.

"I do," the prince replied.

In the torchlight of the ritual chamber, his amber eyes glittered with re-flected firelight, and for the first time in a long time, Kalas felt young and un-sure. He knew and had accepted his destiny from a young age and had lived with it for a long time. A Kralian's lifespan was much longer than those of Earth humans; childhood and adolescence lasted around 500 years. But sud-denly, now the moment was upon him, Kalas felt unsure.

What if he didn't find his fated mate attractive? What would happen if, on meeting them, they hated each other? Kalas had only had one lover dur-ing the course of his life as he'd always known his heart was destiny-bound to another. Another who had not yet been revealed to him. What if whoever Korvarith Thalun had chosen for him just wasn't right?

Kalas shook the thought from his head. He should not be questioning the elder deity. The Twilight Crow had given his people peace and prosperity for a very long time. While other planets warred, mined their resources to de-pletion, or polluted their atmosphere, Kralis was still as beautiful, rich, and resource filled as it had always been, its people living in harmony.

Steeling his resolve, Kalas took the obsidian blade and slashed it across his left palm. Oil-slick, iridescent blood trickled from the wound. Kalas di-rected the blood flow so a few drops landed on the shimmering surface of the pool before his wound sealed itself closed thanks to the Kralians' accel-erated healing factor. With his right hand, Kalas crushed the colour-shifting gemstones to dust and then sprinkled the dust on top of his blood, onto the mirror-like liquid.

The pool shined a bright, blinding white, and for a moment, no one in the chamber could see anything. Even though they were inside, the wind whipped around the gathered Kralians, causing their clothes to flutter.

A piercing shriek filled the air, like the cry of a raptor, and the light filling the chamber changed from a blinding white to a shimmering cacophony of hues similar to the aurora borealis.

As Kalas regained his sight, he stared into the pool before him. Gone was the reflective surface and instead was a vision of a young human woman. She had red hair that made him think of the flame of a candle and green eyes that reminded him of emeralds. He identified her instantly as human by her clothing—a dark cloak wrapped around her upper body and a pair of trousers covering her legs. She was kneeling in a forest in front of a fire and cooking pot, reciting words from a book that looked to be bound in skin.

"A witch," he said to himself, a small smile forming on his lips.

Witches were rare on Earth, though more common throughout the galaxy, and held in high regard the same way Kralians revered their high priests. This made Kalas happy, knowing his fated mate was a woman of intelligence. Not only that, but she was beautiful too. Her skin was milky white and flawless, and she had dark painted lips and dramatic makeup Kalas found appealing.

The gathered courtiers saw the image in the pool too, and someone in the crowd gasped. "A sapien. Is one such as that really suitable for the crown prince?"

Other voices rose to join the first, and a small group of courtiers proclaimed that Kralis was drifting too far from the standards it had once held.

"The bloodlines become more tainted with every passing generation," a Kralian male with swept-back white hair proclaimed.

Kalas frowned. He thought his people were accepting of all races. Was that not the case?

Before he could open his mouth to speak, the high priest said, "We do not doubt the intention of Korvarith Thalun. The union is now bound in the stars."

Those who had objected to Kalas's fated mate being a human began to argue again, and the same Kralian with swept-back white hair said, "Perhaps you do not speak for Korvarith Thalun after all. How do we know this vision is even from Them? You say the Twilight Crow speaks to you directly, but I see no proof of that!"

Other gathered courtiers gasped, but the chamber fell silent when the king bellowed, "That is enough. I will not stand for this behaviour. Those who doubt the word of Korvarith Thalun or Their high priest Varion Drelkar should leave here now."

The group of objecting courtiers, led by the one with the swept-back hair, angrily left the chamber, and it took a few moments for everyone to calm down again.

Kalas looked around the courtiers with uncertainty. Many Kralians had taken partners from Earth and other planets, but this was the first time in millennia that a royal mate had been chosen from anywhere that wasn't Kralis.

"I am sure she will make an excellent consort," his father said, coming to stand behind Kalas and resting his hand on his shoulder.

"She is beautiful, my son," the queen added, taking Kalas's left hand and entwining her fingers with his. "So exotic and different from the Kralians."

"Go, claim your bride," his father encouraged.

The word *claim* caused a weird sensation in Kalas's lower regions, and he gazed again at his intended mate. She really was beautiful. He imagined crushing his lips to hers and felt his heart race. Wondering what it might feel like to stroke her milky, smooth skin or take her smaller frame in his strong arms, Kalas felt himself growing aroused.

Yes, he would claim this fire-haired witch, to the glory of Korvarith Thalun.

Kalas gazed at his parents and smiled at them, his amber eyes shimmering in the torchlight of the chamber. "It would be my pleasure to claim her. I'll transform and leave immediately."

"No need," the high priest interjected. "While typically air and space travel are a matter of a simple transformation for our people, in situations like this, Korvarith Thalun grants a special boon. To travel by lightspeed. All you must do is place your left hand in the pool, and you will be taken to your fated mate."

Kalas swallowed a lump in his throat. So soon? He thought he'd have at least the duration of the journey to Earth to get used to the idea that he'd soon be married.

He glanced at the image in the pool once more. The flame-haired woman was dropping various items into her cauldron as she recited words in the Earth language. He found her positively entrancing.

His doubts faded away as he assured himself this was the path Korvarith Thalun had chosen from him. "Thalunori luminali ethrionth, stellavarien seresth. Aeriathor valiaroni. "By the light of the moon and stars, glory be to The Twilight Crow."

The assembled crowd cheered.

Kalas looked deeply into his parents' eyes for one final time, then turned towards the pool and plunged his left hand into it, just as the high priest had instructed.

Once more, the chamber filled with a bright white light that was pierced by the shriek of a bird of prey, and then the light seemed to be filtered through a prism, reflecting all the colours of the known universe onto the walls of the ritual chamber.

And Kalas, the Crown Prince of Kralis, was gone.

# Chapter Two
# Awaken

He came to me in my dreams. Whispering my name.

*Madelyne.*

The man made of alabaster.

We'd hadn't met, and yet, I knew every plane of his face in detail. I could sketch his features easily from memory. The slightly upturned eyebrow, the smirk pulling at the right side of his mouth, the hint of razor-sharp incisors, and his long and lustrous hair.

The vision in my mind zoomed out and I saw a dark chamber, where the statue stood, and then a series of maze-like tunnels leading out from it. The tunnels were labyrinthine, and I took many wrong turns and twists until I came to a stone stairway that lead upwards.

I followed the stairway and found myself stepping out of a barrow in the middle of a deep, dark forest.

*Madelyne*, the stone-like man called to me again. *Find me. Free me.*

I woke with a jolt still on the hilltop where I'd cast my spell, the candles and camp stove having burned out.

"Hello. Is someone out here?" I called into the darkness, but no reply came.

I switched on the light on my phone and packed my grimoire, candles and the camp stove into my tote bag. I searched the small clearing, as well as the surrounding forest, trying to find the entrance to the underground tunnels I'd seen in my dreams.

But after an hour of searching, I still found nothing.

I sat on a fallen branch and closed my eyes.

'*Where are you?*'

*'Find me. Free me,'* a voice spoke into my mind. I instantly felt drawn to the warm, silky smooth, inviting tone. The sound sent a thrill down my spine, like when I listened to my favourite music.

I knew the spell I'd cast had bought my true love here; I just had to search harder.

Remembering the old legend, I wondered if perhaps there was some truth to it and walked around the circle of blackthorn trees anticlockwise seven times, hoping that might reveal the correct path to me.

But as the stars twinkled above me, still nothing out of the ordinary presented itself.

Maybe I was going mad and the whole thing was just my overactive imagination. In my desperation not to be alone anymore, maybe I had simply dreamed up the stone man in the hidden, underground barrow.

Perhaps my spell hadn't worked.

*'Madelyne,'* the same voice as before whispered on the wind.

But deep inside, I knew what I'd seen was real. I knew my true love and the place I truly belonged was here somewhere, waiting for me.

Perhaps the reason I hadn't found the owner of the voice that spoke into my mind was because they were hidden somehow, and I would need to use my abilities to locate them.

Following my instincts, I walked around the forest until I thought I might be in the right place, and then I concentrated. I focused my magical abilities more acutely than I ever had before, seeing the cells of the plants and trees around me. Actually feeling the dirt beneath my feet.

And as I searched with my supernatural ability, I felt a door. It wasn't visible, and if I reached out like I was opening a regular door, I felt nothing different. But with my magical senses, I was able to grasp an organic material I couldn't see.

Slowly, carefully, I pulled the door aside, and using the light from my phone, I saw the first jagged white rocks of a set of stone steps.

I had found the secret passageway that lead underground.

My heart hammering, I raced down the steps, vines and roots moving instinctively out of my way as if I controlled them with my mind. Soon, I was in a series of labyrinthine earthen tunnels that took a little navigating to find the right path.

Eventually, I found a wide, circular chamber, lit by torches. And there, in the centre, stood a statue of a man that seemed to be made of alabaster.

He was breathtaking, standing at seven-feet tall, with a pale white body that looked to be chiselled and sculpted by the deities. Even though there was no breeze down here, his long hair rippled.

He was perfect.

He had sharp, almost feminine features, with high cheekbones, a long straight nose, almond-shaped eyes, and full lips that were curled in the briefest hint of a smile. As the statue was completely white, I was unsure what colour the eyes were meant to be, but they held me transfixed regardless as I stared deeply into them.

'*Madelyne*,' came the intoxicating voice once more.

Something about the way he called my name and then the sight of his almost naked body made me feel hot and flustered.

As I took more time to study the figure of the man that called out to me, I started to notice things about him that were different. It wasn't just his stunning, inhuman beauty. The way his hair was swept back off his face and held in place by a crown of some sort revealed pointed ears, like an elf. His fingers were unnaturally long and slender, ending in almost talon-like nails.

His inhuman attributes only served to make him more alluring to me. He was different, like I was. I felt a kinship with the stone figure, even though he'd only spoken my name.

'*You found me. Now free me*,' he spoke into my mind.

"Yes, but how?"

Nothing changed in the ethereal features of the stone face, so I walked around the statue, studying it for more information. Though his chest was bare, he wore a long cloak that looked to be made of birds' feathers.

He truly was beautiful, but there was no indication of whether he was alive or not.

"Help me," I said to the figure.

'*Look, see, feel*,' came the reply, and I knew what I had to do.

I was looking with my mundane eyes. I had to search with my supernatural abilities.

I took a deep breath and closed my eyes.

Almost instantly, I heard it; a strong and steady heartbeat that wasn't my own. The statue was indeed alive.

I slowly opened my eyes, and I saw inside the stone. That was when the reality of the situation dawned on me. The alabaster man was alive, but something had transformed his body to rock and imprisoned him.

I had to free him.

I glanced away from the living statue only long enough to pull my grimoire out of my bag and flicked through the pages, hoping to find a spell that would help me.

In the two weeks since casting the initial spell, I had read and re-read the grimoire from cover-to-cover, but I hadn't come across any type of spell or incantation that might help me free someone from stone.

Still, I turned every page slowly, reading the title of each spell.

I came to the final page and noticed something I hadn't in my previous studies of the book. The last page felt thicker than all the others, as though two pages had been bound together.

I channelled my magic into my fingertips, using my innate power to manipulate matter. Telekinesis, Janine had told me it was called.

Using this ability, I was able to pull apart the two pages that had previously been fused together. There, on the new page, was a spell written in a language I'd never seen before.

The letters swam before my eyes as I tried to make sense of them.

"Help me," I begged again, gazing up into the statue's eyes.

Another ability some witches possessed was telepathy, the power to connect to another person's mind and hear their thoughts. Perhaps even share their thoughts with others. I hadn't used it much. As often as I could, I tried to block out the unwanted thoughts of those around me. If I gave into my telepathic abilities, I often heard things I desperately wished I hadn't. Like the fear in my parents' minds when they realised what I was.

But as I gazed into the eyes of the statue before me, I allowed my mind to connect with his. I welcomed his thoughts instead of hiding away from them.

As our minds joined, there was a brief blinding light, followed by a bird-like shriek.

When I stared down at the spell book, the words on the newly revealed page started to make sense, and I read an incantation. In combination with my words, I morphed cells and molecules to my will.

I transfigured the atoms of stone into the cells of living flesh. I remoulded rigid stone arteries into real, living veins. Using an understanding of biology that I didn't consciously possess but that lingered somewhere at the back of my psyche, I transformed the stone organs, muscle tissue, bones, and tendons into real body parts.

My innate abilities combined with the magic ritual from the ancient grimoire, weaved together to awaken something not of this world.

As I read the words of the spell, I understood that the power needed to free the man from his stone prison would require a sacrifice.

From me.

Instinctively, I kneeled down, picked up a jagged rock, and plunged it into my inner forearm. Blood spurted out, splashing on the stone, which seemed to absorb it like a sponge.

My blood trickled onto the newly soft and fleshy body parts, filling them with life. I exhaled a long, slow breath, directing the air from my lungs to flow into the figure's lungs and give him breath.

'*Awaken*,' I commanded.

And as I did, the stone eyes opened, revealing a pair of dazzling yellow eyes that sparkled like amber.

Feeling dizzy from blood loss, I took a few staggering steps backwards as a blinding white light filled the earthen chamber and dust filled my lungs.

As the dust cleared, the figure of a seven-foot muscular being with long, flowing black hair was revealed to me.

Before I had time to gather my thoughts, let alone speak, the figure lunged towards me, their pointed incisors and canine teeth flashing. The being sank its fangs into my arm, lapping at the blood still trickling from the wound I'd made.

And then everything went black.

# Chapter Three
# A Tapestry of Starlight

I didn't know how much time had passed when I regained consciousness, cradled in smooth, strong arms as someone sang to me in a language I didn't recognise but sounded oddly comforting.

Each syllable danced like a feather caught in a gentle breeze, and each word weaved a tapestry of starlight in my mind.

The music had many layers; I could hear the songs of birds intermingled with a voice singing in English, which in turn was overlaid with an unknown language. The melody was light, like the soft caress of a lover, and in my mind bloomed a vision of the vast and sprawling cosmos.

I gazed up into the yellow eyes of the once alabaster man, noticing the way his dark, thin eyebrows quirked.

"My apologies, Madelyne. I did not mean to feed from you without your consent. The journey to Earth and being trapped in stone made me ravenous."

"You drank my blood? Are you a vampire?"

The being cradling me sneered, revealing the pointed incisors and canine teeth. "I'm much more than a vampyre. Those you call vampyre are from this world. I am not."

As I studied him closely, I noticed his skin was almost as pale as it had been when he was imprisoned in stone, only now with a faint, iridescent shimmer. Likewise, what I'd at first taken as simply long, black hair actually shone with a plethora of shades—blue, purple, turquoise—like the feathers of a raven's wings.

"Not of this world?" I questioned, but at the same moment, I became acutely aware that he was still almost naked, wearing only a loincloth secured in place by a leather belt, the feathered cloak, and some metal bracers around his wrists.

He smiled, flashing a brief glimpse of his fangs, and even though he'd fed from me earlier, I didn't feel afraid.

"I am Kalas, from the planet Kralis," he said in the silky-smooth voice I had grown so accustomed to, and yet it still sent a thrill down my spine.

I wasn't dreaming. He was actually real and sitting here next to me.

In not much more than a loincloth.

"We need to get you some clothes."

Kalas chuckled, low and deep, making my stomach flip over. "Does my nakedness offend you?"

"No, it's just that... well... I don't know if everyone from Kralis is the same, but you're kind of hot."

Kalas smirked a little, raising one thin eyebrow. "That pleases me to hear, as we are fated by the stars to be bound together."

Fire blazed through my body. "What do you mean by *bound together*?"

Again, Kalas chuckled. The deep, smooth tone of his voice was almost as enticing as his perfect body just inches from mine. And the implications of his words... Deities... my core tightened just thinking about it.

What would it feel like, baring myself to this exquisite being? A distant part of me thought perhaps I should be afraid of this strange, clearly not-human being, but a bigger part of me screamed to touch him. To taste him. To claim and consume him.

Under the new moon, under the watchful gaze of the Moon Mother, I had cast a spell to bring my true love to me, and She had answered beyond my wildest dreams.

Kalas reached out with surprising tenderness and laid a strong hand on my arm. "Madelyne. My Madelyne. My little witch."

*Oh, Deities. Now he's done it.*

The way he softly spoke my name. The way he called me his little witch. Staring into his amazing amber eyes, all thoughts of propriety left my head, and I leaned in to press my lips against his.

For an instant, Kalas froze, his body going as rigid as when he'd been encased in stone, and I worried I'd done the wrong thing. But then, he took control of the kiss, his hands coming up to cup my face. I melted into him.

His palms felt cool against my flushed cheeks as he deepened the kiss, grazing my bottom lip with his sharpened teeth and causing me to gasp.

Before I could start properly enjoying myself, Kalas pulled back.

Still cupping my face, he stared deeply into my eyes. "Before we begin, there are some things you must know. The act of coupling brings out the wild side of me. The animalistic side. But I won't do anything without your consent. If I do anything that makes you feel uncomfortable, tell me to stop, and I will."

The thought was dizzying, and his implied animalistic side made my heart race with the possibilities. But more than that, to know that I had some degree of power over this exceptional being was sexy and empowering.

"I understand." My voice came out breathy with anticipation, once again causing Kalas to smirk.

He was equal parts infuriating and sexy.

"Don't worry," he said, his voice a soft, husky whisper. "I'll go slowly."

His hands moved down from my face, gently caressing my shoulders before they reached out for my hands and pulled me into his lap.

I nestled in position. All thoughts left my mind as he inclined his head and captured my lips with his.

His hands once more cupped my cheeks, and he gently twisted my head to better suit the angle he wanted, deepening the kiss and sliding his tongue into my mouth. Again, I felt the sharp stab of his fangs and could almost hear the blood pumping through my veins.

I was breathless as Kalas's mouth moved along my throat, and his hands moved down my body to grip my shoulders. Even through the fabric of my cloak and T-shirt underneath, I felt the scratch of his talon-like nails.

With deft hands, Kalas pulled at my clothes, removing them easily and tossing them to the dusty stone ground.

For a moment, I had a shiver of self-consciousness.

Voices from my past flooded my mind: *Freak, unnatural, abnormal.*

*Why would anyone like Kalas want to be with someone like me? Someone tainted?*

"Madelyne, look at me," Kalas demanded, and I did as he asked.

I gazed into his amber eyes, which had now taken on a slightly darker hue.

"You are beautiful. Never worry about that."

"You read my thoughts?" I replied.

'We're connected, you and I,' came the reply straight into my mind, just like when Kalas had called out to me from his stone prison. 'Our entwined destinies are bound in the stars. You were chosen for me by Korvarith Thalun. Your hair is as beautiful as the setting sun. Your eyes like precious gems. And your skin...'

He let out a heavy breath as his fingers trailed down my arm, his long nails scratching the surface of my skin.

He moved in closer again, his lips taking up the path his fingertips had just trailed. He kissed the inside of my wrist, and then worked his way higher, nibbling at my skin as he moved. He grazed my shoulder before dipping down to run his lips across my collarbone.

Meanwhile, Kalas's fingers struggled with my bra.

"Infernal Earth contraption," he muttered against my skin, and I couldn't help but laugh.

"Here, let me." I unhooked my bra easily, throwing it to the ground with the rest of my clothes.

'Why do they make women wear such things?' he asked, speaking directly to my mind again.

'I'm not sure,' I replied telepathically.

Now wasn't the time to get into the history of women's undergarments.

Kalas seemed to agree, as he said nothing more about the subject. He returned his lips to my skin and continued kissing down until he came to my breasts, which he took in each hand, squeezing them together as if enjoying the feel of their weight in his palms. Then he inclined his head and licked the valley between my breasts.

I let out a small squeal at the feeling of teeth against the soft, sensitive flesh, though the sensation wasn't an unwelcome one.

'Did you like that, my little witch?'

If thoughts could be breathless, my desperate 'yes' would have been.

I felt Kalas smile against my breasts as he bit my nipple, his fangs gently piercing the skin like a pinprick, and a jolt of electricity zapped through my body from my nipple straight to my core.

Before I could stop my thoughts running away, I wondered what it would feel like for Kalas to kiss me down there.

He stopped and pulled away from my breasts. "Would my little witch like that?"

"Yes," I panted in reply.

"As you wish," Kalas said, reaching for the waistband of my trousers.

He struggled with these less than my bra, and I idly wondered what clothing his people wore. The question slipped from my mind as he unfastened my trousers, and I kicked off my shoes. He slowly peeled the material from my body, so I was wearing nothing but panties.

Kalas straightened, adjusting himself and removing the metal bracers, shoes, belt, and cloak he was wearing. Now, all that separated our naked bodies were two small pieces of cloth, and I could feel his erection, long and hard, pressed against my thigh.

I gazed into his eyes as my hands caressed the smooth planes of his chest. His body was softer than stone now, and more forgiving, and the colour of his skin changed as it got closer to his fingertips. A steady gradient of iridescent almost-white, turning grey before finally ending in black, along with the black talon-like claws on his hands.

I had so many questions about what exactly he was, but those questions could wait. Now we were so close, nothing else mattered.

Kalas hooked my panties with his clawed nails and tore them from my body, tossing the garment aside like it meant nothing.

He quirked an eyebrow as his gaze travelled to the thatch of red hair between my legs. "They say those with fire-kissed hair are lucky."

I'd been teased at school for being ginger, and later, when the witch hunters came along, I learned it was one of the ways they identified possible witches. But hearing Kalas refer to it as fire-kissed made my stomach flip.

*How can someone like him find someone so abnormal like me special?*

I hadn't even thought about how Kalas could easily read my thoughts like an open book until the reply came. *'Here, let me show you.'*

Lifting me as though I weighed nothing, he stood with me in his arms and then gently laid me down on the ground.

As he stepped back, I could see the outline of his cock through his loincloth, and I was desperate to feel it.

'*Patience, my little witch.*'

Kalas dropped to his knees at my feet and reached out to caress my legs. Once more, his long nails raked at my skin, heightening the sensations already threatening to overwhelm me.

Once he reached my knees, Kalas parted my legs easily, and then nestled between them. He nipped at my inner thigh, his teeth grazing the skin and causing me to squirm. Almost as if intending to hold me in place, Kalas grabbed my upper thighs, his nails digging into the flesh as his mouth moved to my inner folds.

His tongue lapped against my clit. I felt another jolt of electricity zap through my body, and a breathy moan escaped my lips.

Kalas chuckled against my skin and did it again, pressing his tongue harder against my clit this time.

"Oh, Deities," I cried out.

"I will make you beg the deities for mercy," Kalas replied huskily.

Somehow, the switch from Kalas talking telepathically to talking aloud made the moment all the more intimate.

Kalas pinned me in place as his tongue moved down from my clit to my opening and swirled around it, lapping at my juices.

Instinctively, my hips started to rock.

I felt a small, sharp bite against my inner thigh before Kalas's attention once again returned to my clit, and this time, he sucked it into his mouth.

My legs trembled around his head, and his claws pierced my skin as he gripped tighter, holding me in place.

In unison with the rhythm of my rocking hips, Kalas continued to lick and kiss my core, regularly switching from my clit to my opening so I didn't quite know where to expect his mouth next.

My inner walls clenched, and I knew I couldn't hold back my climax for much longer.

"Oh, fuck. Please, I'm so close," I cried out desperately. "I need you inside me. NOW."

In a flash, Kalas moved so his body was braced above mine. I didn't even see him remove the loincloth, but I knew he had, as I felt the tip of his cock press against my entrance.

"Yes, give it to me," I demanded.

With a flash of a smirk, Kalas plunged inside me, his cock long and thick to match his stature, and I felt myself stretching around him as he filled me.

As the first waves of an orgasm crashed over me, Kalas started thrusting. The sensation of him pulling all the way back until his cock almost slipped out of my opening and then slamming back into me sent me over the edge.

The coiled spring inside me was finally released, and I felt the blissful rush consume my body.

I inclined my head, pressing it into his shoulder as the aftershock of the orgasm rippled through me.

Kalas continued moving inside me, and he let out an animalistic growl, his fangs scraping my neck as he found his release.

I opened my eyes for a fraction of a second to see his face had transformed. He was still unnaturally, stunningly beautiful, but he looked more animal than man. His eyes glowed in the dark of the underground chamber. His canines and incisors had lengthened, and I could just make out the glimmer of onyx horns within his dark hair.

As my hands caressed his shoulder blades, I felt soft, downy... I wanted to say fur, but the texture wasn't quite right. It was more akin to feathers. Had he put his cloak back on?

Still, none of that mattered as Kalas's full weight pressed down upon me, and I wrapped my legs around him.

He buried his face in my sweat-dampened hair, speaking in the same strange language I'd heard him singing to me in when I'd first regained consciousness.

The sounds resonated like the song of a distant comet, pure and haunting.

Although I couldn't understand a word he sang, I could feel the meaning. I was his. He had claimed me now, and nothing, not even death, would part us.

# Chapter Four
# My Precious One

I drifted on a blissful cloud, my body more relaxed than it had ever been. For the first time since my abilities had manifested, there were no chattering voices in my head, and I could no longer feel the sometimes-invasive prickle of the natural world around me.

All I could feel was my heartbeat steadily returning to a normal pace.

As my breathing evened out, I opened my eyes.

Kalas lay a little to my left, our legs still tangled together. He looked down at me adoringly as his fingers stroked through my hair.

"Better now, my little witch?" he asked, raising an eyebrow. His eyes glittered with mischief.

"Much, but when we go out there, we really will need to do something about your lack of clothing. You'll get arrested if you walk around half-naked. I'll take you back to my house. It isn't far, and then you can tell me everything."

"Yes, let us leave this place." Kalas stood, and I was only slightly disappointed when he put back on his loincloth and pulled on the leather belt, sandals, and bracers.

As I redressed myself, I glanced down at my naked body and saw I was bruised and streaked with blood from where Kalas had pierced me with his claws.

Noticing my state too, Kalas was at my side in an instant, laying his hands on the marred flesh. "Here, let me heal you."

Before I could protest, he bit his own fingertip, drawing a few drops of blood that he then applied to my various cuts and bruises like a salve, making them vanish instantly.

"I have so many questions," I said, pulling on my clothes. "When we climaxed, I opened my eyes. You looked different. You felt different too. Like you had feathers... and I don't just mean your fantastic cloak."

Kalas let out a light, carefree laugh that sounded like birdsong. "I do. Come, let me show you."

He took my hand and led me from the underground cavern where I'd freed him, back through the labyrinthine tunnels, and then up the stone steps to the entrance of the barrow.

Instinctively, my magical abilities took over, and I reached for the unseen plant-like door that kept the barrow hidden from the rest of the woodlands.

As we stepped out into the harsh sunlight, I realised how much time had passed.

Kalas was even more beautiful in the light of the day. It shone and rippled off his hair, bringing out all the different colours in the blackness—shades of purple, blue, and turquoise. It reminded me of crow feathers.

"Stop!" a commanding voice called, and a moment later, we were surrounded by witch hunters.

I didn't know if it was my repeated use of magic, Kalas crashing to Earth in a shooting star, or mere coincidence, but my worst fear had come true. I knew the witch hunters would lock me away without a second thought. What they might do to someone like Kalas made my blood turn cold.

Using our psychic connection, I told Kalas, '*These people are enemies. We're in danger.*'

'*Do you trust me?*' he asked directly into my mind.

'*Yes!*'

Before anyone could process what was happening, Kalas had wrapped his cloak around me. Feathers appeared across his shoulders and down his arms. As with his hair, they rippled with iridescent shimmers. His hands morphed into clawed talons as his arms transformed into glorious black wings.

"Oh my deities," I murmured.

Even though he looked less human than before, his legs having transformed so they more closely resembled a bird's and the onyx horns I'd spotted earlier peeking through his long hair extended, he was still the most beautiful creature I'd ever beheld.

Not a single ounce of fear inside me, I stepped in closer and looped my arms around his neck tightly.

Kalas extended his wings; they spanned longer than the length of his arms, and he easily took flight, lifting us into the air.

The witch hunters began firing their rifles—rifles I knew were loaded with bullets that could suppress magical abilities—but it was too late. Kalas was already flying high out of their reach.

As the witch hunters below seemed to shrink to the size of ants and the ground grew smaller beneath our feet, I screwed my eyes tightly closed and my heart raced.

'*Where would you like to go?*' Kalas spoke into my mind.

I thought about him taking us back to my home so we could get him some clothes and he could tell me where he came from, but with witch hunters so close by, it was too much of a risk.

Instead, a distant memory of me and my family together, back in the time when they still loved me, flitted into my mind. We'd gone on holiday to Gloucestershire and had visited the Forest of Dean because my dad was interested in seeing the wild boar that lived there.

'*To the Forest of Dean,*' I told him telepathically, letting him see my memories of the place and how we'd gotten there.

'*I will do my best to find it,*' came Kalas's reply, and we soared higher.

He turned east, following the directions from my memories. The wind whipped through my hair and my cheeks grew numb, but it was amazing. The most amazing feeling ever. Well, apart from when Kalas and I coupled, but I was amused to find the sensation was kind of similar. I was breathing heavily, and I could feel Kalas's heart beating rapidly. The air between us crackled with magic, and in my mind's eye, images of a beautiful aurora appeared.

Kalas sang softly, not in the strange language of before, but in a distinctly bird-like way that sounded like a whole chorus of nightingales.

Fighting my fear, I opened my eyes and watched the landscape below us change as the villages and cities faded away, revealing an extensive forested area.

"This is the place," I called.

Kalas flew lower into the trees near a small herd of deer. He was still for a moment, watching the animals closely.

"We will be safe here," he told me, landing gently on the ground.

I unlooped my arms from around his neck and took a step back. "Will we? The witch hunters from before won't have followed us here, but there are wild boar. Even with my magical abilities, they could be dangerous."

"Not to me," Kalas insisted, the feathers covering his body slowly receding into his skin as his claws shortened and his appearance became more human-like. "Besides, I need to hunt. The blood I took from you earlier was not enough."

A cold feeling crept over me. "Will you need to feed from me again?"

Kalas's eyes widened, and he looked offended. "No. I will not take from you again."

"Not even if I give it freely?"

"You've given me so much already. I would never take more. Besides, I don't see you as food."

"That's reassuring to know," I said with a laugh. "What do you see me as, then?"

Smiling down at me, Kalas said, "I already told you. We are bound by the stars, destined to be together."

I had so many questions. About where he came from and who he was. About what he meant by us being bound together. Strangely, the first question that fell from my lips was, "What do you eat?"

Kalas was silent for a moment, shifting back uncomfortably.

"I'm sorry. I shouldn't have asked. If you don't want to tell me, you don't have to."

Kalas bowed his head. "It's not that I don't want to tell you. It's that I don't want you to think I'm a monster."

I'd already seen him transform into a more animalistic creature. Nothing he said or did would make me think he was a monster.

"You think that now, but I'm not sure your reaction will be the same once you know the truth of what I really am," Kalas said, having read my thoughts easily.

"Never," I insisted hotly. "You know I'm a witch, and you've seen how people here react to that. I know we're different, but I feel as though we're alike too."

Kalas gave me a small, soft smile. "Very well. Back on my home planet, Kralis, we feed on animals, but not in the same way you humans do on Earth. We hunt them like predators."

"Like lions and tigers do?" I asked, interested to know more about him and his people.

"Sort of. Perhaps it is better if I just show you. I'll seek out these boars you spoke of. Do you wish me to save some meat for you? You can produce a fire, can't you?"

I shook my head. "Some witches have elemental magic, but not me. My witch friend, Janine, told me I have mental magic. I can hear people's thoughts and move objects with my mind. She could see glimpses of possible futures. Each witch has different gifts."

Kalas smiled. "I understand. Then we will need to find a source of food for you too. But I will need to eat very soon. The journey to Earth, our coupling, and then the flight here has tired me."

"Did you fly to Earth from your home planet?" I asked.

"No, but I will tell you everything about that after I have eaten, if that's okay."

"Of course."

Kalas transformed again, his arms morphing into wings, and his feet taking on the appearance of a bird's. Even his face was more bird-like, with an elongated snout that was almost like a beak if it weren't for the rows of sharp teeth within.

Kalas disappeared into the trees, and I supressed a small shiver.

Without my body pressed to Kalas, I was cold and wrapped both my own cloak and his feather cloak around myself to keep warm. The feather cloak smelled like Kalas, and I inhaled deeply, the scent comforting me.

Even though the forest area was filled with wild animals and a vicious predator, I knew I was in no danger. I could sense Kalas was close by and knew if anything tried to attack me, he'd be there in an instant.

From the darkness came a noise that sounded like a mixture of a raven's caw and the slow, eerie rumbling crocodiles made when they were about to attack. It was followed by the scream of a boar, and then deadly silence.

I shuddered all over.

I almost jumped out of my skin when the bushes around me started to rustle, and then Kalas emerged, dragging a boar carcass with him. He was hunched over now, using his wings and their clawed tips as forelimbs, so he could move on all fours. The dead boar was grasped firmly in his maw, blood trickling from a gash on its throat.

I watched with interest as Kalas released his prey, dropping its body on the ground and then started coughing and hacking. For a moment, I worried he was choking on blood or something, but then a deep yellow liquid gushed from his mouth and covered the dead animal.

I was amazed as the liquid dissolved the boar on the ground until it was reduced to nothing but a bloody, pulpy puddle that Kalas bent over and started lapping at greedily.

I heaved, fighting back the urge to vomit. I'd expected Kalas to feed similarly to how Earth animals did, tearing into their prey with claws and fangs. This was entirely different, and I didn't know how to feel about it.

I suddenly understood why Kalas had been so against telling me how Kralians fed.

Somehow, the yellow liquid had even dissolved the animal's bones, so that Kalas was able to consume every trace of the boar. I wasn't sure if I was sickened or impressed by his actions, and I fought another wave of nausea.

Having consumed what was left of the boar, Kalas straightened and wiped the last of the gore from his maw with one of his wings.

He took a tentative step towards me, tilting his head in a bird-like way, and for the first time since I'd freed him from the stone prison, I saw him as an animal rather than the man who'd held me gently in his arms and sang to me of starlight.

"Maddie. Maddie," Kalas called.

I turned to face him, my vision swimming as I tried to focus on his face. Right then, all I could see was a monster.

"Get away from me!" I screamed. Instinctively, my magic activated, and to my surprise, Kalas transformed back into his 'humanoid' form.

Seeing the heartbreak in his eyes brought me back to my senses, and I dropped to my knees.

At the same time, Kalas said, "In the name of Korvarith Thalun, what have I done?" and collapsed to the ground too.

I sucked in a deep breath, trying desperately to remind myself I was safe. He was the man I'd longed for. The answer to my spell. According to him, we were bound by the stars. He'd never hurt me.

"Maddie, my little witch. I'm so sorry," came Kalas's weak voice, and I glanced up to see shimmering silver tears running down his face.

I crawled on my hands and knees over to him and wrapped him in my arms. "I'm sorry I pushed you away," I sniffled.

"It's okay. It's not your fault. I never should have..." He trailed off, but I caught his thoughts easily *'...consumed the boar in front of you. Now you know what type of monster I really am.'*

"You're not a monster," I said fiercely. I knew what it felt like to have others think you were different, and I didn't want to make anyone feel that way.

Kalas shook his head. "Invarali taleni, my precious one. I can read your thoughts too, remember?"

"I didn't mean it. I was shocked and scared. I don't actually think you're a monster." I stared deeply into Kalas's amber eyes, hoping he saw the truth in my gaze. "Please believe me," I said desperately.

Kalas's resolve crumbled, and his arms tightened around me. "I believe you," he whispered, resting his head on my shoulder.

As I started to calm down and my senses returned to me, I felt terrible for my initial reaction. I shuffled back a little and stared at Kalas, making sure my gaze was on his face. "I'm so sorry I made you feel bad. I was just shocked. Everyone has to eat."

Kalas sighed. "I guess so, but I think from now on, it's best you don't come with me when I hunt."

I heaved out a breath. "Yes. Maybe you're right."

# Chapter Five
# What I'd Prayed to
# the Moon Mother For

Stifling a yawn, I asked, "What do we do now?"

When Kalas had transformed and flown away with me clinging to him for dear life, my only thought had been escaping the witch hunters and getting somewhere safe.

But now we were in the middle of the Forest of Dean, and all I had with me were the clothes I was wearing, the tote bag containing the skin-bound grimoire, and my mobile phone.

"We should go somewhere you can rest and eat in safety, and I will tell you my story. Do you know of such a place close by?" Kalas asked.

I didn't want to risk returning home. After what the witch hunters had seen, they'd be searching the area thoroughly. I was glad Janine had already moved away, or they would have raided her magic shop.

I thought of all the magic-related items back in my home, along with things like my ID. It wouldn't be long before the witch hunters caught up with me. We'd have to lie low until Kalas had told me about who he was and we had decided what to do next.

"Follow me," I said, clambering to my feet. "There are lots of holiday homes near here. I'm sure I can convince the park manager to let us rent one."

As we reached a small park of holiday homes, which also featured a few amenities like a grocery store, laundry, swimming pool, and play park, I told Kalas to wait out of sight for a moment.

"Let me get you some clothes. They've got to have at least swim shorts. Then you'll look less like you're from another planet," I said with a small laugh.

"Don't you worry. From what I've learned about humans, those without abilities like yours don't always notice when something is different. They might be startled by my height, but perhaps nothing more."

He was right. Some humans could sense there was something uncanny about witches, and of course, the witch hunters were aware of our existence, but for the most part, the mundane humans saw what they wanted to see. They dismissed anything different or unusual as simply a trick of their minds. It was how Janine and I had gone undetected for so long. But times were changing, and the propaganda of the witch hunters was becoming more and more frequent. I knew it wouldn't be long before mundane humans realised they weren't alone on the planet. And then what?

Still, Kalas did as I asked and stayed hidden as I approached the holiday park's main office. It was easy to convince the receptionist I was a holiday-maker on a spur-of-the-moment getaway, and they agreed to let me rent one of their cabins for a few days. Thankfully, even though I didn't have my purse, I had online payments set up on my phone, so it was simple to take care of all the financial aspects. I even managed to buy some clothes for Kalas and some groceries so I could prepare food while we were there.

Keys to the cabin in one hand and my bag of shopping in the other, I rejoined Kalas where he was hiding in the trees, and then we hurried to the cabin before anyone saw us.

As I opened the cabin door and turned on the lights, Kalas looked around with interest. "This is my first time visiting Earth," he told me.

"Is it far, your home?"

"It is outside what the humans know as the Milky Way. Kralis is part of a solar system not dissimilar to your own, but with a different star as our sun. And unlike your solar system, almost all of the planets are inhabited. Kralis is one of the smallest, but also one of the most peaceful. My parents are the king and queen, and there hasn't been a serious war since before my great-grandmother's time."

I paused in my unpacking of the groceries and stared at Kalas in amazement. "You're a prince?"

He gave me a small, sly smile. "I am. Does that bother you? If you return with me to Kralis, you will be my consort. One day, you will be queen."

My eyes almost bulged out of their sockets. "But I'm human. And I'm a witch. How will your people accept someone like me?"

"Do not worry." Kalas moved in closer, taking both of my hands in his. "Korvarith Thalun chose you as my mate. No one, not even the king or queen, acts against the word of our deity."

I frowned. "Explain this to me, please. In some Earth cultures, we have arranged marriages, but I've never heard of a deity choosing someone's partner like this."

Kalas settled at the table as I began preparing food for myself. As I cooked, he explained his religion and culture to me.

"The people of Kralis believe the universe was created by an almighty deity named Korvarith Thalun. The Twilight Crow; the deity of the skies, moon, and stars, and of dreaming, who watches over us. It is thanks to Them that our planet has prospered, despite its small size. Korvarith Thalun chose the first Kralian to serve as king of Kralis. Since then, the monarch of Kralis has descended from that bloodline, from first born to first born, regardless of gender. I don't remember the exact history—it wasn't one of my favourite subjects when I was growing up—but it is my understanding that since the beginning of life on Kralis, when the crown prince or princess comes of age, they partake in a sacred ritual where Korvarith Thalun reveals the mate They have chosen for the future monarch."

"And has a human witch ever been chosen before?" I asked, turning away from the stove for a moment.

"A witch, yes, but it hasn't been for millennia that a royal mate has been chosen from anywhere that wasn't Kralis. The last time it happened was with my great-grandmother. Korvarith Thalun chose a witch as her mate too. In fact, if I recall the portraits correctly, my great-grandmother's partner was also fire-haired. They didn't class themselves as male or female, though they presented in a more masculine way. Instead of being known as the prince consort, and then king consort, they were simply known as the royal consort. Korvarith Thalun blessed them with a number of children, the oldest of which was my grandfather."

I listened with interest as Kalas explained more about his ancestors. From the little he told me of Kralis, I was already sensing it was a much more liberal, welcoming planet than Earth.

I had cast a spell to find not only my true love, but the place I belonged. Could Kralis be that place?

"How will we get to Kralis? To me, it looked like you came down to Earth with a shooting star."

Kalas frowned. "I'm not entirely sure. As you know, my people can transform their bodies and fly. To travel from Kralis to other planets, a Kralian's transformation extends further. We can turn into great winged beasts that challenge the ones humans know as dinosaurs."

My eyes almost bulged out of their sockets. "Holy shit! Are you telling me you can transform into a dragon?"

Kalas frowned. "Dragon? I do not know this word."

"Here, let me show you." I grabbed my phone and tapped the screen a few times, bringing up various pictures of dragons from fantasy art, movies, and TV shows.

Kalas chuckled as he studied the images. "Not quite the same. Transformed Kralians don't have scales. They all have feathers, similar to the ones I manifested earlier. And their arms always transform into the wings. We don't have four legs and wings like these creatures."

"Like a wyvern ,then?" I supplied and showed Kalas a picture of the mythical creature.

"Yes, that's closer. But as I said, we have feathers not scales, and our mouths... no, that's not the right word. Our snouts are more pointed, almost beak-like."

"So, kind of like a hybrid of wyverns and birds of prey?" I suggested, quickly searching for images of ravens and other bird species in the genus Corvus, as that was what Kalas's hair and feathers made me think of.

"Yes, closer again. The history books state that my people and the crows and ravens descended from the same source, but we're not exactly the same."

"You have crows and ravens on Kralis?" I asked, serving my lunch onto a plate, and then joining Kalas at the table.

He smiled fondly. "The Kralians are not the only children of The Twilight Crow. Our deity made many creatures, the crows and ravens most revered of all. They are a sacred animal to my people; the only animals we do not hunt. They are our kin."

I smiled fondly. Given Kalas's appearance when he'd transformed earlier, it made a lot of sense that the Kralians held crows and ravens in such high regard.

"And the cloak?" I asked, gently stroking the feathers on the garment that was currently draped on the chair I was sitting in.

"This is a sacred robe, worn for special Kralian ceremonies. It contains the feathers of my ancestors and specific birds my family has bonded with." Kalas reached out and stroked his fingers down the cloak in the same gentle way I was doing. As our fingers brushed, magic crackled in the air, and I noticed a slight change in Kalas's appearance as he took on a more bestial form.

"That's interesting. It seems like my magic might affect your ability to transform."

Kalas nodded. "I do not doubt it. As I have said, we are connected."

I smiled, but I wasn't so certain. Kalas was incredible. Even if he wasn't the prince of an entire planet, I'd still feel inferior. He'd said that Kralians accepted witches, but I'd been living with the fear and hatred of others for a long time now. It was hard to shake the doubts. My own parents had thrown me out of my childhood home the moment I'd turned eighteen because of what I was. Because I was abnormal. Why would a planet of shape-shifting alien beings be any different? Because their deity said Kalas and I were fated mates? I knew religious people held firm in their beliefs, but would their conviction still hold true in the face of an outsider?

Still, that was a long way off yet... we were still on Earth.

"So, you were taking part in a ritual, and then you came to Earth. But not by flying here?" I asked, trying not to let my thoughts distract from the story Kalas had been telling me.

He nodded. "That's correct. I assumed I would transform into my fully bestial form and fly here. When fully transformed, a Kralian can breathe in space and travel at high speeds. But the high priest told me on this occasion that it wouldn't be needed. All I had to do was touch the sacred pool in which Korvarith Thalun had revealed your image to me."

"Wait, you saw me?" I asked, my eyes widening.

"Yes. That is the ritual. The sacred pool is the way Korvarith Thalun communicates with Their people. It is also how the Kralians have avoided war and disaster for so long. The high priests see visions of our future and are forewarned of any threat. The Twilight Crow guides us and keeps us safe."

I was still trying to figure out how Korvarith Thalun fit into my beliefs of the Moon Mother, but it was a comfort to know someone was watching out for Kalas and me.

"Right, okay. I understand," I said, gesturing for Kalas to continue.

"The high priest said I only needed to touch the pool and I would be taken to you. So, I did. And suddenly, I was here, on Earth. I'd travelled far faster than even the most experienced Kralian can fly, but something about entering the Earth's atmosphere at such high velocity changed me. I turned to stone."

"When I couldn't find you straight away, I thought I'd imagined the whole thing. Then I heard your voice in my mind," I said.

"Yes. As soon as I landed on Earth, our minds connected. Your magic enabled you to free me from the stone prison, but I believe it was the will of Korvarith Thalun that allowed such a thing to happen. Perhaps it is The Twilight Crow who gives you your magic. I'm not sure. We don't have native witches on Kralis, only those that join from other planets."

"Other planets? You mean it isn't just Earth that has witches?"

Kalas chuckled. "It's not. There's a planet in our solar system, Valeth, that has a large population of witches."

I almost fell out of my seat. A whole planet of witches? How incredible. "Can we visit there? I mean, once we've gone back to Kralis, and I've met your parents..." I trailed off, getting ahead of myself.

Kalas raised a dark eyebrow. "You've decided then. Will you return with me to Kralis?"

"I have a choice? I thought you said we were fated mates. Won't Korvarith Thalun punish us if we don't marry?"

Kalas bowed his head. "I do not know. No one has ever refused the starlight bond before. But I will not force you to come to Kralis with me. It has to be your choice. It is clear Earth is not a good place for witches, so why not come to Kralis and see how beautiful it is? Once we're at the palace, we can get to know each other properly."

His offer was tempting. We couldn't stay in the holiday home forever. And I wasn't sure we could go back to my home in the village. After what the

witch hunters had seen when Kalas and I escaped, I knew they'd tear the village apart searching for us. I was half convinced that they'd raid every home
in town, and once they found mine, they'd know for certain I was a witch.
From there, it wouldn't be hard for them to learn my identity, and... oh, crap.
I'd used the internet on my phone to pay for the holiday home. That meant
the transaction could be used by the witch hunters to track me here. For all I
knew, they might already be on their way.

Reading my thoughts easily, Kalas said, "If we are in danger, we must act
quickly. We should return to Kralis immediately. But I promise you, Madelyne, if you don't want to marry me, I won't force you. You can remain on
Kralis, or I can take you to Valeth. I will take you anywhere in the universe
you want to go. As long as I know you're safe, that's all that matters."

My body froze, and I sucked in a sharp breath. I couldn't believe what
Kalas was saying. He would give me the choice? He was offering me freedom
from a world that hated people like me. And if Kalas kept his promise, I
wouldn't be trapped somewhere my only purpose was to be someone's wife.

He was offering me the type of freedom and escape I'd longed for since
the moment my magical abilities manifested.

Regardless of whether I wanted to be his wife, Kalas would help me find
where I belonged. This was what I'd performed the spell for. What I'd prayed
to the Moon Mother for.

A jubilant smile covered my lips. "Thank you. I'd love to come with you
to Kralis. Just one question. How do we get there?"

# Chapter Six
# Beauty and Union

K alas looked thoughtful for a moment, and then asked, "I don't suppose your magic extends to allowing you to breathe in space, does it?"

I shrugged. "I'm not sure. I've never had a reason to try. Why, what are you thinking?"

"If we could find a way to ensure you'd be able to breathe in space, I could simply transform, allow you to ride on my back, and we could fly to Kralis."

I imagined myself on the back of a giant wyvern-like raven, and a thrill rippled down my spine. "That sounds amazing. Let me see if the grimoire has a spell that might help me."

Leaving my half-eaten lunch, I stood and grabbed the tote bag that contained the grimoire, but as I placed it on the table, Kalas laid his hands over mine.

"I will read the spell book. Please, continue eating. I know you worry the witch hunters might be able to track us here, but you need to take care of yourself. It was the middle of the night when you found me, and a lot has happened since then. You must be exhausted."

I was touched by Kalas's concern for me, and he was right. I was worn out from all that had happened since I saw Kalas hurtling to Earth.

I pushed the grimoire across the table to Kalas and then continued eating. He picked up the spell book and began reading it with interest.

"I wonder, how are you able to read Earth languages and we're able to understand each other speaking?" I mused as I finished my lunch.

"I believe it is part of our psychic connection. Perhaps one of the reasons Korvarith Thalun chose you as my mate is due to your abilities."

I frowned for a moment. Whenever Kalas spoke about us being together, he said it was because his deity had chosen me as his mate. Was that the only reason Kalas wanted me to accompany him to Kralis? Because his deity demanded it of him? Would he want me as a mate and consort if I hadn't been chosen by Korvarith Thalun?

Kalas's amber eyes met mine, and I knew he'd read my thoughts. Sometimes our psychic connection was helpful, but at times like this, it meant nothing I thought was a secret. That could be a problem.

"Maddie, we are fated mates. Bound by the stars. The hows and whys don't matter. I'd like for you to come to Kralis with me, so we can get to know each other better. Anything else can be decided once we've spent more time together."

His words eased my worries, and I smiled. "That's fair enough. So, have you found anything in the grimoire that might help us?"

"Perhaps. There's an incantation here that will augment the caster's natural abilities. It might be possible that with its help, your telekinetic abilities are strong enough that you could create an air pocket around yourself."

I'd only used my telekinetic abilities to move objects with my mind, and more recently, to alter the stone molecules so Kalas could transform back into a living being. I didn't know if I could trap air, but it was worth a try. And if I couldn't, the incantation to augment my abilities might still be useful.

"Let's give it a try," I said, reaching for the book, but as I did, Kalas reached for my hand.

"I'd prefer it if you rested first. I'm sure performing a spell to augment your magical abilities will be taxing, and you've already been through so much."

I would have argued, but now the adrenaline was wearing off and I'd allowed myself a moment's rest, I could feel the exhaustion threatening to overwhelm me.

"Okay, but let me scan the area first, just to make sure we're still safe here."

"That's fair," Kalas agreed.

I closed my eyes and opened my mind. When my abilities first manifested, blocking out the intrusive thoughts of others was almost impossible, but I'd had almost ten years to get used to the nuances of telepathy. Janine had been a great help in teaching me how to 'turn on' my abilities at will.

Chatter filled my mind as I tuned into the voices and thoughts of everyone in the holiday park. For a moment, it was overwhelming, and because I was tired, I struggled to decipher one thought from another. But, after taking a deep breath, I was able to hone in on individuals. The first mind I focused on was that of the receptionist. She'd likely be the first to know all the comings and goings in the holiday park. Plus, I was curious to know what she thought of me. Thankfully, there were no thoughts about witch hunters, and it seemed nothing about me had stood out to the receptionist. I moved my focus to the next mind, and then the one after, until I'd done a quick mental scan of everyone in the holiday park. There was nothing out of the ordinary to be found in any of the minds of the others. And even more reassuringly, there were no witch hunters nearby.

I opened my eyes and gave Kalas a small, tired smile. "We're good. No witch hunters, and everyone here is thinking about normal stuff. I think it's safe for me to take a nap. But please, if you sense or hear anything strange, wake me up right away."

"I will," Kalas promised, taking my hands. He helped me to my feet, and then with our fingers intertwined, he led me through to the small bedroom.

I hesitated, self-conscious for a moment. Even though Kalas and I had been intimate earlier, that had been in the heat of the moment. Being together now in this small cabin bedroom felt different somehow.

I sighed and dropped onto the bed to remove my shoes. Maybe I'd just sleep in my clothes. It'd probably be safer that way.

My thoughts came to an abrupt halt as I gazed up and saw Kalas removing the Earth clothing I'd bought for him.

"What are you doing?" I blurted.

Kalas chuckled. "Surely sleeping naked is more comfortable?"

"Well, yes, but what if someone comes?"

"We'll hear them first," Kalas insisted, and I knew he was right.

Kalas sat on the bed next to me, and my eyes were instantly drawn to the smooth planes of his chest. "Why are you nervous around me, my little witch?"

I couldn't meet Kalas's gaze and instead fiddled with the end of the quilt. "I wouldn't say I'm nervous."

Kalas laughed again. "No, perhaps that was the wrong word. But I make your body react in a certain way, and you're fighting it. Why?"

"Look at you," I said, gesturing towards Kalas and almost slapping him on the chest by accident. He caught my hand at the last moment, holding it with his own, and stared deeply into my eyes.

I couldn't bring myself to finish my sentence, but Kalas caught my thoughts easily. "Do not worry, Maddie. I think you're the most beautiful creature I have ever beheld."

I felt my cheeks flush and tried to dismiss his compliment. "You're just saying that. I bet back on Kralis there are hundreds of Kralians more beautiful than me."

"But none of them were chosen to be my mate by Korvarith Thalun."

I almost rolled my eyes and couldn't stop myself from asking, "Yeah, but say I hadn't been chosen by Korvarith Thalun. Would you still think I was 'the most beautiful creature you have ever beheld'?"

Kalas gazed at me intently, not a hint of insincerity in his amber eyes. "Without a shadow of a doubt."

Even before my abilities had manifested, I'd always felt like a freak. Red hair, green eyes, and pale skin weren't exactly common, and the kids at school latched onto any difference a person had to make them feel inferior. When I learned I was a witch, I also discovered certain traits were more common among witches. Now, my physical differences weren't just things for my peers to tease me about, they were markers a witch hunter would look for to identify their prey. For a while, I dyed my hair black and even contemplated getting coloured contact lenses to help me blend in a little more. It was Janine who'd shown me there was nothing wrong with being myself. Both physically and in terms of being a witch. Janine helped me realise that changing my appearance because I wanted to was fine, but changing because I disliked something about myself, or because I was trying to hide only led to heartache in the long run.

I'd never felt beautiful, even when I was most comfortable with my appearance. Even when the people I'd slept with had told me I was sexy or attractive.

But staring into Kalas's amber eyes and seeing the genuine affection there, I believed him. I was beautiful.

My confidence renewed, I removed my clothing as Kalas watched hungrily. My body filled with heat and desire as I pulled back the quilt and crawled into position, my head nestled on the pillows.

"If I wasn't so insistent on you resting, I'd show you just how tempting I think you are," Kalas said, coming to lie next to me in bed, his erection brushing against my thigh.

I was more than a little disappointed when he brought the quilt up to my chin, making sure I was adequately covered. But then he leaned forward and pressed his lips to the crown of my head in a surprisingly tender kiss.

"Rest well, my little witch," he said softly, stroking his hands through my hair.

He started to sing in that same strange language I'd heard him sing in earlier. The sound filled me with wonder, its melodic cadence enchanting me and evoking a sense of awe and connection to the celestial realm.

I smiled and lifted my hand to caress his cheek.

"Is that the language of the Kralians?"

Kalas's eyes shimmered for a moment, as though remembering a faraway place, and then he smiled too. "Yes. This is the language of my people. This is an old song my father sings to my mother. It's about beauty and union."

Learning not only the meaning of the song but that Kalas's father sang it to his mother caused my heart to swell.

"Invarali taleni," Kalas murmured.

Kalas continued to sing to me in the language of the Kralians, soft and haunting notes, melodies that rippled like the surface of a cosmic pond, creating fractals of energy.

"Stellavarien ethrionth, lunaviel solemna," he hummed. "Stars weave, moon's embrace."

I closed my eyes and drifted blissfully, my mind filled with images of endless star-filled skies, clouds rolling in a gentle breeze, and the lustrous shimmer of light as it moved through the full spectrum of colours.

I idly wondered if it was just my imagination conjuring up these images or something more. Then, I knew Kalas was projecting these images into my mind when I saw a couple—male and female—holding an infant. The male looked so much like Kalas.

They cooed at the child in their arms, singing the same soft, enchanting melody.

"My mother and father," he told me.

"Thank you for sharing this with me," I replied sleepily, and then I was gone.

I DON'T KNOW HOW LONG I slept for before I was awoken by the feeling of Kalas's lips on my neck.

Warmth radiated from his body, and he moved his mouth to my ear to whisper, "I have been waiting for you to wake."

Heat surged through me, but I did my best to keep my expression neutral as I replied, "Is that so?"

"It seems I have been bewitched." Kalas cupped my head in his hands, his clawed nails lightly scratching my throat and neck as he brought our heads closer together.

I caught the glimpse of fangs as Kalas smirked, and then he crushed his lips to mine. Our tongues swirled together, and I tasted the metallic tang of blood as Kalas nipped my bottom lip. His actions seemed more ardent and hungrier than they had in the underground cavern earlier, and soon, his mouth was moving down my throat and neck.

Again came the scrape of fangs, and I felt his clawed nails digging into my flesh.

"Want you. Need you," he growled in my ear.

"Take me. I'm yours," I panted.

Kalas's mouth moved from my throat to my breasts, and he sucked one of my nipples into his mouth. His hands spread my legs, and his fingertips glided across my clit and core; I was surprised when his talon-like claws didn't scratch my sensitive area.

I opened my eyes and gazed at him intently.

"Is everything okay, my little witch?" he asked in a husky voice.

"Your claws," I blurted mindlessly.

Kalas smiled. "Don't worry, they're retractable, like my sharpened teeth and feathers. It's all part of my ability to transform."

As if to punctuate his point, Kalas opened his mouth, and his sharpened incisors and canine teeth extended.

The sight of them sent excitement through my body, and remembering our psychic connection, I spoke directly to Kalas's mind. *'You know, I wouldn't mind if you were to bite me. I might actually like it.'*

Kalas smirked. As his hands continued to move between my legs, his fangs pierced my nipples, and he bit the tender flesh around my breasts before moving up to my neck. I felt the scrape of fangs against my skin.

Kalas's fingertips pressed against my clit, causing me to rock my hips, and I let out a mewling cry of desperation. He continued to tease me, keeping the pressure slow but steady as his mouth moved over my body, teeth nipping and scraping as he went.

My body shuddered as the pace of Kalas's fingers increased, and they dipped inside my slick opening.

"I'm close," I breathed out huskily.

Kalas moved so fast he was almost a blur, and I barely had time to process what was happening before he was slamming into me, filling and stretching me with his hard, thick cock.

"Fuck!" I cried out, wrapping my legs around his waist so he pounded into me more deeply.

Kalas let out a sound that was somewhere between a growl and the shriek of a bird of prey. I opened my eyes to see his had transformed from amber to black, and his fangs had lengthened again. The feathers along his shoulders and arms were extending through the skin, and I could see his claws transforming more completely into talons.

He clung to me, piercing my flesh, and I cried out, but not from pain.

My cries seemed to spur Kalas on, and he pounded into me harder.

My whole body quaked, and a string of incoherent curse-words fell from my mouth as the orgasm rocked my body and my inner muscles clenched around his cock.

I lay clinging to Kalas as the blissful aftershocks of the orgasm flowed through me. I felt weightless, as though I was floating on a cloud. When I opened my eyes, I saw Kalas's transformation slowly receding and his appearance becoming more human-like. He smiled down at me, his amber eyes studying me reverently.

"How long did I sleep for?" I asked, sitting up a little and looking around the room. The blinds were closed, so I couldn't tell if it was light or dark outside.

"A couple of hours. The sun has just set," Kalas replied, pushing himself into a sitting position.

I sat too, not caring that the quilt fell away from my body. I felt none of the self-consciousness I had when I'd first undressed. In fact, quite the opposite.

"I'm going to take a shower. Do you want to join me?" I asked, getting out of bed.

Kalas raised a thin, dark eyebrow at me. "I'd like that very much, but please let me heal you first."

Just like he'd done in the cave, Kalas bit his fingertip, drawing a little of his shimmering blood, and then applied it to the cuts and scratches on my skin. The wounds closed instantly, not even leaving a scar. He entwined his fingers with mine, and I led him through to the ensuite bathroom, then turned on the shower so the water could heat up.

Kalas's eyes widened, and a huge grin covered his face. "I'm impressed with the facilities on Earth. They almost rival the luxuries we have on Kralis."

"I can't wait for you to show me."

Even though the cabin was on the small side when it came to holiday homes, the shower was more than big enough for me and Kalas.

I reached out a hand to test the water, and finding it was the perfect temperature, I stepped under the hot stream. A moment later, Kalas joined me.

As the water rained down on us, Kalas closed his eyes, tilted his head upwards towards the showerhead, and let out a long sigh of satisfaction.

"This is wonderful," he said reverently.

"Wait until you feel the bathrobe when we get out," I joked, lathering the complimentary loofah with shower gel.

I started working the soapy suds into my body when Kalas opened his eyes and stared at me. "What's that delightful smell?"

I held up the loofah for him to see. I took a step closer to him, rubbing the loofah over his chest and shoulders, causing soap suds to drip down his body. Acutely aware of how close I was standing, heat flashed through me.

Kalas chuckled, and I looked up to see him smirking. "It always comes back to the same thing, doesn't it?"

I blushed. "That wasn't my intention."

I continued lathering soap over Kalas's body and then instructed him to turn around so I could wash his back. "Can I wash your hair?"

"If it pleases you to do so, my little witch," came his husky reply, and a tingle of wanting rippled down my spine.

I reached for the shampoo and lathered it in my hands before stroking it through the lengths of Kalas's hair. The mixture of shampoo and water reflected the light off his hair, bringing out the myriads of colours and creating a stunning oil-slick effect. As the soap dripped onto his body, I saw it had a similar effect on his skin, which shimmered with iridescence.

I carefully cleaned his shoulders where the tips of his feathers just poked out through the skin. "Does it hurt?"

"You bathing me? No. You've got a gentle touch."

I laughed a little and then said, "No, I meant the feathers poking through your skin."

"Does your hair hurt when it grows from your body?" Kalas asked.

"Well, no."

"The feathers are the same. But it does hurt slightly when I transform. Especially if I go a long time between transformations. Thankfully, on Kralis, we're free to transform when we want to. It's common to hold flying contests and tests of our abilities."

"I can't wait to see you transform fully. Though I don't think you should until we're sure I can create an air bubble around myself."

"I agree," Kalas replied.

After cleaning Kalas's body and hair, I moved the loofah back to my own body, but his hand on mine stilled me.

"Let me bathe you now, my little witch," he said softly, taking the loofah from me. "On Kralis, a bound pair will bathe each other. It is one of the many ways we show our mate that we care for them."

"Mate. You say that like we're animals."

"Isn't that what we are at our core?" Kalas asked as he started working the shower gel into my skin with the loofah.

"I suppose so, but it's not how humans see themselves. Many consider themselves above other animals. It's why it's so easy for them to fear and hate anything different."

Sadly, in my experience, humanity saw itself above everyone and everything. All too often there were the sections of the human race that saw themselves as elite. I couldn't imagine an oil tycoon who only cared about profits worrying about the needs of the animals and nature around them.

Kalas shook his head sadly. "This is not the way of Kralis."

When we finished in the shower, I stepped out from under the stream of water and wrapped myself in a fluffy bathrobe and then handed the second to Kalas.

He copied my actions, wrapping his body in the robe, and then sighed in contentment. "This is the softest fabric I've ever felt."

I laughed. "I knew you'd like it. As shitty as this world is, there are still many things to love. I'm sure you'll discover that for yourself."

Kalas reached out and took my hand. His amber eyes sparkled with amusement. "I think I already have.

# Chapter Seven
# Duty and Destiny

We made our way back through to the bedroom and began redressing. As I pulled on the clothes I had now been wearing for almost two days, I wished I'd thought to buy extra supplies from the holiday park store. That was something I could deal with later, though. I wasn't even sure if the shop would be open now.

Once we were both dressed, we made our way through to the living area. After I'd eaten, I practised trying to use my telekinetic abilities to create an air bubble around myself, but I couldn't manage to conjure a pocket that lasted for more than five minutes.

"Even with the spell to augment abilities, I don't think this is going to work." I sighed, pushing the grimoire away.

I was starting to get a headache from using my abilities too much. I'd always found my telekinetic powers harder to use than my telepathic abilities. Hearing others' thoughts came naturally to me. It was blocking them out that I'd struggled with, but moving things with my mind was something I could only do in small bursts. That I'd been able to transform the stone molecules trapping Kalas had been a miracle.

Kalas sighed too. "I wish there was some way I could get a message to my parents. Although Kralians can transform and fly in space, we still have spacecraft for the other species on the planet. I don't know why the high priest didn't consider any of this when he told me to touch the sacred pool."

Kalas's words sparked an idea in my mind. "That I might be able to do. My telepathy is stronger than my telekinesis, and with the augmentation spell, there might be a way to connect our minds and reach out to your parents."

Kalas's eyes widened. "Do you think it's really possible?"

I grinned. "I do, but I'm going to need some ingredients for the augmentation spell. Let me go to the shop and then we can get started."

"Perhaps we should wait until the morning," Kalas suggested softly. "I don't want you overexerting yourself."

I wanted to get started on the augmentation spell straight away. Not only was I still worried the witch hunters would catch up with us soon, but now I had made the decision to accompany Kalas to Kralis, I was excited to begin the journey.

Kalas made a great point, though. Despite my earlier nap and having dinner, I was exhausted again. Practising with my telekinetic abilities had worn me out completely, and I knew attempting any type of magic in my current state could lead to dangerous consequences.

"Yeah, you're probably right. We can get everything we need tomorrow. In fact, it's probably better we don't perform the spell or try to contact your parents here in case someone sees us."

"Tomorrow, I can take us to a part of the forest humans can't get to. We'll be safe there," Kalas said.

Kalas closed the distance between us and pressed his lips to mine. "I wouldn't mind seeing more of Earth before we depart. Despite some of the evil people who live here, the planet is actually quite beautiful."

"It is," I agreed. "It's just a shame about the witch hunters and other closed-minded bigots. It's not just witches who are persecuted. Anyone different is oppressed. It's not like what you've told me about Kralis, where anyone is accepted regardless of race, gender-identity, or sexuality."

"There are planets in the Throvani Ethrionth system whose inhabitants behave in a similar way to the humans of Earth. They are the planets that cause wars. The only planets that experience total peace are Kralis and Valeth. Auroriath is the most war-like planet in the Throvani Ethrionth system. Their beliefs are at odds with the people of Kralis and Valeth, but our respective deities protect us."

I listened with interest as Kalas told me more about his home and the planetary system where Kralis resided. "You've mentioned Valeth before. It's the planet of witches, right?"

"Yes. The people of Valeth are our closest neighbours. Though they do not worship The Twilight Crow, they hold Them in high regard."

"I'd love to visit Valeth. Perhaps learning more about the people from there will help me learn more about witches and myself."

Kalas smiled. "We will visit. As soon as I've presented you to my parents and we've made an official announcement on our intention to bond."

My eyes widened. "But you said you wouldn't force me to marry you if I don't want to."

"And I won't, but certain things will be expected of us when we return to Kralis. A bonded pair is given a period between the announcement of their intention to bond and the actual bonding ceremony."

"Like an Earth engagement?" I asked, then explained the concept to Kalas.

"Yes, it is similar to that. It is our promise to each other, to the people of Kralis, and of course to Korvarith Thalun that we will do our best to honour Their word."

"And if after this I don't want to marry you, I'll be allowed to leave?" I asked, my heart rate increasing slightly.

I wanted to get to know Kalas and to visit the other planets he spoke of, but I wouldn't risk exchanging the threat of the witch hunters' prisons for captivity of an entirely different kind.

"Never in the history of Kralis has this happened. After the pair chosen by Korvarith Thalun has had time to get to know each other, they always choose to make their bond official and permanent."

Kalas's words didn't do much to assure me of my freedom, and I moved back from him. For the first time since I'd freed him from the stone, I felt apprehensive.

"Madelyne, my little witch. Invarali taleni, I will never make you do something against your wishes. Even if that means we are not officially bonded."

"But won't your parents and the people of Kralis object?"

Kalas didn't respond straight away, and I took his silence as hesitation. Could he defy Korvarith Thalun and his parents if he wanted?

I stared into Kalas's amber eyes, and I saw the uncertainty there. He didn't know if his parents would object if I refused the bonding.

"Maddie, I've already promised you, I will never make you do something against your wishes."

While Kalas might not force me to marry him against my wishes, his promise, no matter how genuine, couldn't account for his parents. There were no guarantees. Kalas hadn't even said he would defend my freedom to his parents.

Could I trust that if it came to it, Kalas would take my side? And what would the consequences for both of us be if we defied the king and queen?

I glanced at Kalas cautiously. I liked him. A lot. I wanted to explore whatever this was between us. Who knew, in time, maybe I'd even want to make my bond with him official and permanent.

Not only that, but I wanted to visit Kralis and Valeth. I wanted to experience what life could be like without always having to hide from the witch hunters.

But would I risk his parents imprisoning me—or worse, killing me—for a chance at a different life away from Earth?

The chances of me having a happy life on Earth were zero unless the witch hunters suddenly changed their minds.

Without knowing how Kalas's parents might react if I didn't want to marry their son, I didn't know if I could be happy on Kralis. They might be completely fine with me having freedom. And even if they weren't, perhaps I could find allies before that. Surely, the people of Valeth would offer sanctuary to an Earth witch with nowhere else to go?

Although the future was uncertain, leaving Earth with Kalas seemed like the better option than staying here and waiting for the witch hunters to catch up with me.

I moved closer to Kalas again, looping my arms around his neck and pressing my lips to his. "We'd better get some rest if we want to visit the shops tomorrow and try to contact your parents."

The worry in Kalas's gaze lifted, and he returned my kiss with equal fervour. I snuggled closer, resting my head against his chest, my crown tucked under his chin. I moved my arms so they were loosely draped over him, and Kalas's hands stroked my lower back.

It was like this, our bodies entwined, that we fell asleep.

THE FOLLOWING MORNING, despite how much I wanted to linger in bed with Kalas and how tempting he made the idea of never leaving the room, I finally dragged myself to my feet, showered, and made some breakfast.

When we were both ready, Kalas and I left the cabin, and I asked at reception for directions to the closest town.

The woman stared up at Kalas with a mixture of wonder and apprehension but didn't comment on his appearance and instead turned her attention to me.

The receptionist told me there was a town about fifteen minutes from the holiday park, with a bus that ran frequently between the two.

Once we got into town, Kalas did a wonderful job of hiding his amazement at the new and unusual things in the world around him. True to his earlier assumption, apart from a few glances in our direction, no one seemed to bat an eye at his appearance. I didn't know what the mundanes saw when they looked at Kalas, but it was obviously something very different from what I saw.

Even though I'd been with him almost exclusively since the moment I'd freed him from the stone prison, I still wasn't used to his ethereal beauty. I wondered if I ever would be.

When I stopped in a clothing store to get some supplies, the woman at the till seemed especially interested in Kalas. A blush flushed over her cheeks, and she glanced warily at me. I just smiled back. It seemed at least some people were as affected by Kalas's charms as I was.

When we left the shop, I noticed some women stared at Kalas with obvious lust, while others narrowed their eyes in my direction.

I chuckled to myself.

Fingers entwined with mine, Kalas raised an eyebrow and smirked. "I can read your thoughts easily, my little witch. You like that the women stare at me so wantonly, don't you?"

"I do. I also like knowing you're all mine."

Kalas's smirk morphed into a full-on grin. He paused in the middle of the street and pulled me into his arms. "The feeling is mutual. I can smell the lasciviousness some of the men here feel towards you. But they are also all wise enough to fear me. No one would dare try to steal you away from me. And even if they did, they would never succeed. You are mine."

Heat flashed through my body. "Stop distracting me."

Kalas inclined his head, brushing his lips against mine in the merest hint of a kiss. '*Why? I like distracting you,*' he said telepathically.

Switching to speaking with my mind, I said, '*I like you distracting me too, but if you don't stop, we'll never get everything we need before this evening. And I want to do the spell too if we have time.*'

"Fine. I will control my lust until we've made contact with my parents. But once we know a ship is on the way to Earth, I intend to well and truly ravish you, my little witch."

His husky tone made warmth pool between my legs. "I can't wait."

Finally, we had everything we needed, including a few changes of clothes for both Kalas and me, more groceries, and the items required for the ability augmentation spell. Thankfully, the spell ingredients were all common things, like food items, candles, or crystals, making it easier to avoid suspicion. It would only be if someone searched my shopping bags and were able to put all the items together that they might suspect I was a witch.

The augmentation spell called for turquoise chrysocolla crystals, the stone of the Moon Mother, used by witches to aid in embracing their divine power through strong communication, self-expression, empowerment, and education. The colour blue was associated with communication and clarity, so I bought some candles in that colour. Finally, lemon, garlic, and coriander would help open my third eye, which again, would increase my power.

"It seems spellcasting isn't too dissimilar from cooking," Kalas commented after we'd bought the ingredients from the supermarket.

I chuckled. "You're right. And some witches are especially skilled in the kitchen. I'm sure the same is true on Valeth."

"I would expect so. It certainly seems that way with the witches who live on Kralis, though in honesty, I haven't had much to do with them. I've lived a lot of my life in the palace, being prepared to one day become king."

"That's a lot of pressure to put on someone," I commented as we caught the bus back to the holiday park.

"Is it? I always just accepted it as part of my duty and destiny."

"Have you ever wondered what your life would be like if you weren't the prince?"

Kalas shrugged. "Not really. This is the life Korvarith Thalun chose for me, and I cannot change that."

"But would you, if you could? We don't have to contact your parents. We could stay here on Earth."

"We both know Earth isn't safe for either of us. If the witch hunters who saw us leave the barrow try to locate you, they will want to capture me too. Sometimes, Kralians do come to Earth and live here in disguise, but that is not my destiny."

Part of me wanted to press Kalas further, to find out if he really would challenge his destiny and go against the word of Korvarith Thalun if he thought we could be safe on Earth. But then I realised it was pointless. After what the witch hunters had seen the day Kalas and I escaped, they'd never stop looking for us.

We returned to the holiday park, and after preparing a quick meal, Kalas and I headed into the forest to perform the augmentation spell.

"I'll transform and fly us to somewhere we'll be safe from humans accidentally discovering us," Kalas said once we'd walked some distance from anyone taking an early evening stroll in the forest.

"I wish you could change into your full bestial form, but I'm worried it will draw too much attention. I'd love to be able to fly on your back."

Kalas grinned. "Don't worry. Once we're on Kralis, I will be able to transform freely, and we will fly between the stars."

The thought filled me with wonder and excitement. I was eager to augment my abilities and get in touch with Kalas's parents.

Kalas transformed into his more harpy-like form, and I wondered how much bigger his full bestial form would be. In his harpy-like form, he was slightly larger than when he took on a human shape and could easily lift us both into the air with my arms wrapped around his waist. But he'd spoken of me riding on his back. I doubted I could do that in his current state, which meant his bestial form would be bigger still.

I imagined a glorious, feathered wyvern and couldn't wait to experience the sight in person.

We landed a fair distance away from any humans, closer to where we'd first landed a few days before and Kalas had hunted the boar. I stepped out of his embrace, but he didn't transform back to his human shape as I started setting out what was needed for the spell.

'*In case we need to escape quickly,*' he said telepathically.

As I'd done the night I'd cast the spell to find my true love and where I belonged, I drew a circle and pentagram in salt and then placed the blue candles and chrysocolla crystals at the five points of the star.

I didn't have my camp stove this time but had bought a small incense burner, into which I placed the lemon, garlic, and coriander, so the heat released their oils and a delicious aroma wafted into the air.

Finally, I opened the skin-bound grimoire and turned to the spell that would augment my abilities. If all went according to plan, we'd soon be able to contact Kalas's parents across the galaxy.

# Chapter Eight
## As I Desire
## So Shall It Be

As the intermingled aromas of lemon, garlic, and coriander grew stronger and the candles around the pentagram flickered, I read the augmentation spell.

"I call on the powers of North, East, South, and West. In the name of the Moon Mother, increase my innate telepathic abilities. Let my mind reach across the stars, so that Kalas and I may speak to his parents."

I reached out, taking Kalas's hand in mine, knowing the physical touch would increase the connection between us.

"By the power of the moon and stars above, connect my and Kalas's minds to those of his parents."

My eyelids felt heavy, and my eyes closed. I had just enough strength to finish the incantation.

"By the power of three, I summon thee. As I desire, so shall it be."

For a moment, there was only blackness. All I was aware of was the feel of Kalas's taloned hand in mine. The forest felt unnaturally still around us, as though we'd left it far behind.

Slowly, the darkness gave way, and I felt my spirit leave its body. Beside me, Kalas's spirit did the same. We stood, hand in hand, our physical forms still kneeling in the forest as our astral forms floated higher and higher into the air. My astral self was made from emerald energy that was similar to the shade of my eyes, while Kalas's astral self-reflected light the same way his feathers and hair did, showing shades of purple and turquoise.

The Earth grew smaller beneath us, and then we were walking through the stars. Kalas guided me as we moved through the solar system I was familiar with, passing all the other planets until we moved out of the range of human exploration.

I laughed in delight as we walked weightlessly across the universe until a second sun appeared on the horizon. It was similar to Earth's sun but surrounded by seven planets. The one closest to the sun was the smallest and was a deep, violent red.

'*Auroriath*,' Kalas told me telepathically as we drifted past the war-hungry planet.

The next planet was slightly bigger and looked similar to Earth, with land masses and oceans. The south of the planet glimmered like a full moon reflected in water, and I saw a tall, ivory spired tower.

'*Valeth, and the home of the Witch Queen*,' Kalas said into my mind.

We passed Valeth and approached a planet that might have been its twin, only the oceans glimmered with shades of turquoise, purple, and pink, and the land seemed carved from obsidian. In the centre of the landmass glittered a tall, black tower.

'*The Palace of Kralis*,' Kalas said, and suddenly, we were moving faster, approaching the magnificent obsidian castle, and then phasing through the walls.

Our astral selves stood in a wide chamber, with stained glass windows, and a shimmering pool in the centre. Around the pool were rows and rows of seats, but they were all empty apart from two figures near the front, their hands dipped into the water.

I recognized them instantly as Kalas's parents.

Our astral selves approached the pool, and the king and queen rose to greet us.

"Kalas, is that really you?" his father asked aloud.

They looked very much alike, and there were only a few subtle differences that set them apart. Kalas's father had a few age lines and wrinkles, though he didn't appear to be more than fifty years old. His eyes were a deep purple that were almost black.

Beside him stood Kalas's mother, almost as tall as her husband and just as striking. Her hair flowed down to her waist, and it was a bright, luminous white. Her eyes were the same amber as Kalas's.

The royal couple both wore regalia similar to the clothing Kalas had been wearing when he'd landed on Earth. Their shoulders were adorned with fantastical raven-feather cloaks, and on their heads were crowns decorated with precious gems.

'*Your Majesties,*' I said telepathically, my astral form sinking to its knees in a bow.

Beside me, Kalas did the same. '*Father and Mother, I present to you the one Korvarith Thalun has chosen as my fated mate, the Earth witch Madelyne Grant.*'

"It is a pleasure to meet you," the King of Kralis said, gesturing that we should rise.

"How is it that you're here but you're not?" the queen asked.

'*It is Madelyne's magic. My mind is connected to hers, and we can hear each other's thoughts. On Earth, Madelyne can slip into the minds of others. She used a spell to amplify this ability so that we might speak to you,*' Kalas explained.

The eyes of both his parents widened. "What wonders. It seems The Twilight Crow has blessed you indeed," his father said.

'*Yes. Maddie has many talents. She is much like the witches of Valeth. I cannot wait to introduce you to her in person. Which is why we're seeking your help.*'

Kalas explained all that had happened since he'd touched the sacred pool and that we couldn't leave Earth and return to Kralis without their help.

"Do your best to show us where you are, and we will get one of our best spacecrafts sent to you immediately," Kalas's father said.

I thought of the Forest of Dean and the isolated spot Kalas had taken us to so I could perform the spell. Then I tried to make my thoughts 'zoom out' so the king got a better understanding of where we were. With my mind, I tried to show him where the Forest of Dean was within the United Kingdom, and where exactly the United Kingdom was on Earth.

"We know of Earth and your different countries," the king reassured me.

"I am sure we will be able to use this magical connection to find you and send a spacecraft to the correct location," the queen added.

'*Thank you,*' Kalas said. '*We will all be together soon, and then the wedding preparations can begin.*'

I smiled at the king and queen, while inside, my heart raced.

In many ways, it was flattering that Kalas was so eager for us to be married, but part of me still worried he was only marrying me because he had been told it was his destiny.

Plus, he had promised me that we'd have time to get to know each other before I had to decide if I wanted to marry him or not? Was that just something he'd told me to get me to agree to come to Kralis with him?

Or was he telling his parents the wedding preparations would begin soon, so that they agreed to send a ship to Earth for us?

Not sure what was the correct answer, and unable to discuss it with Kalas at that moment, instead I said, *'It was a pleasure to meet you both. I can't wait to do so in person and see Kralis with my own eyes.'*

"We're excited for your arrival," the king said.

"We'll prepare a feast especially for the occasion," the queen added.

I could feel the presence of the king and queen growing weaker, and then a million voices assaulted my mind, causing me to cry out in agony.

As my shriek of pain filled the air, my and Kalas's spirits returned to their bodies with a jolt.

I gasped for air and felt something warm and wet trickling from my nose. When I wiped it away, I was alarmed to see it was blood.

Kalas noticed too and reached out to me, gathering me in his arms. "Here, let me help you."

Before I could protest, he bit his fingertip and drew a little blood. He dabbed it on my face, just under my nose, but when that didn't stop the flow of my own blood, he pressed his fingers to my lips.

I had no choice but to lap at the blood on his fingers, and as the droplets hit my tongue, I instantly felt clear-headed. Kalas's blood acted like a medicine, healing my body from the trauma of overusing my magical abilities.

"Thank you," I said, wiping the residual blood from my face with the sleeve of my sweatshirt.

"We should go back to the cabin so you can rest," Kalas said, lifting me easily in his arms.

Holding me close to his chest, he strode through the forest and back to where we were staying. I don't know if anyone else saw us, but if they did, no one stopped us to ask what had happened. Perhaps they'd been too intimidated by Kalas's presence.

He laid me in bed, covered me with the quilt, then came to lie behind me and gently stroked his fingers through my hair.

"Rest now, invarali taleni," he said, and then began to sing in the Kralian language.

Even though his blood had helped clear my head and fight off some of the exhaustion I'd been feeling, I had still pushed my telepathic abilities to the absolute limits. Nothing could have prepared me for sending my and Kalas's minds across the universe and speaking to his parents.

Knowing I was safe and that sleep was the best thing for me at that moment, I allowed my heavy eyes to close and lost myself in the beautiful visions Kalas's singing created.

WHEN I WOKE UP WITH Kalas beside me, sleeping softly, I knew we'd both been asleep for a long time. Not only was it dark outside again, but my body felt fully refreshed. That would only be possible if we'd slept through much of the day and into the evening. I probably would have slept longer still if I didn't need to visit the bathroom and have something to eat.

Careful not to wake Kalas, I got out of bed and used the bathroom before padding through to the living area. I'd left my phone on the dining table, so I grabbed it to check the time. Almost twenty-four hours had passed since I had begun the power augmentation spell and we'd made contact with Kalas's parents.

"Damn," I muttered, realising the grimoire wasn't here. Kalas must have forgotten to grab it when he took me back to the cabin. I was sure it would be okay, though. We'd gone to a secluded location to cast the spell. Still, I would need to retrieve it just in case. Plus, it was too valuable a resource to lose.

But first, food.

I was just dishing up breakfast, or dinner, or whatever meal it was, when Kalas entered the living area.

"Why didn't you wake me sooner?" he asked, sitting at the table.

"You looked so peaceful," I replied. "Do you want anything?"

"Just water, please. I intend to go hunting shortly."

"Will you bring back my grimoire, please? We left it in the forest yesterday," I said, sitting down opposite him with my plate of food.

"Yes, of course."

"How long do you think it will be before the spacecraft your parents sent arrives?"

"Kralian spacecrafts can travel much more quickly than anything Earth has ever created, but it will still take a couple of days, I'd imagine. I'll have to watch the skies for its arrival."

This alarmed me a little. "What if someone else sees it?"

"Don't worry, I'm sure my parents will cloak it so that only a Kralian can detect the craft."

"Well, that's a relief. The last thing we need is to draw attention to ourselves. I think we've managed to shake off the witch hunters for now, but reports of a UFO would bring them here instantly."

"Soon, you will never have to worry about those monsters again," Kalas promised.

Knowing I'd soon be free of the witch hunters was a relief, but I was still unsure about everything else that was about to happen.

Speaking to Kalas's parents and hearing him discuss making wedding plans made the whole situation hit home for me. Yes, I wanted to leave Earth, but what would my life be like then? Would the King and Queen of Kralis really accept a witch as their prince's bride? What about the other Kralians? What if our marriage caused some sort of civil war? That was if I even married Kalas. I wanted to explore our feelings for each other, but marriage was a huge step to take so soon.

Kalas gave me a soft, understanding smile. "I know your worries, Maddie, and I promise you, they're all unfounded. Please. You trust me, don't you?"

I gazed into Kalas's amber eyes, and I knew the answer instantly. No matter what other doubts I had, one thing was certain.

"I trust you," I said, laying my hand over his.

Kalas covered our hands with his other and then leaned across the table to press his lips to mine. When he pulled back, his eyes had darkened, and I could feel the desire radiating from him.

"You should hurry up and go hunting, so I can drag you back to bed," I said, unashamed of my passion.

Kalas smirked, then released my hand and stood up. As he did, I noticed the tightness in his trousers. "I'll be as quick as possible."

When Kalas left the cabin, I finished eating and then headed straight through to the bathroom and freshened up so I'd be ready for when he returned. Now the idea was implanted in my mind, I was desperate to feel his body against mine and could think of nothing else.

# Chapter Nine
# Was That
# What I Wanted?

Waiting for something to happen was usually agonising, and the same would have been true of the wait for the spacecraft from Kralis if it weren't for Kalas.

We spent almost all of our time in bed, only venturing into another room if we needed to eat or use the bathroom.

For the first time since my powers manifested when I was a teenager, I felt at peace. The usual psychic feedback I experienced on a daily basis had lessened so much that I barely noticed it.

I was completely unaware of what was going on in the world outside of the cabin. All that mattered was me and Kalas. The way he made me feel. The things he did to my body.

When we weren't exploring each other's bodies, he was telling me more about his parents and the royal palace. Of Kralis and its culture. Of the neighbouring planets, and all the adventures we would go on after we were married.

He'd just been telling me about a planet on the edge of his solar system called Valoriani Ealuna that was entirely inhabited by non-humanoid, less intelligent beings. The Earth translation for the planet was animal kingdom, and from the way Kalas explained it to me, it sounded like a planet completely free from intelligent, humanoid interference. Kalas had said that while the people of the Throvani Ethrionth system were often at war, especially the beings from Auroriath, all had agreed to leave Valoriani Ealuna untouched.

"But won't your parents expect us to stay on Kralis and attend to royal duties?" I asked as Kalas and I lay in bed together.

"Not at first. A Kralian's lifespan is much longer than a human's. In your years, I am 500."

"You're what?" I sat bolt upright in bed, but Kalas only chuckled.

"Do not worry. In terms of a Kralian's lifespan, I am not much older than you are."

My eyes narrowed. "I'm only twenty-four."

Kalas shrugged. "Which isn't much beyond a quarter of your total lifespan, correct? That is the same for me. As to what I was saying, given a Kralian's longer lifespan, there will be no hurry for us to step into our royal duties. Probably not until you've borne at least one child."

"Wait..." All the blissful feelings lingering from our earlier sex evaporated as soon as I heard phrases like 'a Kralian's longer lifespan' and 'not until you've borne at least one child.' "If Kralians have a longer lifespan, won't I grow old and die before you're even middle-aged?"

"Do not worry. There are talented potions makers both on Kralis and Valeth. As you know, a Kralian's blood has certain healing properties. When combined with the right ingredients, that blood can be used to make a powerful elixir that will slow your aging to match my own. If you become my consort, you will live from anywhere between 1500 and 2000 years. As will I."

My eyes widened. "That long? What will we do with all that time?"

Kalas chuckled in response. "Live. As I said, we will adventure through the Throvani Ethrionth system. We may want to live on Valeth or visit Valoriani Ealuna for a time. And then there are the other star systems in this universe. Perhaps we will return to Earth and see how much or how little things have changed here. Then, when we are both ready, we will start a family."

"Is that even possible?" I asked in wonder. Once, a long time ago, I'd dreamed of being a mother. Then my magical abilities had manifested and I could never imagine bringing a baby witch into a world so hostile towards them.

"Of course. Don't you remember, I told you my great-grandparent was a witch from Earth? They and my great-grandmother had three children, my grandfather included."

My mind boggled at the possibilities. The more Kalas told me of life on Kralis and what it would be like to be his consort, the more I realised I actually could have the life I'd always dreamed of as a child. I could have a happy family and go on adventures. And best of all, I wouldn't have to give up my magical abilities and identity as a witch to do so...

Would I?

I still couldn't shake the feeling that everything Kalas offered me was too good to be true. That at some point, someone would proclaim I wasn't worthy of this beautiful prince and the amazing life he was offering me.

And deep in my heart, I feared that, despite what he said, Kalas only cared for me, only wanted me to be his bride because Korvarith Thalun had written it in the stars.

I turned away from Kalas, trying desperately to block the psychic connection between the two of us. To stop him from easily reading my thoughts. And it was working.Since the power augmentation spell, my telepathic abilities had been heightened. Now, I could sense the thoughts of people hundreds of miles away. In fact, I'd even been able to make contact with Janine. She'd been startled when my mind connected with hers, but after getting over the shock, we'd been able to converse psychically. She told me she had stopped practising magic and was living life as a 'normal' human. Because of this, her daughter had eagerly welcomed her back. Now, she lived in her daughter's guesthouse and looked after her two young grandchildren when her daughter and son-in-law were at work.

I wasn't sure how I felt about Janine giving up her magic to be with her daughter. I knew I'd never do the same, even if my parents begged me to return. But Janine had been on her own for much longer than I had. And with the increasing witch hunter raids, it made sense that she'd willingly sacrificed her powers for more safety and security. I didn't agree with her decision, but I'd never begrudge her happiness.

Janine had read in the newspaper that the village where we'd both once lived had been raided by witch hunters and her former magic shop razed to the ground. She was relieved when I told her I was safe and had escaped the village before the witch hunters could catch me, but I knew it was only a matter of time before they found me again. If they'd investigated the village and burned down Janine's former magic shop, they likely had my identity and were tracking me even now.

Janine was shocked when I told her about Kalas and everything he'd told me. The only thing that didn't seem to surprise her was learning that out there in the universe, there was a whole planet of witches. She said she'd heard legends of such a place, and that they worshipped a deity named Vesper. Janine even theorised that Vesper could be the same Moon Mother the witches of Earth worshipped, and that there might be a connection between the witches of Earth and the witches of Valeth. I was more excited than ever to visit Valeth with Kalas and promised Janine that once I left Earth, I'd try to reach out to her again if I could. It was my hope I would be able to either recreate the power augmentation spell or that the witches on Valeth or Kralis might have some way of increasing my abilities.

My hopes and dreams for the future warred in my mind with the doubts that lingered, and my fear that sooner or later the happiness I had experienced since Kalas came to Earth would be snatched away from me. Just like the love and happiness I'd experienced as a child was disregarded when my parents threw me to the kerb like rubbish once my abilities had manifested.

Parents were supposed to love their children unconditionally, but mine hadn't been able to look past what I could do and failed to see who I really was.

If a mother could turn her back on her only daughter, what was stopping a prince from another planet walking away from a woman he barely knew? What would prevent a whole race of ethereal beings from turning against someone they deemed not good enough?

I desperately tried to push the doubts from my mind and turned back to Kalas's warm and comforting embrace. As my gaze met his, Kalas's eyes widened, and I feared he'd easily picked up on my insecurities.

Instead, he said, "The spacecraft my parents sent is approaching the Earth's atmosphere."

Any other emotion I was feeling was pushed aside by a mixture of excitement and worry. What if the spacecraft wasn't as well disguised as Kalas hoped?

Not caring that we were completely naked, I threw open the curtains and looked up into the sky.

It was early evening, and the moon and stars were just beginning to appear. The moon was now a thick crescent, bright, white, and comforting. For an instant, I thought I saw something fly across the surface of the moon.

Was that the spacecraft from Kralis?

"Come, let's get ready and head into the forest. The ship will land soon," Kalas said, climbing out of bed.

I followed him, but more slowly. Now that this was really happening, I needed a moment to process everything.

I sat on the edge of the bed and watched Kalas pull on the simple Earth clothing he'd been wearing since our impromptu shopping trip.

I did the same, dressing in something casual and non-descript, then I packed the suitcase I'd bought when Kalas and I had ventured into the nearby town. I wasn't taking much with me, just my grimoire and a few changes of clothing. I packed Kalas's Kralian regalia into the case too, and the other Earth outfit I'd brought for him. We were leaving everything else. I always washed up straight after I ate, and the toiletries I used had been provided by the holiday park owner. I felt bad leaving without giving the cabin a proper clean, but we had no time. Instead ,I left all the money I had in my purse, along with a note that simply said,

*Thank you for letting us stay. We're moving on now. M&K*

Once everything was packed, Kalas picked up the case with ease, and I checked to make sure all the lights and appliances were switched off.

It was growing increasingly darker as we left the cabin, and people in their own holiday homes were sitting out on their decks, enjoying a late-night drink.

One couple nodded in our direction, but aside from that, no one paid us any attention.

Kalas and I were able to leave the holiday park and walk into the Forest of Dean unnoticed. Due to the hour, there were no hikers in the forest, and we made our way to the secluded location.

"Oh my God!" I gasped as we stepped into the clearing where I'd performed the power augmentation spell.

Shrouded in a shimmering, colour-changing aura was a... Well, it didn't look like an Earth air or spacecraft. It was about the width and length of two holiday cabins but shaped like an elongated rhombus, with the top and bottom tips being narrower than the middle. The whole thing appeared to be made out of the same colour-shifting material the jewels and gems on Kalas's Kralian regalia were made from. The spacecraft emitted a soft, low hum, reminding me of the sound a giant fan would make.

"This is incredible," I said breathlessly, taking a tentative step towards the spacecraft.

Kalas gently grabbed my wrist. "Wait. Let me approach first, just to make sure my parents didn't equip it with any weaponry or alarms."

Kalas approached the shimmering spacecraft, and as he did, he bit the tip of his forefinger to produce a small pool of blood. He swiped the blood on the surface of the spacecraft, and for a moment, it shone so brightly I feared someone would notice.

As the lighting returned to normal, I saw an opening that was just big enough for a person. Well, more accurately, a Kralian, to fit through.

Kalas strode towards the opening, pausing as he stepped onto the threshold. He turned, looking the most handsome I'd ever seen him. Even though he was still dressed in human clothing, something about the spacecraft had changed him. His skin shimmered more clearly, and even in the darkness, the turquoise and purple hues in his hair were unmistakable. Kalas's eyes shimmered like amber.

He extended his clawed hand to me, the skin on his forearm having turned black up to his elbow. "Come, Maddie. Let's go."

My hand clutched the suitcase, but my feet didn't move. This was it. The final moment I had to turn back. I could walk away now and pretend Kalas had never landed on Earth.

I met his gaze, and through our psychic bond, I knew—Korvarith Thalun's will or not—if I turned away now, Kalas wouldn't stop me. He was prepared to give me my freedom, in whatever form it took, and return to Kralis alone if that was what I wanted.

But was that what I wanted?

I imagined Kalas telling me Korvarith Thalun had made a mistake, and I wasn't his fated mate. The thought broke my heart. Pain akin to when my parents had disowned me wracked through my body.

Blinking away the thought, it was replaced by a vision of the king and queen telling me I wasn't good enough for their royal son and banishing me from Kralis. Again, my heart shattered, and tears welled in my eyes.

I contemplated walking away, living on Earth alone with only my memories of Kalas and our amazing time together. But despite all we'd shared, I knew the memories would be hollow without him by my side.

From the moment I'd seen the shooting star and then freed Kalas from the stone encasing him, life became meaningless without him.

I'd prayed to the Moon Mother. I'd cast my spell. And she had answered. She'd sent Kalas to me.

I wasn't sure how Korvarith Thalun played into all of this, and I definitely knew I wasn't ready for marriage yet, but despite all my worries, I knew without a doubt that walking away from Kalas now would be the biggest mistake of my life.

I wanted to explore the growing feelings between us. I wanted to get to know him better. I wanted to see his home and meet his parents in person. I wanted to adventure in far off galaxies with him.

Clutching the suitcase more tightly, I took a decisive step towards Kalas and the spacecraft.

"Yeah, come on. Let's get out of here."

# Chapter Ten
# Come For
# Your Prince

I took Kalas's offered hand and followed him through the spacecraft door-way and into the main interior of the ship.

"Oh my God!"

The inside of the spacecraft was amazing, like the most futuristic private jet I could imagine. Everything was made of a sleek, black material that glimmered when the light caught it. It reminded me of the precious gems on Kalas's royal regalia.

"What is this made from?" I asked, stroking my hand across the smooth, hard surface of an end table.

"It's nyxorith. It's the main resource on Kralis, and what many of our buildings and architecture are made of. Nyxorith is a gift from The Twilight Crow. The old history books say They forged nyxorith from inside a volcano."

Nyxorith being forged in a volcano made sense, as it looked almost like obsidian, but with an iridescent sheen.

As I passed the end table and stepped further into the spacecraft's cabin, I saw that not everything was made of nyxorith. There were also softer mate-rials, like seat cushions and plush carpet under my feet, but everything had the same aesthetic. The aesthetic of Kralis; black that shimmered with pur-ple, turquoise, and magenta hues.

Kalas sat down on a two-seater sofa, and I joined him, pleased to feel the fabric was luxuriously soft and comfortable.

"How long will it take to get to Kralis?"

Kalas pursed his lips for a moment as he thought. "Perhaps a week in Earth time. But don't worry, my parents will have ensured we have everything we need. There's a sleeping chamber, a bathing chamber, and I'm sure they will have provided food for you."

I smiled, feeling my body relax, and I reclined on the sofa. "It all sounds wonderful. I can't believe we're actually travelling through space. It doesn't feel like we're moving at all."

Kalas flashed me an indulgent smile. "The wonders of Kralian technology." He moved in closer, taking my hands in his, and stared deeply into my eyes. "So, you have no regrets about leaving Earth?"

"None at all," I said, leaning in and pressing my lips to his. "All that was left for me on Earth was fear and hatred. With you, I can start over. I can have the happy future I always imagined."

Kalas let go of my hands so he could cup my face in his palms. His long claws were gentle as he stroked my cheeks. "I promise, I will always do my best to make you happy and give you the life you deserve. You will be my consort, and eventually, my queen, and I intend to treat you as such."

His words caused warmth to flood my body, and my knees felt weak. Raising an eyebrow, I playfully asked, "So, how will we spend our time until we arrive at Kralis?"

Kalas caught my meaning instantly, and a predatory grin covered his lips. The sight of his pointed incisors made my heart race, and I longed for the feel of his mouth on my throat.

Kalas smirked and raised his brows. "My little witch gives orders and expects me to answer obediently. Have you forgotten that I am a prince?"

Kalas's teasing tone caused heat to pool between my legs, and as I squirmed, my eyes widened.

Kalas slowly removed the shirt he'd been wearing, revealing his perfectly sculpted body to me. Like with his hair, the play of light on his skin was mesmerising. Although I'd now seen him naked multiple times, the sight of him without clothing never ceased to take my breath away.

Obviously enjoying my rapt attention, Kalas continued his strip show and removed his trousers with equal teasing languor.

His dick was hard and ready for me, and I had to stop myself from climbing out of bed and jumping on him instantly.

*'No. I am in control now, my little witch,'* Kalas told me, having easily read the desire from my mind.

His words only served to entice me more, and I clutched at the sheets in desperation.

Kalas kept his eyes fixed on mine as he slowly crossed the bedroom and then pulled back the quilt.

"You're entirely too clothed," he muttered. "I must remedy that."

With lightning speed, Kalas was on the bed, tearing my nightclothes off my body, but he did it in such a careful way that his fingers barely brushed my skin. I ached for him and tried to press my starved body into his touch, but his hands only lingered for a moment.

"Please," I begged breathlessly.

"I have already told you, I am in command now. If you are to be my bride, my consort, you will learn patience. But if you are a good girl, I will gladly give you what you beg for."

His words caused heat to blaze through my body, and I pressed my legs together as my core burned.

Knowing exactly what effect he was having on me, Kalas smirked and stood from the bed.

I studied his body with fascination, still unable to quite believe this stunning, otherworldly prince was mine. I watched the skin on his hands darken as his talons extended and feathers pierced the skin along his shoulder blades.

"Perhaps you will behave yourself if you're restrained," Kalas said, reaching into the dresser for some clothing he could use as a makeshift restraint.

Under any other circumstances, being tied down would have terrified me. But this was Kalas. I trusted him with my life and knew he only intended to do deliciously wicked things to me.

Still, I played along with his game and struggled a little as he bound my hands and legs.

"Behave yourself," he said, giving my ass a firm slap.

I let out a squeal that caused Kalas's dick to twitch, and the heat raging through my body increased.

"Now to see how well you can obey me," Kalas said, pulling me into a sitting position. He moved me to the edge of the bed and then stood directly in front of me, so his thick cock was perfectly level with my mouth. "Open up."

I did as he commanded, licking my lips as I opened my mouth and took in his whole length. I fought my gag-reflex, knowing if I did a good job pleasuring him, I would be wonderfully rewarded.

Kalas gripped the back of my head with both hands, guiding me, as he fucked my mouth. I had to stretch my jaw to capacity, but it was worth it to feel him twitch against my tongue. And the sounds he made... oh my God. They started off as grunts that morphed into groans as I sucked harder, gently grazing his dick with my teeth. As I felt him coming closer to climax, I swirled my tongue around the tip of his cock, and Kalas let out a desperate, breathy moan that almost sent me over the edge too.

"Thalunori luminali ethrionth," he muttered, and my mind easily understood the meaning; 'by the moon and the stars.'

Kalas's grip on my head loosened, and he let out a cry that was akin to a bird's shriek as his hot seed hit the back of my throat.

I swallowed it down eagerly and then opened my eyes and gazed up at him with a barely disguised self-satisfied smirk.

"You did well, my little witch," Kalas praised, gently stroking my cheek. "Now, let me repay the favour."

He pushed me back into a lying position and loosened the bindings on my legs so he could nudge my knees apart and nestle between them. He lowered himself into the perfect position and gripped my ass in his hands. His talons pierced the skin of my butt cheeks, and I let out another squeal.

Kalas chuckled and lifted my mound to his face, his tongue darting out to gently lap at the sensitive flesh.

My hips started to rock involuntarily, and I was just getting into things when Kalas lowered my body back onto the mattress.

I let out a desperate whimper, to which he replied, "Patience, invarali taleni."

Kalas's fingers lazily stroked up my thigh to the apex and danced around my sensitive area, barely skimming near my clit. Again, my hips jerked, desperate for more.

*'You will have more when I decide you're allowed more,'* he said directly into my mind.

His words made the coiled spring inside me tighten, and I eagerly anticipated his next touch.

Kalas continued to work his way up my body, his talons gently breaking the skin and drawing a faint line of blood. He circled my breasts before lowering his head and claiming one of my nipples in his mouth. As his fangs pierced one nipple, he pinched at the other with his talons, causing it to stiffen to a hard peak.

My chest heaved as my breath came out more heavily. I relished the pleasurable-bordering-on-painful sensations Kalas was causing within my body.

His mouth moved up from my breasts to my neck, and he easily found the pulse point there.

*'Even though I fed earlier, I hunger for something more specific,'* he spoke into my mind, and I caught his meaning instantly.

He wanted to drink my blood.

*'Take it. It's yours. I'm yours,'* my mind screamed in response.

I swooned as Kalas's lengthened incisors and canine teeth pierced the sensitive flesh on my neck, and I felt the blood spurt out. He lapped at it hungrily, letting out a moan very similar to the one he'd made when I'd had his dick in my mouth.

"You taste exquisite," he told me breathlessly.

He sucked on the vein in my neck again, and I started to feel lightheaded. My vision dimmed slightly, but before he got carried away and took too much, Kalas moved from my throat to my lips.

He tasted of blood, of my blood, as he kissed me. Then a moment later, a different flavour filled my mouth, and I realised he'd nipped his own tongue. My mouth filled with Kalas's blood, and I swallowed it down just as eagerly as I had with his cum. The effect was instantaneous, and the light-headedness I had experienced a moment before vanished, as did any pain in my body where he'd scratched and pierced me.

It was intoxicating.

It felt like my whole body was vibrating on a different plane as Kalas's mouth moved from mine, trailing back down my body until he came to my mound again. This time, there was no gentle teasing. He grabbed my ass, lifted my body up to meet his face, and then all but devoured my pussy. His tongue lashed against my clit until it was throbbing, and my hips jerked erratically.

"Yes, yes. That's it, my little witch. That's it, invarali taleni. That's my good girl. Come for your prince," Kalas said, his fingers replacing his mouth as two digits easily slipped into my opening.

It only took a couple of thrusts before my inner walls were clenching around his fingers and my body was shuddering as the orgasm claimed me.

I saw fireworks. Or what I thought was fireworks, until I studied the vision more closely. My and Kalas's minds had connected, and I saw what he saw. He was watching me steadily, his usually amber eyes now completely black, just like the skin on his arms all the way to the elbows. And there I was, lying before him, as bright and dazzling as a star exploding into a supernova.

# Chapter Eleven
# Your Happiness
# Is My Happiness

I was lounging in the living area of the spacecraft, reading one of the many Kralian books onboard, when Kalas's excited voice pulled me from my thoughts.

"Maddie, you have to come and see; Kralis has just appeared on the horizon."

My heart hammering, I put down the book and made my way through to the control deck. The spacecraft had an autopilot function that Kalas's parents had already programmed to take us to Kralis, but sometimes he went in there just to check we were still on course and that there was nothing to be aware of.

The control deck consisted of four seats in two rows of two, like in a car, although with less division between the front and rear seats. Each seat was similar to a computer chair and had the ability to swivel around. Additionally, in front of each seat was a computer that showed various data streams about the journey and if there was any incoming debris we needed to avoid.

At the front of the ship was a massive window that offered a panoramic view of the galaxy sprawled out in front of us. I'd spent many hours in here, watching as we left the Earth's solar system, and then as we journeyed through space. It was fascinating, and I had made pages and pages of notes that I asked Kalas about and also planned on studying once we reached Kralis.

Kalas was standing right at the front of the ship, his gaze fixed on a sun not dissimilar to Earth's, only with a more magenta hue than the one I was used to seeing. Orbiting the sun were four distinct planets, two of which were the smallest and similar in size, about as big as Mercury. The twin planets were like yin-and-yang, despite their similar sizes. One was a deep, dark purple that shimmered with the same colour-shifting iridescence that the nyxorith Kalas wore did. Around the planet shimmered an aurora that was the same colours; purple, magenta, and turquoise.

I instantly knew it was Kralis.

"It's more beautiful than I imagined," I told him, coming to stand beside Kalas and entwining my fingers with his.

"It's more beautiful than I remember," he agreed, then pointed towards the glittering haze. "And there, look, you can see some Kralians in their bestial form, flying around."

I watched closely, and though the creatures were no bigger than specks in the sky, I could see their massive feathered wings and long feathered tails.

"Amazing."

I watched the flying Kralians for a time before my focus moved to Kralis's twin, the shining silver orb. The surface of the planet looked like it was made from moon opals, reflecting shades of peach, rose, lilac, and mint.

Just as surely as I knew the darker planet was Kralis, I immediately knew its twin, Valeth, the home of the witches. Similar to Kralis's aurora, Valeth had its own aurora, this time in the same shades that were reflected from the surface.

"As soon as we've spoken to my parents and an official announcement has been made, I promise, I will take you to Valeth," Kalas said, easily guessing my thoughts.

"Thank you."

My gaze drifted from Kralis and Valeth to a third planet which was bigger than the first two, about the size of Earth. It was a bright, angry red, similar to Mars, and seemed to radiate fire. Wisps of orange flickered from the planet, and I sensed a foreboding aura.

This had to be Auroriath.

"The home of the Auroriathian," Kalas confirmed for me. "And no, we won't be visiting."

"Good. I wouldn't want to." My focus moved from Auroriath to the final of the four planets orbiting the magenta sun. This one was the largest of all, at least double the size of Earth, and was a rich, verdant green.

"So, this must be Valoriani Ealuna," I said, remembering what Kalas had previously told me about the Throvani Ethrionth Star System and the planet that was home to only animals.

"It is indeed," Kalas said. "We will spend our honeymoon there, if you wish."

A strange sensation washed over my body at his mention of our honeymoon. It was equal parts apprehension and excitement, and the two conflicting emotions warred inside me.

I let out a slow, steadying breath and said, "One step at a time, okay?"

Kalas smiled down at me. "Of course. As my little witch wishes."

We remained in the control room, watching Kralis draw closer and closer until finally Kalas stood.

"We will land in about an hour. We should prepare ourselves. I will need to change into my royal regalia to greet my parents. You should dress appropriately too. My mother will have left some options in the closet for you."

My chest tightened. I'd been so transfixed by the beauty of the Throvani Ethrionth Star System that I'd completely forgotten what would happen when we landed. I would be presented to Kalas's parents, the King and Queen of Kralis, and the rest of the Kralian court.

I wasn't ready. I didn't think I'd ever be ready.

Kalas said he loved me, and that his family and the people of Kralis would too. But what if they didn't? What if my being a witch or a human was a problem for them?

It was a conversation Kalas and I had had numerous times on our journey here, and he always reassured me, telling me that his parents were excited to meet me, and that the people of Kralis would follow the word of Korvarith Thalun, but still, some feelings were difficult to shake.

I'd spent all my life on Earth feeling *different*. When I was a teen, I'd found out why. I *was* different. I was a witch. And as my abilities had manifested, and I'd accidentally read the thoughts of those around me, I quickly became aware that everyone else knew I was different too. And they were scared of me. Even my own parents feared what I was so much that they'd thrown me out of my childhood home.

The only person who had ever treated me like an equal was Janine, but she'd given up her magic to be accepted by her family.

Despite Kalas's words of reassurance, twenty-five years of knowing you were different and then becoming aware that people feared and even hated you for your differences was hard to shake. Even if most of the people on Kralis accepted witches, I was certain not everyone on the planet would.

Kalas moved in closer to me, cupping my face in his large hands and tilting my head up so that our gazes met. "I don't need to read your mind to know what you're thinking. I promise you, Maddie, everyone will love you. And anyone that doesn't, I'm sure you will win over once they get to know you and they see how amazing you are."

I stood on my tiptoes and pressed my lips to his. "I'm trying to be brave. But even without the whole witch thing, I'm still a human. What if I say or do the wrong thing? What if I make some awfully embarrassing mistake and that's everyone's first impression of me?"

"I will be by your side, guiding you. And even if you do accidentally get something wrong, people will understand. Besides, you're the intended bride of the crown prince. No one would dare speak a word against you."

I stifled a small giggle. I wouldn't allow myself to think that way. That sort of power could be intoxicating and dangerous.

"Don't worry, it won't be all royal banquets. Later, after you've been formally introduced, we can go flying. Once you're in the sky with me, nothing else will matter."

The thought of riding on Kalas's back as he took to the skies helped chase away my fears about what arriving on Kralis would entail. I focused on that and the wonderful man beside me, holding my hand.

Fingers still entwined, Kalas led us through to the sleeping quarters and opened the large closet that stood opposite the bed. From inside, he withdrew his royal regalia and then stepped back.

"Come choose what you wish to wear," he said, gesturing to the array of outfits his mother had selected for me.

I was instantly drawn to the glittering strands of nyxorith and carefully pulled them from the closet to find that they were similar to an Egyptian Usekh or Wesekh.

"This is the most traditional garment for someone of your status and is similar to what my mother will be wearing."

My eyes widened. "But it's practically see-through."

Kalas shrugged. "It's traditional."

I sucked in a breath. If I was going to do this, I was going to do it properly. "Okay, I'll wear it."

Kalas grinned and pulled a semi-transparent long black skirt from the closet. "You can wear it with this. During the ceremony, I will present you with your ceremonial circlet and cloak."

My mouth gaped open. "What? Like yours?" I asked, my voice coming out as a squeak.

Kalas chuckled. "Don't worry, my little witch. You won't be expected to dress like this every day. Tomorrow, I will summon Kralis's greatest tailor to the palace, and they will create anything your heart desires."

"This is a lot to get used to," I said, feeling a little lightheaded. I sat down on the bed, and Kalas was instantly at my side, caressing my shoulders gently.

"I know, my precious one, but you will soon get used to it. And it won't be *all* the time. The first week or so will be busy as we attend to various royal duties, but then we will have time to ourselves."

Knowing this craziness wouldn't be forever helped a little, and I still had visiting Valeth to look forward to.

"And don't forget my promise. If at any time you change your mind about me or us being together, all you have to do is tell me., I want us to be together, Maddie, but I will not make you my prisoner."

I let out a long breath and laid my head on Kalas's shoulder. "What if I want you, but not all this?" I gestured to the royal regalia as an indication that I meant all the responsibilities and pressure that came with being the crown prince's betrothed.

Kalas took the regalia from me and tossed it to the floor as though it were a used rag and not some important royal garment. "Then we will leave Kralis and go wherever you'd like. I want to be with *you,* Maddie, regardless of anything else. If you do not wish to be my consort or you do not want to be a princess, just tell me. I will do whatever you want. Your happiness is my happiness."

"Even if it meant your parents disowning you?"

I saw the hesitation flicker in Kalas's eyes, and he didn't answer my question. Instead, he stood, picked up the regalia, and said, "We will be arriving soon. We should get ready."

I turned away from Kalas. I *wanted* to push him – to ask if he really *would* put my happiness above what his parents wanted. But I knew now wasn't the time or place. I hadn't even stepped foot on Kralis yet. For all I knew, everything would be perfect and I'd love being Kalas's princess and eventually queen. I was getting ahead of myself and creating problems that didn't even exist.

*One day at a time*, I reminded myself and took the regalia from Kalas with a smile.

# Chapter Twelve
# Witches

I took my time getting ready, pleasantly surprised that Kalas's mother had thought to supply makeup in case I wanted it. I wasn't sure what makeup the Kralians wore, but I had been wearing makeup since I was twelve. Of course, back then, I hadn't developed the skills to apply it properly, and I'd always had 'raccoon eyes' and over-painted lips.

My makeup was still dramatic now, leaning on the Gothic side, but I'd refined the techniques over the years. It was one of the masks I wore. If people wanted to think I was weird, I'd give them something to look at. While many other women my age followed trends, I always kept my own fashion sense. I figured I'd lean into what made me different.

Kalas seemed to like it and smiled approvingly as I painted my lips a dark plum shade. "It's like you were made to wear nyxorith," he said, gently stroking his hand through my curly red hair.

"I'll admit, I was a little nervous about wearing the royal regalia at first, but seeing it all together, with you by my side... well, we make a striking couple, don't we?"

I stared at our reflections in the mirror, admiring how we looked like we belonged together. For the first time in my life, I didn't feel like a freak. I felt powerful.

If I wanted, one day, I would be queen of Kralis. That was quite an achievement for the girl her mother wished she'd 'gotten rid of.'

I couldn't take my eyes off Kalas. I'd grown so used to seeing him in human clothing that seeing him in his Kralian regalia startled me. The sight of him brought me back to when I'd first discovered him in the stone chamber under the barrow. He looked otherworldly. He *was* otherworldly. Taller than any man I'd known on Earth, and with pale, iridescent skin. His fangs were just showing at the edge of his parted lips, and remembering the feel of them piercing my most sensitive areas sent a shiver of longing through my body. He looked resplendent in the nyxorith threaded loincloth and cloak made from the feathers of his ancestors.

My perfect prince.

"You look good enough to eat," Kalas murmured, and I glanced up to see him smirking.

"Behave yourself. You can't be distracting me like that when we're about to meet your parents."

"I'm sorry," Kalas replied seriously before the mischievous smirk returned momentarily. "But later, when we're alone, you're all mine."

My heart fluttered. "I will hold you to that."

Kalas extended his hand to me and we entwined our fingers. "Come, let's go back to the control room to watch the descent."

Through the large window in the control room, Kralis looked closer than ever. Closer than the moon was to the Earth.

"We'll be landing soon. There's a space port on the western side of Kralis, and I imagine my parents will send an escort to accompany us to the palace. From there, we will meet my parents in private before being introduced to the court at large. After, a feast with music and dancing will be held. I missed the feast held for my coming-of-age as I was on my way to Earth to meet you. Tonight will be a double celebration."

I was equal parts excited and nervous, but Kalas's reassuring presence by my side helped me fight back the worst of my worries.

I'd *chosen* this. I'd known Kalas was a prince when I'd agreed to return to Kralis with him. Meeting Kalas's parents and being introduced to the court of Kralis would be difficult, but I'd been through other challenges in life before. I could do this.

The spacecraft landed smoothly in the port, and I looked out of the window with interest. The dock was almost full of various spacecraft that were all so distinct that I got the impression people from planets across the galaxy had travelled to Kralis.

"Is it always this busy?" I asked, watching a group of small, imp-like creatures with mottled blue skin descend from a neighbouring craft and scurry across the port.

"Kralis is one of the busiest planets this side of the galaxy, welcoming guests from all over the universe. But there does seem to be more people than usual. I imagine word of our arrival has spread far and wide. Everyone will be eager to get a glimpse of the crown prince's betrothed."

"No pressure then," I said with an uneasy laugh.

"I'm here," Kalas said, squeezing my hand lovingly.

I inclined my head, about to press my lips to his, when a knock at the door of the spacecraft startled us both.

"That will be the escort my parents have sent," Kalas said, letting go of my hand and crossing the control room.

He strode to the main door of the spaceship, and I followed, knowing it wouldn't look good for his future bride to dawdle.

As Kalas opened the door, his eyes widened. "Savrion?" he questioned.

I glanced at who he was speaking to and saw a male Kralian who looked about the same age as Kalas. However, they were as different as Kralis was from Valeth. Savrion had long, silver-white hair, and eyes like amethysts. He was handsome, undoubtedly, though nothing compared to my beloved. He wore similar royal regalia to Kalas's clothing, though far less lavish.

"Greetings, Your Highnesses," Savrion replied with a polite bow.

"Please, come in," Kalas said, stepping aside. "I thought you'd left Kralis. You must tell me why you're here now."

Savrion smiled and entered the ship, and it was then Kalas and I noticed someone was behind him.

A female, with green skin and green hair. She was dressed in simple clothes that were plainer than Savrion's. She curtsied politely and then avoided my and Kalas's gazes.

"This is Josain. She is to be your betrothed's handmaiden," Savrion explained.

I was taken aback to hear I was to have a handmaiden. "I'm already dressed. I don't need any assistance, thank you," I said before I could remember my proper courtesies.

Savrion smiled. "I'm sure you don't, Your Highness, but the queen insisted, and Josain comes highly recommended."

I glanced at the green-skinned woman Savrion indicated to. She was petite, about my height, with pointed ears and lightly freckled skin. She looked like a woodland nymph from fairytales, and I wondered about her background.

She offered me a kind, warm smile. "It is my pleasure to meet you, Your Highness."

Being called 'Your Highness' when Kalas and I hadn't even announced our intentions to marry was weird, but I guessed it was all part of courtly life. I smiled back.

"It's good to meet you too, Josain. I look forward to getting to know you."

"I'm sure you didn't just come to introduce my betrothed to her handmaiden," Kalas said, watching Savrion closely.

There was a familiarity between the two Kralians, but it seemed strained.

"You're correct, My Prince. I have returned to my family's home, and upon my father's recommendation, I have been appointed head of your retinue."

Kalas's eyes narrowed. "I thought you and your father had fallen out?"

Savrion shrugged. "Times change. I found a reason to reconsider."

The suspicion lifted from Kalas's gaze, and a genuine smile covered his face. "Well, I won't say it isn't good to see you again, old friend."

He opened his arms, and the two Kralians embraced. I watched them closely, noticing the look of relief that flashed across Savrion's face. Had he not expected Kalas to welcome him?

"I am to escort you and your betrothed to the palace," Savrion said as he and Kalas pulled away from each other.

"Then please, lead the way," Kalas said, gesturing towards the door.

Savrion took the lead, with Kalas and me following, our arms interlinked as we exited the spacecraft.

Josain followed, keeping her head bowed, and I felt bad for the other woman. I didn't like the idea of handmaidens and servants, but I supposed that was part of Kralian tradition. I wondered if, after I'd settled in, I could speak to Kalas about it and see if having a handmaiden was really necessary.

In the meantime, I wanted Josain to know I wasn't someone to be feared. I glanced over my shoulder and offered her a friendly smile, which she returned.

Together, the four of us left the spaceport and made our way out onto the streets of Kralis. I was not surprised to see that many of the roads and buildings were made from nyxorith and other similar materials like obsidian and jet.

As we crossed the city, the streets grew wider until the area opened out into a huge marketplace, where countless people lingered, all watching us closely. There were numerous Kralians, as well as other species, including humans, those imp-like beings with the blue skin, and finally, my gaze fell on a pair of women with fiery red hair and green eyes just like mine.

I knew who they were instantly.

"Witches," I whispered in awe.

The witches noticed me too, and both raised their hands. "Greetings to the prince's betrothed," they called out.

I waved and smiled back.

Kalas inclined his head and whispered, "That is Luna and Phoebe, witches from Valeth. I will introduce you to them at the feast."

"Thank you," I said, giving his hand a grateful squeeze.

As we made our way through the market square, more and more people appeared to witness our arrival. Everyone had smiling faces, and some people called out well-wishes or greetings.

*So far, so good*, I told myself, but I knew this was only a small percentage of the people on Kralis, and certainly not anyone who'd have any power at court.

Finally, Kalas's home, the obsidian palace, came into view, and I gasped. It was more beautiful than he'd described. It was a many-turreted building, with the highest point at least a hundred metres tall. It was entirely black, but when the light caught it, it shimmered with hues of magenta, purple, and turquoise, just as nyxorith did.

It made my head spin to think that if I accepted Kalas's offer and became his wife, this would be my home.

While I was still trying to process the magnitude of it all, my gaze fell on the couple standing in the palace entranceway. Having already spoken to Kalas's parents via our psychic connection, I recognized them immediately.

The King and Queen of Kralis were breathtaking. Kalas looked like a younger version of his father, the only noticeable difference being their eye colour. While the king's were a deep purple, Kalas's were a bright amber, just like his mother's. In contrast, the queen had the same silver-white hair that Savrion had. I'd noticed as we'd made our way through the marketplace that Kralians fell into two distinct categories—those with black hair and those with white. So far, the split was almost equal, with the dark-haired Kralians being slightly more common.

The royal couple's regalia was the most splendid I had seen, with the king dressed much like Kalas, wearing a loincloth and feathered cloak. Just like Kalas had said, his mother was wearing rows upon rows of nyxorith beads that looped around her neck, spilling down onto her chest, all the way to her midriff and almost completely concealing her breasts. Like me, on her bottom half, she wore a semi-transparent black skirt, and like her husband's loincloth, it was threaded with silver and nyxorith.

Both wore circlets on their heads, again adorned with nyxorith, their onyx horns extending upwards through their hair to act almost as part of the ornamentation.

Remembering my manners at the last moment, I dropped into a low curtsy in front of them and gazed up into their sharp eyes.

Beside me, Savrion bowed, and then Kalas did the same. The king quickly dismissed Savrion, who stepped to the side, pulling Josain with him.

The king studied his son for a long time, and the gathered crowd held their breath. Finally, he grinned, exposing his pointed incisors and canine teeth.

"Welcome home, my son," he said, wrapping Kalas in a tight embrace.

I remained in my curtsy position on the ground as the king hugged his son and then gently passed Kalas over to his mother, who embraced him too.

As Kalas and his mother reunited, the king's gaze fell on me, and a small smile covered his lips.

"You are even more beautiful than the vision from Korvarith Thalun showed," he said, extending his hand to me. "Please rise, Madelyne of Earth, and welcome to Kralis."

# Chapter Thirteen
# Welcome to Kralis

I carefully took the king's hand, and as best as I could while holding it, rose to a standing position. He held me at arm's distance for a moment, studying me closely, and I took the same opportunity to take in all his features.

Up close, I noticed even more subtle differences between Kalas and his father. While both dark-haired, Kalas's features were much more delicate. Not quite feminine, but certainly less masculine than his father. Kalas had an androgynous feel to him, and with both male and female Kralians being much taller than the average human, I imagined he'd be able to present as either masculine or feminine if he wished.

I wondered what the king thought of me as his deep purple eyes met my emerald ones. Was he reminded of his own ancestor who had also been a red-haired witch?

Finally, a grin covered the king's face, and he pulled me into a tight embrace. As his arms wrapped around me, those gathered outside the Obsidian Palace erupted into cheers.

The king held me tightly against him for a moment, and I could feel his slow and steady heartbeat before he released me and gently passed me over to his wife.

I immediately bowed before Kalas's mother, once again dropping into a low curtsy.

Unlike her husband, the queen didn't immediately offer me her hand and instead watched me closely. After a moment, she reached out, but instead of helping me to stand, she wrapped a lock of my hair around her fingers and inclined her head as though presented with the most interesting thing in the universe.

A small smile covered her lips, and she said, "It's coarser than a Kralian's hair, but still very beautiful." She unravelled her fingers from my hair and offered me her hand finally. "Welcome to Kralis, Madelyne."

As I stood, the queen pulled me into an embrace, but this one felt stiffer than the king's, Kalas's mother not fully relaxing into the hug. She waited just long enough for the gathered crowd to cheer and then lowered her arms and gently manoeuvred me to Kalas.

Kalas instantly entwined his hand with mine, rubbing the pad of his thumb over the back of my hand.

The king whispered something to Savrion, who in turn whispered to Josain, and then the royal couple entered the palace.

Kalas and I followed them, and out of the corner of my eye, I saw Josain scurry away to some part on the western wing of the palace. Savrion remained outside, and I just caught the beginning of his speech as the doors closed.

From the entrance hall of the palace, the king and queen led Kalas and me to the east, and as we walked the obsidian hallway, the king turned around to make conversation.

"How was the journey from Earth?"

"Fantastic," I replied, unable to keep the smile off my face. "Thank you for sending a ship and making sure it was fully stocked with everything we needed. It was incredible being able to see some of the galaxy as Kalas and I travelled here. Though nothing we saw along the way prepared me for the magnificence of Kralis."

The king smiled, but I swore out of the corner of my eye I saw the queen roll her eyes. I didn't have a moment to dwell on it, as the king went on speaking.

"When I was Kalas's age, I visited Earth. It was some 600 years ago."

I did the quick calculation in my mind, estimating that the king had visited Earth around the 1300s. "Did you visit England, where I'm from?"

The king thought for a moment and then shook his head. "England is part of Europe, to the east of the Atlantic Ocean, correct?"

"Yes, that's right," I replied.

"Where I visited was to the west, and further south than Europe. They built massive square-topped pyramids and conducted blood sacrifices to their deities. When the humans of the time encountered me, they thought I was one of their deities come to Earth. They called me Quetzalcoatl."

I gasped. "They thought you were Quetzalcoatl?"

Ahead of us, the queen chuckled quietly. "Yes, it seems the easiest way for humans to comprehend what we are is to believe we're their deities or rulers. I've visited Earth countless times and posed as some pharaoh or countess."

My mind boggled at the implications, and I filed it away in my mind as a question to ask Kalas later, when we were alone.

We'd come to what looked very similar to a sitting room on Earth, with large comfortable seats and a low table in the middle. The king gestured that Kalas and I should sit, and Kalas led me to a loveseat to the left of the room. His parents occupied the loveseat across the table to the right.

After a moment, a Kralian wearing simple clothing, their dark hair tied in a long braid, entered the room carrying a tray laden with four obsidian goblets decorated with nyxorith gems.

The Kralian with the tray offered a drink to the king first, then the queen, and next Kalas, before finally, one goblet remained for me.

I took it with a murmur of thanks and watched Kalas closely. I knew Kralians didn't typically eat human food and hunted live prey. While Kalas had been on Earth with me, I'd only ever seen him drink water. He took a sip and let out a small sigh.

Figuring it would be rude not to take a sip myself, I brought my goblet to my lips and inhaled the aroma. It was like a good red wine, though richer and with a hint of spices. The consistency was thicker than wine too, being slightly more viscous, and for a moment, it made me think of blood.

*Surely, it's not, right?*

Aware that the king and queen were watching me closely, I took a sip. The taste was pleasant, like spiced cherries, and it coated my tongue like syrup.

"This is delightful. What is it?" I asked.

*Foolish child.* The thought flashed quickly in my mind, and I could see the queen still watching me. A blush covered my cheeks.

I hadn't accidently slipped into someone else's mind and read their thoughts for years. Either I was less in control of my abilities due to travelling halfway across the universe, or the queen had purposely projected her thoughts to me.

I glanced away as the king said, "It's a gift from Queen Celestia of Valeth. It's a drink the witches make for special celebrations. When she heard of Kalas's coming of age and your imminent arrival to Kralis, she sent an envoy with gifts and her well wishes. There is a letter for you in Kalas's chambers."

I had a letter from the Witch Queen of Valeth?

I desperately wanted to know what it said, but I figured running out of the room would look rude, and well... with the thoughts I'd picked up from the queen, I didn't want to give her any more reasons to dislike me.

Instead, I quietly sipped my drink and let Kalas take the lead with his parents.

"We intend to visit Valeth soon," Kalas said. "Maddie understandably wants to get to know other witches. I said I would introduce her to Luna and Phoebe at the feast."

The king smiled. "Quite so. And will we be announcing a wedding date later at the feast?"

Kalas glanced at me quickly, and then said, "Maddie and I have decided to have a prolonged engagement, so that we can get to know each other better, and she can adjust to life here on Kralis."

"Your father and I were married within a moon's turn of Korvarith Thalun revealing me to your father," the queen said.

"Yes, but you are from Kralis too. You didn't have a new culture to get used to. I'm sure all this is quite a shock for Maddie," the king said. "My great-grandmother had an extended engagement, and their spouse was from Valeth, so they were more familiar with our customs. Give Maddie a chance to acclimatise herself. There's no rush. We're not going anywhere."

"There are certain expectations," the queen insisted.

"Expectations be damned. I am the King of Kralis. If I say Kalas and Maddie are having an extended engagement period, then the people of court will just have to accept it."

The queen opened her mouth to speak, but the king gave her a hard glare that silenced her.

Ignoring the waves of tension radiating from his wife, the king turned to me and asked, "Did you leave family behind on Earth?"

"No one that will miss me," I admitted, and as the king continued to stare at me steadily, I elaborated. "My parents disowned me as soon as they were legally able to due to my magical abilities."

"Disgraceful. Please, rest assured, Maddie, the people of Kralis don't think the same way. All are welcome here, and we would never disown our child."

The king's words reassured me and gave me hope that if I decided I didn't want to marry Kalas and become queen, he'd be supportive. I wasn't certain the queen would feel the same, though.

She gazed at me for a long moment, but I used all the willpower I had not to read her thoughts. Over the last seven years, I'd gotten quite good at only using my telepathic abilities when I wanted to. I didn't want to know just yet if Kalas's mother disapproved of me or not. Knowing she disliked me would have been too difficult to deal with right now.

Finally, her eyes shifted from me to Kalas, and a smile covered her face. "As lovely as this is, the people of court will be waiting. We must make the official announcement of your engagement and then begin the feast. I shall summon a messenger."

From a side table beside the loveseat she was sitting on, the queen picked up a nyxorith bell and rang it. The clear, high note echoed through the room and reverberated off the walls.

After a few moments, there was a knock at the door, and the king called out, "You may enter."

When the door opened, the same Kralian that had brought the refreshments appeared and bowed to us all.

"We're ready to begin the official betrothal ceremony. Please inform the priest and gather the people of court."

The messenger bowed. "Of course, Your Majesty," he said and then hurried from the room.

"We still have some time before everyone is gathered in the ritual chamber," the king said once the messenger had left. "Which is the perfect opportunity to prepare you for the ceremony. The priest will summon the power of Korvarith Thalun to bless your union. You are both to make an offering to the sacred nyxorith pool. Then a formal exchange will be made. Maddie, as you know, the people of Kralis are able to consume the blood of others. As part of the Kralian betrothal ritual, you and Kalas are expected to exchange blood. This is usually done orally in the form of a kiss."

I didn't know why this surprised me. Kalas had drunk my blood on a few occasions, and he'd used his own blood to heal me when needed. Still, knowing it was part of the Kralian betrothal ritual was a little startling. What would happen if Kalas and I exchanged blood, but then I later decided I didn't want to marry him? Would the blood exchange act like some sort of spell and cause some harm to us if we didn't fulfil the marriage contract?

I stared at Kalas, hoping our psychic connection would allow me to share my worries with him without alerting his parents.

'It's okay, my love,' Kalas's voice spoke in my mind. 'Yes, this is a sacred ritual, similar to what you would call magic, but no harm will befall us if we don't marry.'

I want to believe what Kalas was telling me was true, and that the ritual wouldn't cause either of us harm. He said he cared about me, so surely he wouldn't let me do something dangerous, right?

"Thank you for telling me, Your Highness. I suspected we'd have to do something like this."

The king smiled. "It's good to know my son isn't an idiot and you're not completely unprepared."

The comment broke the tension in the room, and we all laughed.

"I'm afraid you won't be able to sneak away directly after the ritual. You're expected to make an appearance at the feast and get to know the people of court," the queen said.

I raised my chin and met her gaze directly. "I expected no less."

We lapsed into a slightly tense silence until the messenger returned and announced, "Everyone is gathered in the ritual chamber, and they await your arrival."

The king and queen stood and entwined their fingers. "We will enter the ritual chamber first."

# Chapter Fourteen
# Your Mother
# Hates Me

With the messenger leading the way, the king and queen left the sitting room hand in hand. As they disappeared along the corridor, Kalas stood and offered me his hand.

"You did well, my little witch," he said, his hand caressing mine as my palms pressed together.

I huffed out a breath. "Your mother hates me."

Kalas frowned. "Nonsense. She's just a little more forthright than my father."

I didn't have the heart to tell him I'd accidentally read her thoughts and heard her calling me a 'foolish child'. Right before a sacred ritual and massive feast was not the time to have that discussion.

Putting on my best smile, I gazed up at him and said, "Yeah, I'm probably being silly."

"You are." Kalas leaned in and briefly pressed his lips to mine. "You were perfect, and I'm sure they love you already, just as the rest of the people will."

Hand in hand, Kalas and I walked further along the corridor, away from the sitting room, until we arrived at a massive nyxorith archway covered with a curtain that an attendant was holding open.

I quickly peered through the archway to see the room on the other side was a massive amphitheatre full of people. Most of them were Kralians, though I easily spotted the witches from Valeth by their red hair, and some other species I didn't know the name of.

I was interested to notice Savrion sitting near the front, just one row behind the king and queen. To his left was an older Kralian with short, swept back white hair. They had an air of similarity about them that made me certain they were related, though the older Kralian was much sterner.

To the right of the older Kralian was a female I estimated to be of a similar age to Kalas's parents. She had a look on her face that told me she was smug at being seated so close to the king and queen. To her right was another female who was closer in age to Kalas. From the way she was staring intently at him, I knew there was a history between them.

*An ex-lover?* My stomach dropped as I studied her. She was beautiful. Almost as stunning as the queen, with long silver-white hair decorated with nyxorith and eyes that seemed to shift from magenta, to purple, to turquoise depending on how the light hit them.

A nasty voice at the back of my mind that sounded disturbingly like a mixture of my mother and the queen asked, "Why didn't Korvarith Thalun choose her to be Kalas's intended bride?"

I glanced at Kalas, who wasn't even looking at the beautiful woman seated behind his parents and instead was watching me closely.

A small smile curled his lips, and through our psychic connection, he asked, *'Are you okay, invarali taleni?'*

I stroked my thumb over his and gave him a genuine smile. *'I am now.'*

*'Let's do this,'* he said and then took a step through the archway.

I could feel hundreds of pairs of eyes watching us as we walked through the archway and crossed the platform until we stood in front of a massive reflective pool, beside which stood an old male Kralian. I assumed from the way he was dressed he was the priest the king had spoken of.

He gestured that Kalas and I should stand to his left, and then the king and queen rose to stand to the right of the priest.

He gave us all a brief nod of recognition before lifting his gaze and addressing the room as a whole.

"Faithful of Korvarith Thalun, it is wonderful to see you all gathered here. Before you is Crown Prince Kalas, returned safely from his journey to Earth. With him, the one The Twilight Crow has chosen as the prince's fated mate, the Earth witch, Madelyne Grant."

The priest paused briefly, and there was applause from those gathered on the stone benches around the amphitheatre. I caught a glimpse of Josain, who was sitting near the witches, and was heartened to see her clapping vigorously.

It seemed I had at least one ally here at court.

In fact, the only people who didn't look happy with the priest's announcement were the older Kralian with the swept back hair, his female companion, and the younger female Kralian to her right.

The one I assumed was an ex-lover of Kalas had stopped looking at him and was now glaring at me with more venom than a black mamba.

I stared right back, forcing a smile onto my lips, and only gazed away when the priest began speaking again.

"With the blessing of Korvarith Thalun, Crown Prince Kalas and his intended bride, Madelyne, will now be bound in starlight."

The priest reached into a small pouch attached to his belt and withdrew a handful of nyxorith, which he divided between Kalas and me. Next, the priest handed Kalas a nyxorith blade.

*Just copy what I do,*' Kalas's voice spoke into my mind.

He crushed the precious gems in his palm until they were dust and then sprinkled the dust into the reflective pool we were standing in front of.

I did the same, squeezing my palm tightly closed around the nuggets of nyxorith and infusing my fist with a little of my magical abilities to help me crush them. When I felt the dust form in my palm, I opened my hand and sprinkled the debris into the reflective pool, just as Kalas had.

Next, Kalas took the blade and slashed it across his left palm, drawing a pool of blood that looked like an oil slick on water. He allowed the blood to flow from his hand into the pool, and then his Kralian abilities healed the wound.

He handed the blade to me, and I copied his actions, wincing as the impossibly sharp knife sliced into my skin. I allowed my blood to flow, and it ran down my arm as it fell into the pool.

I turned to Kalas, whose fingertips glistened with his own blood, and he smoothed them over my palm, healing the cut instantly.

I opened my mouth to ask what we were expected to do next when a blinding white light erupted from the pool and filled the room.

I could see nothing, and the air had grown thick, like in the moment before a storm. The only thing that stopped me from freaking out was Kalas's reassuring presence next to me.

Slowly, my eyes adjusted to the brightness, and I was able to make out a hazy figure in the distance. Someone stood before me, taller than any Kralian I had encountered. They were completely naked but covered in feathers. Their legs were the legs of a bird, and their arms were wide, magnificent wings.

The being before me had a raven's head, and it opened its beak wide. As it did, a piercing cry that sounded like the call of a raptor filled the air. The light intensified again, and when my vision returned, the raven-headed being was gone, and I could see the amphitheatre clearly again.

*What the hell?*

I glanced at Kalas, but his expression was impassive. Looking around, everyone gathered seemed unperturbed, and I didn't know if they'd seen the figure or just the blinding light.

"Praise be to The Twilight Crow, whose call signifies that their blessing has been given to this union," the priest said to all gathered. "All that remains is for the union to be bound."

I didn't have time to process the priest's words, as Kalas grasped my waist and tugged me flush against his body.

*'Now we exchange blood,'* he said through our psychic link. *'Kiss me, and I will bite my tongue, and then yours. Let the blood mingle and then swallow it.'*

Kalas gazed down into my eyes, and I knew he wouldn't begin with blood exchange without my consent. This was my last chance to back out if I wanted to.

I wasn't sure what would happen if I declined. Would the raven-headed figure appear and smite me? Would the king and queen banish me from Kralis? If they did, would Kalas leave his family to come with me?

I stared back, all the questions passing from my mind to his in an instant.

*'I am always yours, no matter what. The choice is yours.'*

Knowing I had the freedom to choose, that the exchange of blood would have no negative ramifications and only served as an official signal of our engagement, I stood on my tiptoes and pressed my lips to Kalas's.

Time seemed to move in slow motion as Kalas raised his hands to cup my head, his claws gently scratching the base of my skull. I felt his tongue slide into my mouth, and then the taste of his blood, followed by sharp pin pricks to my own tongue as his fangs pierced the organ.

As our mouths moved together, it was easy to forget that we were in a room full of people, with his parents and a priest standing just feet away.

Despite my worries, this felt right. This was where I was meant to be. With Kalas by my side, nothing bad could happen. I wanted this. I wanted us. I wanted the time and freedom for us to get to know each other better and eventually plan our wedding.

Someday, I wanted to be Kalas's queen.

I felt Kalas's erection poking my thigh, and I stifled a giggle.

*'Behave,'* I said through our psychic connection.

*'How can I when I know exactly how good you taste?'*

He nipped my tongue again, and then I tasted his blood mixing with my own. I swallowed, relishing the thought that we were united in this way. I couldn't wait to unite with him in other ways too.

The sound of the priest clearing his throat finally caused us to break apart, and when I did, both Kalas and I were flushed.

Over Kalas's shoulder, I spotted the king, who was smirking, and the queen, who was scowling.

Quickly drawing the attention away from us, the king stepped forward and addressed the room. "Kalas and Maddie have informed me that they wish to take a long engagement to allow Maddie the chance to get used to life here on Kralis. A date for their wedding will be announced in due course. Now, please join us in the great hall for feasting and celebration."

Everyone in the room rose to their feet and started applauding, and I was surprised when some people called out.

"Korvarith Thalun's blessing to Crown Prince Kalas and Princess Consort Madelyne," someone shouted.

Slowly, those gathered in the room slowly filed out until only Kalas and I remained, along with the king and queen, and the priest.

The priest pressed his palms together and bowed to us. "Korvarith Thalun's blessing to you," he said, and then moved to the other side of the once-more reflective pool.

The king and queen left the amphitheatre first, but Kalas and I lingered for a moment, Kalas inclining his head to kiss me again.

"Are you okay?" he whispered.

Before I could respond, a near-hysterical giggle escaped my lips. "I think so. I could do with some food and wine, though."

"Come, then. Let's officially introduce Princess Madelyne to the people of Kralis."

Holding my hand firmly, Kalas led me from the amphitheatre, through the corridors of the obsidian palace,until we were almost at the entrance hall again. There, he turned east, and down a short walkway until we came to a massive ballroom, where everyone who'd been at the ritual was now gathered.

At the far end of the ballroom was a raised dais, with regal chairs the king and queen were seated on. To the left were two additional seats, which I assumed were for Kalas and me.

The room was dotted with tables and chairs, and that was where everyone else from the ritual chamber was gathered, splitting into smaller groups. I spotted Savrion sitting with the older Kralian I assumed was his relative, as well as the older female Kralian and the one I thought was Kalas's ex-lover.

"Who is Savrion sitting with?" I whispered to Kalas as we made our way across the room.

"His father, Lord Darakon, the Lady Voritha, and her daughter, Thalyn," Kalas whispered back, nothing in his tone indicating his feelings towards any of them.

As we passed their table, I felt Thalyn's venomous glare on me again.

# Chapter Fifteen
# You Can Do This

I did my best to keep my head held high as Kalas and I approached the royal table. The king smiled broadly, an expression I had already become accustomed to seeing on his face. The queen looked a little more reserved, though I was relieved to see she didn't seem unhappy. Kalas bowed and I curtsied as we stepped onto the royal dais, earning a nod from the king, while the queen barely inclined her head in recognition.

We took our places at the royal table, and I hadn't even had a moment to adjust my clothing when a server approached carrying a tray holding goblets. As when we'd spoken with the king and queen in their sitting room, we were served spiced cherry wine from Valeth. I wondered, were the others gathered drinking the same? Or was this a treat reserved for royalty only?

As I sipped my drink, the king stood, raising his goblet. "I'd like everyone to join me in toasting the happy couple, Crown Prince Kalas and his consort, who will henceforth be known as Princess Consort Madelyne."

"To Crown Prince Kalas and Princess Consort Madelyne," those gathered around the room said, all raising their own glasses and goblets in toast.

I gazed back, trying to familiarise myself with the faces of the Kralian court. It was easy to recognize the witches of Valeth due to their hair, and I'd already been introduced to Savrion. Despite their differing hairstyles, Savrion and his father were similar enough in appearance that there was no doubt they were related. Though Savrion had softer, friendlier features than Lord Darakon. Something about the way the older Kralian had gazed at me with equal parts contempt and lechery made me uncomfortable. Beside him, Lady Voritha looked equally unimpressed, and her daughter, Thalyn, continued to glare at me like I'd murdered her best friend.

These would be people I'd have to win to my side. I'd have to gain their approval, and that would begin this evening by making an extra effort with them.

Many of those sitting at the lower tables smiled up at me, their expressions holding nothing but curiosity and kindness. I'd have to make sure to speak to these people too; they could be useful allies if my being Kalas's betrothed became a problem in court.

It was dizzying trying to keep up with it all, and I longed to be alone with Kalas. I wanted him to wrap me in his arms and keep me safe from everything. I had thought leaving Earth would make life easier, and in some respects, it had. I was no longer being chased by witch hunters, but I had traded one set of problems for another.

I could only hope that whatever animosity some courtiers had towards me was short-lived and non-lethal.

*You haven't even been here for twenty-four hours. It will take time to get used to this new way of life. But it won't be forever.*

I remembered Kalas's promise that once we'd seen to our royal obligations, we'd be free to take a step back, perhaps even visit Valeth and spend quality time getting to know each other before we announced an official wedding date. With that thought firmly in mind, I laid my hand on Kalas's arm, which was resting on the table, and raised my head higher.

I was here to stay. I wanted to be with Kalas and all that entailed. If anyone had a problem with that, they'd find I wasn't some pushover to be easily cowed.

After the king's toast, serving platters were brought out, and I was unsurprised to see the menu heavily featured meat, especially boar, in thick, rich sauces that could almost have been mistaken for blood.

The queen took a few delicate bites of her meat, but she barely swallowed a mouthful, and I assumed her actions were more for show than anything else.

The meal was a little too rich for my tastes, but I ate what I could, focusing on the freshly roasted vegetables.

I was delighted when the main course was followed by dessert. I didn't know if Kalas had told the king to prepare something especially for me or if it was a coincidence, but I gasped as the server presented me with a huge slice of Black Forest gateau.

"My favourite!" I took the fork and dug in with relish.

Beside me, Kalas gave me a knowing smile.

*'So, you did arrange this especially,'* I said through our psychic link, while my mouth was full of rich, chocolatey cake and tart cherries.

*'For you, my little witch, I would move the stars. Making sure the baker knew to prepare this recipe from Earth was nothing.'*

I squeezed Kalas's hand, the dessert tasting all the sweeter knowing he'd arranged it especially for me.

There was a short interlude after the dessert plates were cleared, and then light music filled the hall. All around the room, guests got to their feet and coupled off to dance.

"I would very much like to dance with you," Kalas said, getting to his feet. "But first, it is expected that I introduce you to the people of court. If I may?"

He offered me his hand, which I readily took. I wanted to dance too but knew what was expected of me, and so I did as he asked.

I wasn't surprised when the first table we approached was that of Lord Darakon. He was obviously an important member of the court.

"My Lord Darakon, it is good to see you," Kalas said, bowing to the older Kralian. "And I am pleased to learn you and Savrion have reconciled."

The smile Lord Darakon gave Kalas was almost a sneer. "Yes, my son has finally come to his senses."

Lord Darakon's eyes drifted to me, and he studied me closely. His gaze was intense, and if I hadn't known better, I would have thought he was trying to probe my mind. Even without psychic abilities, his stare made me feel vulnerable and like I was about to be judged for a crime I hadn't committed.

Finally, he extended his hand to me. "Ah, the Earthling. I haven't had the pleasure of meeting one of your kind before."

The hatred radiating from him was palpable, and I almost flinched away. But I'd dealt with people like Lord Darakon, including my own parents. People who passed judgement on you simply because of the circumstances of your birth before even trying to get to know you.

I plastered a fake smile on my face, took Lord Darakon's hand, curtsied politely, and said, "It's a pleasure to meet you, My Lord."

Lord Darakon kept hold of my hand only for as long as it wouldn't seem rude to dismiss me before turning away to join the conversation of a different group.

As his father moved away, Savrion gave Kalas and me an uneasy, apologetic smile. "Please, don't let my father's cool welcome concern you. He isn't the type for small talk."

"No, he never was," Kalas agreed, his demeanour changing as he and Savrion embraced. "But please, tell me about your return to Kralis. We didn't get a chance to properly catch up before the ceremony."

Savrion shrugged. "There isn't much to tell. It was time to come home."

My gaze danced between the two Kralians, wondering what the history was between them.

Sensing my curiosity, Kalas said, "Savrion is one of my oldest friends. We played together as children. We were as close as brothers until Savrion's mother unfortunately passed away. After Lady Elara's death, Lord Darakon fell into a deep depression and withdrew from court. He and Savrion fell out over something, and Savrion left Kralis."

"I'm sorry to hear you lost your mother," I told Savrion, genuinely sad for him. In my own way, I had lost my parents too, and I knew how difficult that was.

"Thank you, Your Highness." Savrion offered me a small, sad smile. "And congratulations on your betrothal. I hope you and Crown Prince Kalas will be very happy together."

I took Kalas's hand, entwined our fingers together, and smiled at Savrion. "We are."

Savrion's smile brightened. "I'll leave you to greet the rest of your guests, but no doubt we will be seeing a lot of each other around court."

"You can count on it," Kalas said, reaching out to embrace Savrion for a second time.

From Savrion, Kalas and I moved onto Lady Voritha and her daughter, Thalyn. Both women regarded me coldly, though not with the same hostility as Lord Darakon had.

"It's a pleasure to see you, Lady Voritha," Kalas said, bowing. "And Thalyn, you're looking well. Please allow me to introduce my betrothed, Princess Consort, Madelyne."

I curtsied and smiled at Lady Voritha and Thalyn.

Lady Voritha extended her hand to me. "An honour to meet you, Your Highness. I've not met an Earthling before. Are they all as interesting as you are?"

The way she said *interesting* sounded distinctly like an insult and reminded me of the way people on Earth spoke about witches when they wanted to make it clear they were offended by the witch's presence without being outright rude.

I felt the heat rise up in my cheeks, and I quickly replied, "All Earthlings vary, like you see with the people here on Kralis."

"Hmm, quite so," Lady Voritha replied, turning her head. "I serve as a lady-in-waiting to Queen Seraphina. I hope to expect the same courtesy from you in regard to my daughter, Thalyn."

"Yes, of course," I answered without thinking.

"Excellent. Well, we will give you a few days to 'settle in' and then I expect an invitation to join you in your parlour for refreshments."

"Of course," I said again, making promises I was hesitant to keep.

Lady Voritha stepped away without another word, joining with Lord Darakon and the group he was speaking to.

Only Thalyn remained, and she continued to stare at me ferociously.

"Thalyn, it is good to see you," Kalas said stiffly. "I hope there are... erm... given the circumstances. I'm sure you understand."

I didn't need magical abilities to know the smile Thalyn gave Kalas was completely fake. In an equally phony saccharine sweet voice, she said, "Of course not. The word of Korvarith Thalun is law, after all."

I offered my hand to Thalyn, who looked as though taking it greatly pained her, though her mouth remained locked in the fake smile. "It's a pleasure to meet you, Your Highness."

"Likewise," I replied, trying to inject some warmth into my tone and show this woman she had no reason to hate me.

Thalyn's hand barely touched mine before she pulled it away and stalked off to join her mother.

*'What was that about?'* I asked Kalas through our psychic link.

*'Thalyn and I used to be lovers,'* Kalas admitted.

*I knew it!* Only an ex would behave towards me the way Thalyn had.

*'And let me guess, she hoped Korvarith Thalun would choose her to be your consort?'*

Kalas shrugged helplessly. *'When we were together, she always understood it might not be forever, that my fated mate would be chosen for me by Korvarith Thalun. But, well, I guess the reality is harder for her to accept.'*

I felt bad for Thalyn. She hadn't asked for any of this, and for all I knew, she might still be in love with Kalas. Did he still love her? Would he want to marry her instead if he had the choice?

'Invarali taleni, you are the one Korvarith Thalun chose for me. You are the one I will marry. That is all that matters.'

Kalas's response didn't answer my question, but I chose not to push the issue. In the middle of a royal ball was not the right time to have that sort of conversation. Plus, I'd only just arrived on Kralis. Perhaps after we'd both had time to settle in, Kalas would be more open about his feeling towards me.

# Chapter Sixteen
# A Letter From
# Queen Celestia

I was pleased when the next people we approached were Luna and Phoebe, the witches from Valeth. Looking at them was like seeing a long-lost relative for the first time, and I was struck by the similarities between the three of us.

"Your Highness, it's a pleasure to meet you," Luna said, offering me her hand. She was the slightly taller of the two, with deep green almond-shaped eyes. I estimated her age to be early thirties.

"It's a pleasure to meet you too. Kalas has told me so much about Valeth, and I can't wait to visit. I also want to thank you for the gifted cherry wine. It's delicious."

Phoebe, who was shorter and curvier than Luna, with downturned seafoam-green eyes, offered me her hand. "Believe us, Your Highness, the pleasure is ours. For a witch to be chosen as the crown prince's fated mate is a great honour. The people of Valeth remember the Late Royal Consort Aster fondly."

I glanced at Kalas, who answered my question. "The Royal Consort Aster was the partner of my great-grandmother, Branwynn. I will show you pictures of them later, when we retire to my chambers."

I smiled. "I can't wait to see."

"We have much to tell you about Valeth and Earth's witches' connection to our home," Luna went on. "Queen Celestia has requested that you speak with her directly."

Given that the king had already mentioned I had a letter from Queen Celestia, this news didn't surprise me.

"And I would be delighted to meet with her. Kalas and I plan to visit Valeth as soon as we're able. I'm sure you understand we have many obligations to attend to first."

"Of course, Your Highness," Phoebe said, with a small smile of understanding. "We will remain here on Kralis until you're ready to travel and then act as your escort and guides to Valeth."

"I look forward to it. I'm excited to learn more about Valeth and its people. You mentioned a connection to the witches of Earth. Am I right in guessing that your Deity Vesper is the same Moon Mother the witches on Earth worship?"

Luna grinned. "Yes, you're correct. I haven't visited Earth for a long time, so I was unsure if they still paid tribute to Vesper. But that's not the only connection. The people of Valeth travelled far and wide across the universe, and it's our belief that some eventually came to settle on Earth. On Valeth, it's a popular theory that the witches of Earth are the descendants of those who left Valeth."

My eyes widened. What Luna told me made a lot of sense, especially considering our similarities. "That's amazing. Is there any way to confirm this?"

"Yes. We have a ritual on Valeth that can be undertaken to trace your bloodline. We will even be able to discern which witch you descended from, and you'd be welcome to review the old record books at length."

"I can't wait. I'll make it my priority to visit as soon as possible. Where will I find you both when I'm ready to visit Valeth?"

"We have a house west of the marketplace, not far from where the transformation grounds are. Prince Kalas will know the place."

"I do indeed," Kalas agreed.

"I'd love to talk with you all night, but duty calls," I said, extending my hand to Luna. I was surprised when, instead, she pulled me into an embrace.

"Blessings of the Moon Mother to you and the crown prince," she said, pressing her lips to my cheek.

"Blessings of the Moon Mother to you too," I replied.

After embracing Luna, I then embraced Phoebe, and we exchanged the same farewell. As Kalas and I stepped away from the witches, I felt lighter. I was not only excited to visit Valeth and find out about my ancestry, but it seemed, if I didn't take to life on Kralis, there might very well be a place for me on Valeth. I could finally live alongside others like me without fear of persecution.

Hours passed as Kalas and I toured the great hall, visiting with every guest in attendance. In addition to the Kralians and witches, I met some Earthlings who had travelled here, either from other planets, or due to meeting a Kralian on Earth Though, the number of Kralians who married Earthlings was low, with the percentage estimated at around five.

Finally, we had spoken to everyone in attendance. I was pleased to find that the majority of guests seemed either happy or indifferent to my and Kalas's betrothal. While there were a few Kralians who were cold towards me and barely spoke to me and Kalas, none were as openly hostile as Lord Darakon.

The behaviour of Savrion's father continued to baffle me. Was he simply some older Kralian, stuck in his ways, who didn't care much for anyone and his disdain for humanity had been exacerbated by the passing of his wife? Or was there more to his dislike of me?

How to win Lord Darakon's endorsement still eluded me. I only hoped Savrion might have some useful information about his father he could share. He seemed close with Kalas, and I got the distinct impression we could trust him.

Lady Voritha and Thalyn's attitudes towards me had an obvious cause—Thalyn's previous relationship with Kalas. I just wasn't sure if she still had feelings for him. Or was the mother and daughter's dislike of me caused by the fact they were social climbers who were disappointed at Thalyn not being chosen as Kalas's fated mate?

I hoped that whatever feelings Kalas and Thalyn had for each other were in the past and that Lady Voritha wasn't still hoping her daughter might someday become queen consort. It would be nice to make genuine friends on Kralis. But at this early stage, and not knowing anyone properly, I couldn't take anything for granted. Either way, I knew I'd have to be careful around them.

Having spoken to all the guests, Kalas and I were then free to join the others who were dancing. The Kralian music was similar to Earth's ballroom waltzes, with a variety of string instruments and piano melodies.

I'd never been to a formal dance before, but it was easy to follow Kalas's lead as he wrapped one arm around my waist, and with the other, held our hands out extended. My unoccupied hand rested on his shoulder, brushing the feathers of his cloak.

Even though we were surrounded by people, it was easy to lose myself as I stared up into his amber eyes. Especially as we could still communicate without words.

*'You did well, my little witch, as I knew you would,'* he said through our psychic bond.

*'I was worried at first everyone hated me,'* I replied.

Kalas's hand caressed the exposed flesh on my waist, and he scratched the skin lightly with his claws. *'If anyone hates you, they will have to face me.'*

His words reassured me a little, but I couldn't help asking, *'Even your own parents?'*

*'I know my father, and it's clear he approves of you. My mother is just a little stuck in her ways. She wasn't born on this side of Kralis, and her being chosen as my father's fated mate was contested by some. Perhaps she's worried about history repeating itself. Or perhaps she's just being over-protective. Either way, I'm sure she will come around. She won't defy the word of Korvarith Thalun.'*

*'Do you think anyone would?'* I questioned, thinking immediately of Lord Darakon.

*'They would be foolish to. Doing so would be high treason and mean their execution.'*

Kalas's words didn't entirely ease my concerns. What if I decided I didn't want to marry him after all? He said he'd let me choose, but would that mean I was going against Korvarith Thalun? I wasn't Kralian, and They weren't my deity so would I be directly going against Them if I walked away, and as such, be executed?

Once again, it didn't feel an appropriate time to raise my concerns. I needed some space to think before I broached the subject.

After dancing with Kalas, his father stepped in to dance with me, while Kalas danced with his mother.

The king was in high spirits as we danced, asking me how I was enjoying my first night on Kralis and checking if everything was to my liking.

"Everything is wonderful, thank you. And special thanks for the dessert. Kalas told me he arranged it especially, and I imagine he had to get your approval."

King Eldarion chuckled. "Yes, he contacted me while you were travelling here. He said he wanted something to help you feel at home."

I beamed in response. "He is a good man. And very crafty."

"It is obvious my son is besotted with you. You will make each other very happy. And hopefully, in the years to come, produce lots of beautiful fire-haired grandchildren for the queen and I to fuss over."

I flushed discussing such things with my future father-in-law, but I humoured him and said, "In time. We have to marry first. And before then, I intend to visit Valeth."

"Yes, I thought you might. Luna tells me there is some possibility you're descended from the witches there."

"That's right. She told me there's a ritual I can undertake to find out for certain. I very much want to know who my ancestors were. When my abilities manifested, my parents didn't approve and kicked me out of the house once I came of age. I don't have any other family."

"You have Kalas, and by extension, the queen and I," King Eldarion insisted. "But I understand your desire to know where you came from. History is very important to the Kralians too."

When I finished dancing with the king, Savrion asked me to dance, and I readily accepted, eager to get to know Kalas's friend better and learn more about what Kalas had been like as a child.

"So, you and Kalas grew up together?"

"That's right. My father was close to the king and often visited to advise him on various matters, and my mother was one of the queen's ladies-in-waiting, meaning I was left to play with the prince. Neither of us had siblings, and due to our status, we weren't allowed to play with just anyone."

"You say your father was close to the king. Is he still, or did something happen?"

Savrion shrugged. "Lots happened, most importantly, my mother's death."

"I'm sorry. That must have been very hard for both of you."

Savrion shook his head. "You have no idea. It changed my father, and not for the better."

"But you've reconciled now, right? You said you were living with him again."

"All is not as it seems, Your Highness, and you'd do well to remember that," Savrion replied.

I filed that piece of information away for later, intending to discuss it with Kalas once we were alone.

As Savrion and I danced, I noticed he kept staring over my shoulder, as though looking for someone.

"Do you wish I was someone else?" I teased.

Savrion flushed, his pale skin taking on a lilac hue that matched his brows. "Am I that obvious?"

"Only a little." I laughed lightly, and Savrion smiled. "Who do you wish was here in my place?"

Savrion shook his head. "It's best I don't speak of such things. But yes, there is someone I wish I was dancing with. Not that you're not an excellent dance partner."

"But I'm not the one you long for. I understand. I hope you get a chance to dance with them before the night ends."

When Savrion and I parted ways, I was reunited with Kalas. As we had during our first dance, we said nothing, and instead spoke with our minds.

*'How was dancing with Thalyn?'* I asked.

*'Awkward. The last time we saw each other was before my coming-of-age ceremony. Before Korvarith Thalun showed you to me.'*

*'Did you love her?'*

*'In my own way, yes. But this was some time ago now and we both knew our relationship might not be forever. In the lead up to my coming-of-age ceremony, I spoke to her about our previous relationship, and she seemed to understand it was all in the past. Besides, dancing with her just now, after having held you in my arms made me realise the feelings I had for her pale in comparison to what I feel for you.'*

Kalas's words warmed my heart. *'That's good, because there is no one else I would rather be dancing with.'*

*'Even Savrion?'* Kalas teased. *'You seemed to be getting along well.'*

'*We did, but even if I were interested in Savrion, his heart belongs to another,*' I said, which had Kalas raising a brow in questioning. '*We will speculate on that in a minute. First, I need to tell you what else Savrion said to me. He warned me that all is not as it seems and that I'd do well to remember that. What do you think he meant? Do you think it's to do with his father?*'

'*Perhaps. Lord Darakon voiced his disapproval when you were revealed as my fated mate and my father had him removed from the ritual chamber.*'

'*That's something to keep an eye on.*'

'*I already told you, anyone, even Lord Darakon, would be foolish to try anything. A move against you is a move against the royal family.*'

I wanted to believe Kalas that the threat of losing his life would be enough to keep Lord Darakon in line, but in the back of my mind, I couldn't shake Savrion's warning. All was not as it seemed.

# Chapter Seventeen
# The Royal Portrait

The dancing and celebrations went on well into the night, and I was exhausted when the great hall finally started to empty of guests.

As much as I wanted Kalas to show me more of the obsidian palace and Kralis, I was too tired to contemplate doing anything else. All I wanted was to retire to our quarters in peace.

After all the guests had left, Kalas and I walked in companionable silence with the king and queen through the obsidian palace, this time heading to the opposite wing from where the great hall was located.

There was a wall constructed entirely out of nyxorith, with a massive silver door in the centre and an attendant guarding the entrance way. I assumed the door led to the royal quarters.

"Your Majesties," the attendant said, bowing as the king and queen approached.

"Good evening, Taeral," the king replied as Taeral opened the door to us.

Through the door was a long hallway lined with a rich, thick carpet, and on the wall opposite the entrance was a galley wall of portraits. I instantly recognized the king and queen, as well as Kalas. I assumed the other pictures were the previous monarchs of Kralis.

"This is my grandparents," Kalas said, pointing to slightly smaller portraits below the ones of his mother and father. The king's father looked exactly like him, and the king's mother had been another dark-haired Kralian with eyes that were almost black.

The dark colouring continued through the generations as Kalas pointed out his great-grandmother, who also looked a lot like the king, only with feminine features.

What really caught my eye was the late Queen Branwynn's partner, Aster. They were dressed in the Kralian style, with a feathered cape, rows upon rows of nyxorith, and an onyx circlet on their head. They were the most androgynous of the royal portraits, and I guessed they could have presented as either gender if they chose. But what *really* stuck me about them was how similar they looked to me.

It was almost like looking in a mirror. Aster's hair was shorter than mine, reaching to their shoulders, where mine flowed down to my mid-back. But it was the exact same shade of burnt orange and formed in the same voluminous curls. Additionally, our eyes were identical shades of forest green. I looked more similar to Aster than I did my own mother.

I reached out, stroking the picture. "It can't be," I whispered in awe.

As my fingertips touched the image, my mind filled with visions.

A young Aster of around three, on Valeth, playing happily with two others who looked almost identical to them, the only difference being their ages. Aster was the youngest of the three, and the oldest appeared to be about twelve in the visions. From their appearance, they could only be siblings.

The vision quickly changed, showing the trio of siblings, only older this time. The oldest now appeared to be in their early twenties, Aster was around eleven, and their middle sibling was about fourteen or fifteen.

It was the oldest sibling's wedding, and she looked resplendent in a silver gown embroidered with moon and star symbols. On her head, she wore a magnificent crown that seemed to be made of opals and moonstones.

Before I could get a chance to see who the oldest sibling was marrying, the vision changed. Aster and their older sibling were hugging the middle one, who was wrapped in a travelling cloak that looked to be woven from the galaxy itself.

"You have your place as queen," the middle sibling said to their older sibling, before saying to Aster, "and soon, you will marry Branwynn and move to Kralis. Vesper told me that my destiny is on Earth."

I pulled my hand away with a gasp to find Kalas and the king and queen all staring at me with concern.

"Are you okay, invarali taleni?" Kalas asked, his hands coming up to hold my face as his eyes scanned my body.

"When I touched that portrait of Aster, I saw psychic visions of them with their siblings. One was the Queen of Valeth, and the other was going to Earth. Do you know anything about these witches?"

"Aster was before my time," Kalas said. "But from what I remember in the history books, they were indeed the youngest of three. I don't remember what happened to the other two, though. Do you, Father?"

"Aster's oldest sister was Queen Andromeda, the ancestor of the current queen, Celestia. I don't recall what happened to their other sibling. We might have records of them, and if not, Luna and Phoebe certainly will."

"In the visions, they spoke of going to Earth. I think they might be *my* ancestor," I said, slowly piecing the visions together.

Kalas's eyes widened as realisation dawned on him. "That would mean we share a common ancestor, Aster's parents. Which might be why Korvarith Thalun chose you as my fated mate. Kralis and Valeth are considered two sides of the same coin. They're called twin planets."

"Yes, I can understand why. They're almost like yin-and-yang," I said, wishing my phone worked on Kralis so I could access the internet and show Kalas the Chinese symbol. "Do you have a library? Maybe there are books there that will give me more information."

Kalas chuckled. "The private royal library is just along this hallway, past our chambers. But weren't you complaining a moment ago about how tired you are?"

"That was before I touched Aster's portrait and had that vision. Don't you think it's weird how much I look like them?" I gestured back to the royal portrait.

Kalas studied it for a moment then smiled. "You do. I never considered it before, but yes, you look very much alike."

"And Aster's siblings in the vision looked the same too. If it weren't for their age differences, I would have assumed they were triplets."

"We will visit Luna and Phoebe tomorrow, and you can ask them about it," Kalas suggested.

"Actually," the queen began, "I promised that we would meet with Lady Voritha and Thalyn. As I'm sure you're aware, Lady Voritha is one of my closest friends. I thought perhaps you and Thalyn could become friends."

I didn't know what I was more frustrated by. That the queen had made arrangements for us both without asking me first, or that she was suggesting I befriend her son's ex-lover. Yes, I had already thought about befriending Thalyn, but I wanted the choice to be mine. I suppose having decisions made for me was all part and parcel of being the crown prince's betrothed, though.

Plastering a smile on my face, I replied, "Of course, Your Highness."

"Meeting with Lady Voritha and Thalyn shouldn't take all day. We can always visit Luna and Phoebe afterwards," Kalas said.

"I hope so," I replied, eager to get to know the witches.

There was so much I wanted to do. Kalas had promised to take me flying, and I was curious to search through the royal library, but I feared there would be other royal duties I'd need to attend to first.

"We will see you both in the morning," the king said, and I could tell by the way his eyes were drooping that he was eager to get to bed too. I was exhausted, so I could hardly imagine how he felt.

"Goodnight, Father," Kalas said, and the father and son embraced.

After letting Kalas go, the king pulled me into an embrace too. "Goodnight, aelrion vethara."

Having psychically learned the language of Kralis from Kalas, I instantly understood the king's meaning—cherished daughter—and warmth spread through me.

"Goodnight, aelrion thalor," I replied, which caused the king's eyes to widen, and then he beamed at me and hugged me tighter.

After the royal couple departed to their rooms, Kalas and I continued along the hallway, past a bathing room and dressing room, until we came to what had previously been Kalas's quarters but would now be our shared chambers.

As we walked through the door, I was a little startled to find Josain waiting beside the doorway.

She bowed to us and said, "Greetings, Your Highnesses. I am here to assist the princess consort in getting ready for bed."

I was about to open my mouth and tell Josain that it was fine, and that I could change for bed myself, but Kalas looked at me intently. Even without our psychic bond, I didn't need telling. To refuse Josain's offer would be seen as rude. Letting someone wait on me like this felt completely contradictory to my nature, but it was what was expected.

I followed Josain out of the room and along the hallway to my and Kalas's bathing quarters. There was a massive tub that water from a vessel affixed to the wall flowed from, as well as a slightly smaller basin. I couldn't see a toilet, but I imagined there would be one hidden away somewhere. There was also a vanity table with a large mirror and a cushioned seat. It was to this vanity table that Josain led me.

"Would Your Highness like me to braid and wrap your hair for sleep?" Josain offered.

I wasn't sure if I could trust Josain yet. For all I knew, she had been appointed my handmaiden so she could spy on me for the queen.

With this in mind, I decided it was best to follow tradition, at least for the time being. "Thank you. That would be greatly appreciated."

Josain moved in closer, gently untangling my curls before separating my hair into smaller sections so she could braid it. As she worked on my hair, I noticed a nyxorith feather pendant around her neck that looked oddly familiar. Had someone at the ball been wearing the same necklace?

"I love your necklace," I said as Josain wrapped my braids in strands of silk. "Where did you get it from?"

Colour flushed across Josain's green cheeks. "Someone I care about deeply gave it to me."

Eager to know Josain better to discover if she was trustworthy, I asked "Anyone I might know?"

The way Josain's blush intensified told me that it was.

"I must not speak of it, Your Highness," she said quickly.

"I'm sorry. I shouldn't have pried."

Josian shook her head. "No, it's not that." She looked around nervously, as though anyone could be hidden in the bathroom and listening in. "But our relationship is *unusual*, and all isn't as it seems in the obsidian palace."

I frowned. Josain was the second person who had given me that warning. What did she and Savrion know that I didn't?

Others with my abilities might have been tempted to read Josain's thoughts, but the idea repulsed me.

I wanted Josain to genuinely like and trust me, so instead, I asked, "I don't know much about the universe and other solar systems, only what Kalas told me. But you're not from the Throvani Ethrionth Star System, are you?"

I'd never seen anyone from either Kralis or Valeth with green skin. I knew Valoriani Ealuna was inhabited only by animals. From everything Kalas had told me, it seemed unlikely that someone from Auroriath would be serving in the Kralian royal court.

"No, I'm not. My parents were born on the planet Sylvethia, which was sadly destroyed by the Auroriathians before I was born. I grew up in an orphanage on Naltariana, a planet in another star system that welcomes all people from across the universe."

"I'm sorry to hear that Sylvethia was destroyed. From what Kalas has told me, the people from Auroriath are very war-like. He said Kralis and Valeth have been fortunate to avoid conflict with them."

"That's right, Your Highness. Though Kralis and Valeth are smaller planets, and the Auroriathians are known for preying on those that seemed lesser than them, Kralis and Valeth are often united. Like two sides of the same coin, some might say."

I smiled, Josain's comment almost exactly the same as what I'd said to Kalas earlier. "Yes, I thought the same. Are you familiar with the Earth concept of yin-and-yang?"

"I am. I was an avid reader back on Naltariana. I've never had very much of anything, but one thing that costs nothing is knowledge."

I grinned. It seemed Josain and I were kindred spirits, in that regard, at least. "I quite agree. Due to the planets' colouring, Kralis and Valeth make me think of the yin-and-yang symbol."

Josain contemplated my words for a moment as she covered my wrapped braids in a silk bonnet, and then said, "Yes, I can see what you mean. It's like they're twins, or maybe lovers."

Her words gave me a lot to think about in regarding the two planets, and their respective deities. It's something I wanted to know more about, and definitely a matter I wanted to discuss with the witches from Valeth when I had the change.

# Chapter Eighteen
# Moon Mother
# Are You Still There?

Josian's comments left me much to think about. After the handmaiden had helped me remove my makeup and change into a light nightdress, I padded into what was to be my new bedroom, my head even more full than it had been earlier.

Kalas wasn't in the room, and I assumed his equivalent of a handmaiden had taken him to prepare for bed.

Alone in the room, I took the opportunity to look around. The bed was massive, at least a king-size, with black sheets, and a fluttering canopy around it. Opposite the bed was a dressing table, where a few jewels lay discarded. The bed was neatly made, and nothing much in the room gave a hint of Kalas's personality. I'd have to add my own personal touches.

I lay down on the bed, pleased to find the covers and pillows were extremely soft and luxurious. At least we'd sleep in comfort.

From my position, if I looked to the left, there was a large window open to the night. The sky was ink black and dotted with stars I didn't recognize. The moon was smaller than the Earth's and had a curious purple tinge to it, just as the Throvani Ethrionth Star System sun was more magenta than the Earth's.

Even though the moon was a different colour from the one I was familiar with, the shape was almost the same, and I found that oddly comforting.

As if praying, I said in my mind, *'Moon Mother, are you still there? Can you hear me? Are you the one the witches of Valeth call Vesper?'*

No reply came, but my memory drifted back to earlier in the day, when Kalas and I had been in the ritual chamber. After we'd allowed drops of our

135

blood to fall into the metallic pool, a blinding light had filled the room, and in the light, I had seen a figure.

Who was it? Had I glimpsed the deity Vesper? Or perhaps, for some reason, Korvarith Thalun had shown Themself to me.

It was a lot to think about in addition to everything else on my mind. I hadn't even been on Kralis for twenty-four hours yet, and I already had so much to process and no idea where to begin.

I wanted to start with finding out more about Aster's older sibling, and if I could be descended from them. If I could have, I would have visited Luna and Phoebe first thing the following day. Not only did I want to discuss my possible relationship to Aster's older sibling, but I wanted to speculate on the connection between Kralis and Valeth that Josain and I had noticed.

As my thoughts turned to Josain, I wondered about the lover she'd alluded to. Had *they* given her the feather necklace? And where had I seen one similar?

I racked my brain, trying to remember the details of everyone I'd met that day, but there were just too many people for me to keep track of.

Instead, my mind drifted to Lady Voritha and Thalyn. It was obvious the queen was close to them, so befriending them would hopefully improve my relationship with my future mother-in-law. I couldn't help thinking of the old saying 'keep your friends close and your enemies closer.' If Thalyn *did* still have feelings for Kalas, or if Lady Voritha *was* disappointed her daughter hadn't been chosen to be Kalas's consort, it was better to have them in my favour than not. Maybe once they got to know me, they'd be more hesitant to plot against me.

That was if Kalas was wrong. Maybe the threat of punishment for treason would be enough to prevent anyone from challenging my and Kalas's marriage.

I shook my head. I was acting like I'd already agreed to marry him when that wasn't one hundred percent the case. I'd agreed to the official betrothal ceremony, mostly to appease Kalas's parents and Kralian traditions, but I wanted Kalas and I to get to know each other fully before I committed to becoming his wife.

I needed to know he loved me for me, and not just because Korvarith Thalun had decreed us to be fated mates.

I WASN'T SURE HOW LONG I'd slept for when I was awoken by gentle knocking at the door.

"Yes?" I called out, my voice hoarse.

Opening my eyes, I saw that light filtered in through the open window. I felt well-rested and refreshed. I'd just had the best night's sleep of my life.

"May I enter, Your Highness?" came Josain's voice.

I quickly scrambled to find what remained of my nightdress and pulled it on before calling out, "Please come in."

Josain entered the room, wheeling in a trolley laden with food. When she saw the state of my nightdress, she smirked and said, "Let me get you a robe. It's chilly this morning."

I took the offered robe and wrapped it around myself, then sat up in bed to see what had been brought for breakfast. Next to me, Kalas stirred.

I was pleased to see the trolley held not only a jug of iced water, but also a platter of food including fresh fruit, what looked like yoghurt, some simple grain crackers, nuts, cured meat, and cheese.

I took a handful of what I assumed were raspberries and popped them in my mouth, delighted by their sweet, slightly tart and juicy flavour. They were similar to raspberries in the same way strawberries were, but these fruits had an unfamiliar, though not unpleasant taste.

"They're nekka-nekka berries," Josain said, answering my unasked question. "They're native to Kralis and cultivated for their unique flavour. They also make a refreshing drink when blended into a juice."

I took another handful of berries and savoured the flavour slowly. "Yes, I can see how these would make an excellent drink. Especially in warmer months."

"The queen instructed that I should ensure you're fed and dressed before I accompany you to the parlour, where you and the queen will host Lady Voritha and Thalyn."

"Thank you, Josain."

The green-skinned woman gave a polite bow and then settled quietly in the corner as she waited for me to eat breakfast.

I turned to Kalas, offering a nekka-nekka berry to his lips, which he ate with a lazy smile.

"Do you want anything else?" I asked, gesturing to the trolley.

"No. My father and I plan on going hunting with Lord Darakon and Savrion while you and Mother host Lady Voritha and Thalyn."

Out of the corner of my eye, I noticed Josain looking in our direction at the mention of Lord Darakon and Savrion. That was an interesting piece of information I mentally filed away for later.

"Do you think you'll be long?" I asked Kalas. "I hoped we could visit Luna and Phoebe later."

"Hunting will take a couple of hours, knowing Lord Darakon. He likes to draw that sort of thing out and 'play' with his food. And believe me, whatever mother has planned could likely last all day."

I groaned internally. I didn't want to spend all day hosting Lady Voritha and Thalyn. Not only was I anxious to speak to Luna and Phoebe about the vision of Aster I'd had, but I still wasn't sure what to make of Kalas's ex-lover and her mother. And of course, there was the queen. I was convinced she hated me.

Still, this was the life I had agreed to when I'd left Earth with Kalas, and he'd promised our royal duties wouldn't last forever. Soon, the novelty of my arrival would wear off, and we'd be allowed to come and go more freely. I just had to get through the next... well, I hoped it was only for days and not weeks.

"As soon as I have finished hosting Lady Voritha and Thalyn, I'll return here and wait for you," I said, closing the distance between Kalas and me so I could press my lips to his.

Kalas growled low in his throat, his hands clawing at my nightdress, but I quickly pulled away.

'Behave yourself,' I said through our psychic bond. 'We're not alone.'

Kalas flushed as he remembered Josain was in the room with us. "Josain, would you please find Kaelivar and ask him to come to the chambers?"

"Of course, Your Highness," Josain replied, bowing politely before exiting the room.

The moment the door closed, Kalas grabbed my hand and moved it to his hardened cock. "This is what you do to me, my little witch."

Heat erupted through my body. "Behave," I chided again, though I couldn't help but give his erection a teasing squeeze.

"I will make you pay for that later," Kalas said, and the air crackled between us.

Pushing all indecent thoughts aside, I focused on my breakfast and waited for Josain to return with Kaelivar.

Kaelivar was a male Kralian with long, dark hair tied back neatly. He was dressed similarly to Josain in a simple yet refined way. Nothing about their outfits made Josain or Kaelivar stand out as part of the royal court, but it was clear from the quality of the material they were wearing that they were more important than other servants. I assumed Kaelivar was the one who'd help Kalas dress and get ready for the day.

Kaelivar handed Kalas a robe similar to the one Josain had given me earlier. It was long and thick, black, and like much Kralian clothing, threaded with nyxorith.

Kalas wrapped the robe around himself, then leaned in to quickly press his lips to mine.

"I will see you later, my love," he said, getting out of bed. "I hope you have a pleasant time with my mother, Lady Voritha, and Thalyn."

"Thanks, I'm sure I will," I replied, anything but sure. But for Kalas's sake, I smiled and then added, "Enjoy your hunt."

# Chapter Nineteen
# I'll Wear The
# Black Dress

After breakfast, I followed Josain through to the dressing room I'd used the night before. As she started running a bath, I couldn't help saying, "Please, you don't have to wait on me like this."

It was a risk, dismissing Josain's services when I still wasn't sure I could trust her, but I just felt too uncomfortable having someone assist me in this way.

"But, Your Highness, it's my job," Josain replied.

I sighed. "I know, but I didn't grow up in royalty, and honestly, the idea of having someone be my servant makes me uncomfortable. I don't want either of us getting into trouble, so in public, I suppose we should keep up appearances, but when it's just the two of us, can we just, you know, hang out?"

Josain offered me a small, hesitant smile. "If that is what you wish, Your Highness."

I was about to insist she call me Maddie instead, but I thought I shouldn't push my luck too far. I smiled back and took over readying the bath for myself.

The water was divine, and I longed to spend the whole day lounging around. My body ached deliciously all over from my and Kalas's lovemaking, and the heat of the bath soothed me.

As I lay in the water, Josain sat on a stool nearby.

"What should I wear while I host Lady Voritha and Thalyn with the queen?"

"The queen has had some of her old robes altered for you. She's having someone send them here as soon as possible. There will be a variety for you to choose from."

I wasn't sure if I was relieved or not. I hadn't packed much when I'd left Earth, as Kalas had promised everything would be provided for me once we reached his home. The royal regalia I'd worn for our 'engagement' ceremony was beautiful, but not something I could wear every day. While I appreciated that I was being given traditional Kralian clothing, I wished it was something of my own, not passed down from the queen. But I guessed I could visit a tailor when Kalas and I had fewer duties to attend to.

"How long have you worked at the palace?" I asked as I washed my hair.

"Not long. I came to Kralis on the day of the crown prince's coming-of-age ritual, looking for work. I was fortunate that there'd soon be an opening for a royal handmaiden."

"Ah, so you might not know all the inner workings of the court yet?" I asked, hoping she might be able to shed some light on the distinct tension I'd felt at the ball last night. "Do you know much about Lord Darakon?"

At my question, Josain glanced away. "I'm afraid not, Your Highness."

I sensed Josain was withholding something from me, but I knew I needed to earn her trust first. I just hoped that if Lord Darakon did turn out to be a problem, it was one Kalas and I could handle. Thinking of Kalas hunting with Lord Darakon and his son, I was curious about the younger Kralian.

"What about Savrion? I danced with him last night, and he seemed much friendlier than his father. Kalas certainly speaks highly of him."

A flush covered Josain's cheeks, and she lowered her voice. "I don't know Savrion well, but from what I have seen, he's a good man. He will be a loyal friend to the prince."

That set my mind at ease, though I did wonder why Josain was so sure of Savrion and had flushed at the mention of his name. Could he be her secret lover? Savrion had mentioned wishing he could dance with someone at the ball. Given their status difference, it would make sense that they'd hide their relationship.

I didn't want to pry too much into Josain's private life, though. I hoped she'd grow to trust me and tell me about her relationship when she was ready. Instead, I asked, "And what are your thoughts on Lady Voritha and Thalyn?"

"I haven't had the pleasure of meeting them yet," Josain said.

I sighed. "That's a shame. I know Thalyn and Kalas were once lovers, and I wondered if you knew anything about when they were together."

Josain shook her head. "I'm sorry, I don't. As I said, I only arrived on Kralis recently."

"That's okay. I appreciate you telling me what you do know," I said as I reached for a large towel and stepped out of the bathtub. "Life on Kralis is all new and confusing, so it's nice to have someone to trust."

"You can count on me, Your Highness," Josain said.

Nothing in Josain's voice suggested she was lying to me, and something about the woman endeared me to her. I could have used my magical abilities to probe Josain's mind, but that felt like a huge violation, and so I took her at her word.

We moved to the dressing table just as there was a knock at the door.

"Please come in," I called.

The door opened and a female Kralian who looked a few years older than me with long white hair entered with a bundle of clothing in her arms. "Her Majesty sent me with these, Your Highness."

"Thank you," I replied, searching the woman's face.

She curtsied. "Taena, Your Highness. I am Her Majesty's personal hand-maiden."

I extended my hand to Taena, who took it and shook it firmly. "It's nice to meet you, Taena. If you could please hang the clothes on that rail."

"Of course, Your Highness."

Taena did as I asked, arranging the five garments neatly on the rail, and then leaving a stack of what looked like underwear on a table nearby. She curtsied again and then left the room.

I moved from the dressing table and sorted through the clothing the queen had provided. All were in wonderful condition, and if I hadn't been told otherwise, I would have assumed they were new. It seemed daily wear on Kralis was similar to what ancient civilizations like the Egyptians, Aztecs, and Mayans had worn. There were five loose cotton robes in a range of colours from deepest black to a bright magenta that would clash with my hair. Each different robe came with a complimentary belt to cinch in the waist, as well as other decorations like necklaces and bracelets. I was drawn to the black, as dark colours were my usual preference.

I glanced at Josain. "Do you know if there's a specific colour I should wear or avoid? I don't want to offend anyone by making the wrong choice."

"I'm not sure, Your Highness. I haven't noticed any specific trends." She joined me and browsed through the robes I'd been provided with. "These are all colours I've seen the queen wearing, and she did give them to you, so I assume they meet whatever standards there are on Kralis."

I pursued my lips. Ordinarily, what Josain said would have made sense, but something in the back of my mind wondered if the queen was testing me somehow by sending these specific garments.

"Have you had much contact with the queen?"

Josain shook her head. "Not really. It was sort of a last-minute decision to hire me as your handmaiden. I spent a few days shadowing Taena, but my contact with the queen was limited."

"What do you think of her?" I asked, hoping I'd gained enough of Josain's trust that she'd be honest with me.

Now it was Josain's turn to purse her lips. Finally, she said, "I'm not sure. She's never openly hostile to me, but she's certainly cold. Though, that makes sense given our status difference. I find her much more difficult to read than the king."

I sighed. Yes, that was exactly how the queen seemed to me too. Perhaps this was how she was with everyone.

Realising I'd already taken so long bathing and I still hadn't decided what to wear, I pushed the thoughts aside until I had the proper time to dissect them.

I held my head up. Regardless of what anyone thought of me, I was Kalas's fated mate. I'd been chosen for him by Korvarith Thalun. That meant something.

"I'll wear the black dress," I said with renewed confidence.

I put on the undergarments I'd been provided, and then dressed in the robe, securing the waist with a purple belt that was threaded with nyxorith strands and dotted with the precious, colour-shifting gem. I also wore nyxorith jewellery that complemented the outfit. I was pleased to discover that Kralis had cosmetics similar to those from Earth, and I applied my usual 'gothic' makeup, with dark eye makeup and deep purple lipstick that was almost the same colour as the belt around my waist.

The combined look was imposing and dramatic; exactly what I was aiming for, and it made me feel even more confident. I defined my curls with some scented oil, and then I was ready to go.

Before leaving the dressing room, I took Josain's hands in mine. I wasn't sure if we were breaking rules by being so familiar with each other, but I squeezed Josain's fingers, letting her know I appreciated her talking with me so freely.

Before I'd left Earth, I'd only had one friend, and Janine had her own life to lead, reuniting with her daughter and granddaughter. While I missed her, I didn't feel terrible for leaving Earth. We were both walking our own paths now.

I hadn't expected to make new friends so quickly after arriving on Kralis, but I felt I'd already formed friendship with the witches of Valeth simply because we all had magical abilities.

I could feel a tentative kinship between Josain and me too. We were similar in many ways, both outsiders on this strange new planet. Phoebe and Luna had a home on Valeth to return to; they had somewhere they belonged. Josain and I didn't have that. We just had ourselves, our lovers, and maybe each other.

"Thank you for your words of reassurance. I feel like you at least understand what I'm going through being new here."

Josain smiled, her hand subconsciously raising to hold the nyxorith feather she wore around her neck. "I do. Enjoy your time with Her Majesty, Your Highness. I will be here later if you need anything."

"Please, don't wait around for me. As soon as Kalas is done hunting, we plan on visiting the witches from Valeth. Take some time for yourself. Maybe see if you can sneak a few moments with your lover."

A blush flushed Josain's cheeks. "Thank you. I will."

I left the dressing room and followed the corridor to the main door that separated the royal quarters from the rest of the palace. The moment I stepped through the ornate door, a male Kralian servant with long white hair was at my side. I recognised him as the one who had escorted Kalas and me to the ritual chamber the previous day and assumed he was here to do the same now.

# Chapter Twenty
# Even The Strongest Will
# Can Falter In The Face Of
# The Challenges Ahead

As I hadn't memorised the layout of the palace yet, I followed the servant as he strode confidently through the hallways. Finally, we came to the parlour where Kalas and I had chatted with the king and queen the day before.

I peered inside the room to see the queen was the only one there.

"I have brought the Princess Consort Madelyne, as requested, Your Majesty," the servant said, bowing in the doorway.

"Thank you, Ashryn. Can you please escort Lady Voritha and Thalyn?" the queen said, dismissing the servant before addressing me. "Madelyne, please, come and join me."

I crossed the room but paused as I reached the seating area. The day before, Kalas and I had sat on one sofa across from the king and queen, who'd been seated on the other. Now, the queen occupied the same position she had the day before, but I wasn't sure where I was meant to sit.

The queen watched me closely, raising one thin white eyebrow but didn't answer my unspoken question. Even without my ability to read minds, it was clear this was a test. I had to choose the correct place to sit.

I thought for a moment, finally deciding my place was beside the queen. I was to be princess consort. While that didn't make me equal to the queen, it certainly meant I was on a level closer to her than either Lady Voritha or Thalyn.

Tucking my robe under me, I sat down next to the queen, making sure to leave enough space between us that our bodies didn't touch. I didn't know what the protocol was here on Kralis, but I imagined touching the royal family without their permission was a big no-no.

The queen's expression remained neutral, giving me no indication of whether I'd made the right choice. The room lapsed into tense silence until Ashryn appeared in the doorway again. This time, Lady Voritha and Thalyn followed him.

"As requested, I have brought Lady Voritha and her daughter, Thalyn, Your Majesty," Ashryn said.

The moment Ashryn made the announcement, the queen's expression morphed, and a saccharine smile covered her lips. I mirrored the expression as best I could, convincing myself that having refreshments with Lady Voritha and Thalyn was the highlight of my day.

"Your Majesty," Lady Voritha said, coming to stand before the queen and then dropping into a low bow.

The queen offered Lady Voritha one of her many-ringed hands to kiss, and the other woman brought it to her lips briefly.

As the queen withdrew her hand, Lady Voritha straightened and then side-stepped so she stood before me. She moved into the same low bow, and I copied the queen's actions, extending my hand to the courtier.

Lady Voritha pressed her lips to my knuckles, but the contact was much quicker than with the queen, as though touching me caused her great discomfort.

Unbidden words flashed through my mind— unworthy, unsuitable, not deserving—and I realised I'd unintentionally read Lady Voritha's thoughts.

I quickly closed off my mind and withdrew my hand.

Lady Voritha stood and moved away to the sofa opposite the queen and me, leaving Thalyn to greet us in the same way.

Thalyn first bowed and kissed the queen's hand and then moved to me. When I extended my hand to Kalas's ex-lover, I tried my hardest to keep my mind closed, refusing to even pick up the hint of a thought from the young Kralian woman.

Thalyn joined her mother on the other sofa, and a moment later, a servant appeared with a tray of refreshments that held four iridescent glasses filled with a pinkish-purple liquid. From the colour alone, I knew we weren't served the same cherry wine from Valeth that we'd enjoyed yesterday.

The servant offered the tray to the queen first, and then me, before moving across the room to Lady Voritha and Thalyn.

I brought the glass to my lips, taking a tentative sip, and instantly recognized the flavour as the same one I'd tasted at breakfast. Nekka-nekka berries. I remembered Josain telling me the fruits were often made into a sweet and refreshing juice. It was delicious, slightly sweeter than raspberries, with an additional flavour I couldn't quite place. If anything, it tasted like pure starlight itself.

Despite the pleasantness of the drink, I sat stiffly on the edge of the sofa, one hand resting on the curved arm of the seat, while the other grasped the glass.

While the previous day, with Kalas at my side, I'd felt relaxed even under the watchful gazes of the king and queen, today, the parlour felt oppressively grand. Its arched windows framed the otherworldly violet sky and magenta sun. Overhead, I saw wyvern-like creatures chasing each other through the turquoise clouds.

I idly wondered if it was Kalas hunting with his father, Lord Darakon, and Savrion. I would have given anything to join them.

It wasn't only the alien luxury that unnerved me, it was the company.

Lady Voritha lounged opposite me, the flickering light from the crystalline chandeliers catching in her angular features and gleaming along the polished ridges of her elaborate nyxorith necklace. Her lips curved into a smile that didn't reach her deep, lilac eyes. Beside her, Thalyn mirrored the expression, her younger face no less calculating.

The queen sat beside me, her elegant, midnight blue robes flowing around her as though magically animated. Her expression was serene, though her silence carried weight.

"It must be quite an adjustment for you, Your Highness," Lady Voritha began, her voice smooth as silk but with the faintest bite beneath. "A human... among us. Your kind rarely has the fortitude for such... unique environments."

Thalyn tilted her head, her tone syrupy. "Yes, and such a burden for someone with no prior experience in our ways. It's admirable, truly." She leaned in slightly. "But are you certain you're up to the challenge?"

My stomach tightened, but I used every ounce of will within my body to keep my expression neutral. I was used to people talking down to me, even on Earth.

I met Thalyn's gaze head-on, my lips forming the barest of smiles. "I wouldn't be here if I didn't think I could handle it."

"Of course," Lady Voritha said quickly, her voice rising in mock concern. "Still, I imagine there are... doubts. Understandable, of course. You don't have the benefit of centuries of tradition guiding you." She sipped her drink, her eyes lingering on the glass in my hands. "Even the strongest will can falter in the face of the challenges ahead."

"Believe me, I've faced challenges before," I said, forcing calm into my voice, despite the way my heart raced. "I'm not afraid of what lies ahead."

*This is nothing,* I told myself. *They can't hurt you. You are Kalas's fated mate. Chosen for him by Korvarith Thalun.*

Thalyn let out a soft, almost musical laugh, exchanging a glance with her mother. "Oh, no one's questioning your courage. It's more... your compatibility. The balance of power here is delicate, you see." Her voice dropped to a murmur. "Sometimes, it's better to bow out gracefully than risk upsetting the harmony."

I felt heat rise to my cheeks, picking up Thalyn's emphasis on the word *compatibility*. No doubt she'd used it to hint that she and Kalas were once lovers. I forced myself to focus. I brought my glass to my lips and took a deliberate sip.

The cool sweetness of the nekka-nekka berry juice refreshed me, and I straightened my shoulders. Lowering the glass, I turned my gaze to Lady Voritha before glancing back at Thalyn.

I was pleased my voice held firm as I said, "I understand the stakes better than you think. And I'm here because Korvarith Thalun decreed it so. Whether you agree with that or not doesn't change anything."

Lady Voritha's smile tightened, the corners of her mouth drawing ever so slightly downward. Thalyn's fingers tapped against the arm of the sofa, a faint, irregular rhythm that betrayed her annoyance.

The queen shifted slightly, her inscrutable gaze falling on me. "A bold statement," she said softly, her voice like distant thunder, calm yet commanding attention. Her expression revealed nothing of her thoughts. "Conviction is a strength. But strength can be tested." She paused, letting the silence stretch. "I trust you're prepared for the weight of what you've agreed to."

My throat felt dry, but I refused to let the tension show. I inclined my head, smiling pleasantly at Kalas's mother. "I am."

"Then we shall see," the queen said, her tone remaining neutral.

All it would have taken was simply opening my mind and using my abilities, then I'd have known exactly what the queen thought of me and if she was on my side or not. But I refused to use my powers like that. I was too scared of what the truth might reveal. I'd already heard one mother admit their fear of me. I wasn't ready to experience that for a second time.

Instead, I turned my attention back to Lady Voritha and Thalyn, whose smiles had taken on an even sharper edge.

Even without my mind-reading abilities, I knew they didn't want me here. That much was clear. But I wouldn't let them see me falter, not now. Not ever.

As the conversation shifted to trivial pleasantries, the tension beneath remained palpable. I did my best to remain polite, firm, and quietly determined. But deep down, I knew Lady Voritha and Thalyn were not my allies. And whatever tests awaited me, I couldn't count on the queen. Without Kalas by my side, I would face them alone.

As the queen, Lady Voritha, and Thalyn chatted about the previous evening's ball, my gaze once more drifted to the window. I searched the skies for a sign of the wyvern-like creatures I'd seen earlier, but they were nowhere to be seen.

While with the queen, Lady Voritha, and Thalyn, I had been reluctant to open my mind, now I needed reassurance. I needed to connect with Kalas.

Allowing a little of my magic to open up the psychic bond between us, I asked, *'Is the hunt going well?'*

*'It would be if Lord Darakon wasn't playing with his food,'* Kalas replied. Even the mention of the other lord sent a chill down my spine, and I remembered Josain's earlier words.

I wondered, had Lord Darakon and Lady Voritha conspired to draw the morning's activities out for as long as possible, thus keeping Kalas and me apart?

I sighed. *'I miss you.'*

*'I miss you too, invarali taleni.'*

The Kralian term of endearment warmed my heart and chased away some of the tension still lingering within my body.

"Madelyne." The queen's cold voice severed the connection between Kalas and me, and I turned to face her. Her yellow eyes were narrowed. "I was just telling Lady Voritha and Thalyn that you received a letter from Queen Celestia of Valeth."

I wasn't sure what they'd been talking about, but I took the opportunity to reveal my possible connection to the sovereign of the neighbouring planet.

"That's right. Kalas and I plan to visit her as soon as possible. As you know, the Late Queen Branwynn was married to a witch from Valeth by the name of Aster. Last night, when I touched the royal portrait of Aster, I saw visions of them and their siblings. It is my belief that I am descended from Aster's older sister, who left Valeth and travelled to Earth."

Lady Voritha and Thalyn's eyes widened to comical proportions, while the queen's face remained as impassive as ever.

Finally, Lady Voritha trained her expression back into that fake, overly sweet smile. "It's good that you have a place to go should things not work out here."

Ignoring her jab, I replied, "Yes, it's good to know I have people who support me."

# Chapter Twenty-One
# Kissed Away My Doubts

Relief and exhaustion warred within me as Ashryn returned to escort Lady Voritha and Thalyn back to wherever they were staying and I was left alone with the queen.

She remained as enigmatically silent as ever, and I focused on the churning of my stomach to keep me from accidentally slipping into her mind.

My exhaustion gave way to excitement as I heard familiar voices approaching, and a moment later, Kalas and his father appeared.

The king was in good spirits and greeted his wife with an embrace and a kiss to the cheek. I stood and was about to move over to the other sofa when the king threw his arms around me.

"Good day, Madelyne. I trust you slept well and had a pleasant morning?"

"I did, thank you, Your Majesty," I replied, offering an awkward curtsy while still embracing the king. "Was your hunt enjoyable?"

Kalas's father sighed. "It would have been if Darakon hadn't taken so much time chasing his prey. I much preferred it when he was less active in courtly affairs."

It eased my fears to know that the king, at least, wasn't a fan of Darakon's.

After the king released me from his embrace, I crossed the room and sat on the couch beside Kalas. His hand instantly reached for mine, and he entwined our fingers. Tugging me closer, he pressed his lips to mine but kept the kiss brief as we were in the company of his parents.

"How was hosting Lady Voritha and Thalyn?" the king asked the queen.

"As expected," she said, revealing nothing of her feelings.

*'Everything okay?'* Kalas asked through our psychic bond.

*'Well, nothing terrible happened, but it was obvious Voritha and Thalyn hate me,'* I replied.

*'They'll come around,'* Kalas reassured me, but I didn't have his confidence.

"If you will please excuse us," Kalas said, addressing his parents. "Maddie will need to have some lunch, and then we plan on visiting Luna and Phoebe."

"Of course," the king said with a relaxed smile. "Please do keep us up to date with your discussion with the Valethians. I'm very interested to know if you too descend from the same line as Aster."

"I will be sure to come and speak to you once we've visited Luna and Phoebe," I promised.

I was glad he didn't seem to disapprove of me wanting to meet with the Valethians or find out about my ancestry. If I was descended from the same line as Aster, that meant I shared a common ancestor with both Kalas and the king.

We stood and bowed to the king and queen before departing the parlour and heading along the hallway back to the royal chambers. As we drew closer to the sectioned off area of the palace, I was surprised to see Savrion waiting near the entranceway.

Kalas seemed shocked to see his friend so soon again too, as his eyes widened. "Everything okay?" he asked.

"Of course, Your Highness. I wanted to check in with the princess consort and ask how she's settling in."

I smiled up at Savrion, touched by his concern for me. "I'm well, thank you."

"And everything is going smoothly with your handmaiden?"

"Yes. Josain is fantastic. I don't know what I'd do without her."

"That's good to know," Savrion said, and I noticed the necklace he wore. It was made up of several nyxorith feathers, though one was missing.

My eyes widened. "That's a beautiful necklace. Where's it from?"

Savrion's cheeks flushed, and he hastily tucked the necklace into his shirt out of view. "It was my late mother's."

I barely heard as Kalas and Savrion said goodbye to each other; my mind was swirling as I made a connection.

As soon as Kalas and I stepped through the door to the royal quarters, I turned to him. "I think Savrion and Josain are secret lovers."

Kalas raised a thin, dark eyebrow. "What makes you think that?"

"Well, they've both mentioned having a lover, and Josain wears a nyxorith feather necklace just like Savrion's. And did you notice his had a feather missing? I think that's because he gave it to her."

Kalas was thoughtful for a moment. "Well, that would certainly explain the earlier tension between Savrion and his father."

"What do you mean?" I asked as we entered our chamber and settled on the bed.

"There's been a rift between them since Savrion's mother died. And then, for a while, he left Kralis. I wondered whether perhaps they'd put their differences aside since Savrion has moved back into the family home, but it didn't seem like it earlier. In fact, Savrion acted as though being around Darakon was torture."

"Do you think he found out about Savrion and Josain's relationship and doesn't approve because she isn't a Kralian?"

"That's entirely possible," Kalas agreed.

"If Darakon doesn't approve of Savrion being with Josain because she isn't Kralian, does that mean he doesn't approve of you and I marrying?"

"Maddie, invarali taleni," Kalas said, cupping my face in his hands. "I already told you, it doesn't matter how Darakon, or anyone else feels about us being betrothed. You are my fated mate."

"I know, I know, but something doesn't feel right. Voritha and Thalyn weren't outright hostile towards me, but they made thinly veiled comments about 'compatibility' and the challenges I'll face by agreeing to marry you. And your mother... she's impossible. She didn't say anything either, but I'm certain she doesn't approve."

"Give it time," Kalas said, bringing his lips to mine. As our mouths moved together, Kalas kissed away my doubts. When we were joined like this, nothing else mattered. Being with him was where I belonged.

Kalas deepened the kiss, slipping his tongue into my mouth as his pointed incisors nipped at my bottom lip. I knew exactly where this was headed, and despite how much I wanted it too, I pulled away. Kalas let out a frustrated growl.

"Don't look at me like that," I chided playfully. "We said we'd visit Luna and Phoebe."

"The witches aren't going anywhere," Kalas insisted, his eyes darkening.

I laid my hand on his. "And neither am I. I will make it up to you later." I sealed the promise with a quick kiss and then stood and straightened out my robes.

Kalas stood too, righting his own clothing. "You still owe me from earlier."

"Don't worry. Once we return from speaking to Luna and Phoebe, we won't leave our chambers again until tomorrow."

This answer seemed to satisfy Kalas, and he took hold of my hand. "Do you want something to eat before we visit Luna and Phoebe?"

"I was thinking I could grab something from the market on our way."

"As you wish," Kalas said, and together, we left the royal quarters.

I wasn't sure if it was typical for the royal family to leave the palace unaccompanied, but no one challenged us as we left and made our way to the market.

The market was much livelier than it had been when we'd arrived the day before, with numerous stalls selling a variety of wares. Young Kralians ran around laughing and squealing. As Kalas and I walked past the vendors, everyone paused what they were doing to call out greetings and blessings to us.

"Long live the Prince and Princess Consort," someone shouted.

"Blessings of The Twilight Crow," another voice added.

It reassured me to know that, even if not all the courtiers approved of my and Kalas's betrothal, the general population of Kralis didn't seem to have a problem with it.

We passed a stall that sold food very similar to Greek gyros from Earth, and the smell was divine. My stomach rumbled, and I tugged on Kalas's hand to slow down his pace.

"This is what I want for lunch, please."

"Of course. Anything for my little witch," Kalas replied before turning to the vendor. He brought me some pork, char-cooked on a skewer and served in a thin bread similar to pitta, along with some sliced vegetables. To accompany the food was a tall glass of nekka-nekka berry juice.

I ate and drank everything there on the street beside the vendor, and it was exquisite. The pork was perfectly seasoned, and the vegetables so fresh and flavourful that I was certain they'd been harvested that very day. Nekka-nekka berry juice was fast becoming a favourite of mine.

"Thank you for the wonderful food," I said, returning the now empty glass to the vendor and gladly accepting a cloth napkin to wipe my fingers and lips with.

"It was an honour to serve you, Your Highness."

From the market, it wasn't difficult to find where Phoebe and Luna were staying while on Kralis. The Valethian witches had procured a large manse in an affluent area that housed a handful of similar estates.

One in particular caught my eye, as it was almost as grand as the royal palace with a tall nyxorith fence enclosing the entire property.

"Who lives there?" I asked.

"Lord Darakon," Kalas replied.

I rolled my eyes. "Of course."

We walked away from Darakon's home and approached a much more modest home that, like all the others, was made almost exclusively from a mixture of nyxorith, obsidian, onyx, and jet.

Kalas knocked firmly on the door, and a moment later, it was answered by Luna, whose eyes widened when she saw us.

"Your Highnesses, we didn't expect you so soon," she said, smiling broadly. "Please, come in."

Luna escorted us to a large, airy sitting room that had all the windows open to the world around it. Phoebe lounged on a plush, upholstered loveseat as we entered, rising to her feet to curtsy and greet us.

"You should have told us you were coming. We would have arranged refreshments," Luna said, gesturing for Kalas and me to sit down.

"It's okay. I stopped for lunch at the market on our way here," I said as Kalas and I sat down on the couch opposite Phoebe.

"Can I get you some drinks at least?" Phoebe offered.

"I wouldn't say no to a glass of nekka-nekka berry juice if you have it. I've never tasted anything so amazing before."

Phoebe smiled as she crossed to a modest kitchen. "I'm the same. We don't have it on Valeth, and I was completely obsessed with the fruit when we first visited Kralis."

Phoebe carried over a tray with glasses of nekka-nekka berry juice for all of us and then settled on the loveseat opposite Kalas and me, where Luna sat. The two women entwined fingers, and I finally realized they were more than just travelling companions.

"You're together?" I asked, hoping my tone didn't sound accusatory.

Luna smiled. "Yes. Valeth doesn't have laws against different genders or species being in relationships, as you likely know due to the late Queen Branwynn's marriage to Aster, sibling of Valethian Queen Alsephina."

"That's right. I actually wanted to speak to you about that." I took a sip of my nekka-nekka berry juice and then relayed to Phoebe and Luna what had happened the night before when I'd touched the portrait of Aster.

Both women's eyes were wide as I finished speaking. "You saw Princess Andromeda?" Luna asked.

"Is that the name of Aster and Alsephina's other sibling?"

"Yes. She was the second of Queen Ursula's three children. As you know, Alsephina became Queen of Valeth upon her mother's death, and it is from her that the current Queen Celestia descends. Aster was chosen by Korvarith Thalun to be Branwynn's fated mate. With her two siblings married or betrothed, Andromeda was unsure of her place in the world and so decided to venture to Earth. It is the belief on Valeth that the witches of Earth descend from Andromeda and any children she had," Phoebe said.

"This history appears to have been lost," I said. "The witches on Earth have no idea where their magic originates from. They don't even know Vesper's name, and refer to her simply as the Moon Mother"

Luna gave me a sad smile. "It is a shame the true history has been forgotten."

"It is. I assume Earth witches stopped talking about where our magic comes from to keep our abilities secret," I said, agreeing with Luna's sentiment that the true history being forgotten was sad. "I saw her. I felt her. There was a connection, I know it."

"Yes, I believe that due to your magical abilities and the blood connection, when you touched the portrait of Aster, you were able to see their family line. This confirms what we thought. You and the other witches on Earth are indeed descended from Andromeda. You would not have seen the visions through Aster's memories otherwise," Luna said.

I glanced at Kalas, whose expression told me he was following along with what the witches had told us and had come to the same conclusion as I had.

"We share a common ancestor; Queen Ursula," he said.

# Chapter Twenty-Two
# The Royal Family of Valeth

Knowing I was descended from the royal family of Valeth, and that Kalas and I shared a common ancestor, made our betrothal feel even more destiny bound. I had cast a spell to find where I belonged, and it had been answered. I'd found the origin of my bloodline and my fated mate.

"I wonder if this is what Korvarith Thalun intended all along," I mused. I told Luna and Phoebe the theory Josain and I had come up with that Vesper— the deity of Valeth—and Korvarith Thalun were somehow connected.

"Yes. There are those on Valeth who share the same theory," Phoebe confirmed. "It's one of the reasons Luna and I came to Kralis. Queen Celestia shares the belief too and sent us here as envoys. When she learned that Korvarith Thalun had chosen a witch from Earth as Prince Kalas's fated made, she became even more certain the theory is correct. She'll want to speak to you both immediately. How soon do you think you can visit Valeth?"

"We'll have to get permission from my father, but I don't see why he won't grant it. Aster was his ancestor too, and the royal family of Kralis has always had a good relationship with the royal family of Valeth. I'm sure he'll be thrilled to know that Maddie and I share a common ancestor. And of course, he will be curious about this connection between Korvarith Thalun and Vesper."

"I will write to Queen Celestia as soon as you leave. She will want to know about your vision, and I imagine she will want us to return to Valeth as soon as possible, bringing you with us if we can," Luna said.

"Yes, of course. As soon as we get permission from the king," I said, hoping Kalas was right, and that his father would have no objections. "But how will we get there? Do you have a ship in the dock?"

"No. Those from Valeth have their own, unique method of interstellar travel, granted to us by Vesper. We will be happy to share this with you, of course. And well, the crown prince can simply transform and fly to Valeth," Phoebe said.

"If you'd prefer, you can ride with me when I fly," Kalas suggested, and I was torn. I desperately wanted to fly with him in his wyvern-like form, but I was also curious about this Valethian mode of transport.

"We can discuss all the finer details as soon as the king grants his permission for you to leave Kralis," Luna suggested.

"Yes, we need to know we'll actually be allowed to visit Valeth before we make any more plans," I said, trying to stop my thoughts from running away from me. "Can we ask him now?"

Kalas chuckled. "We could, but it might be best for Luna and Phoebe to contact Queen Celestia first." Through our psychic bond, he added, *'Besides, I remember a certain witch making a promise that we wouldn't leave our chambers again today.'*

Heat flashed through my body as my mind filled with images of Kalas's lips, tongue, and teeth ravaging every inch of me.

"We can send your father a note asking that he and the queen meet us tomorrow morning," I said aloud before psychically saying to Kalas, *'And don't worry, I intend to keep the promise I made.'*

"That should give us plenty of time to hear back from Queen Celestia," Phoebe said. "Why don't you come by tomorrow for lunch? I'll prepare something special for us all, and then we can discuss the details of our journey."

"That sounds perfect. Thank you. We will send you a note if anything changes, and otherwise, we'll see you tomorrow," I said.

Kalas and I placed our empty glasses on the table and then stood to leave. As we did, Luna and Phoebe joined us, accompanying us to the door of the manse.

Before taking our leave, the witches pulled me into a warm embrace. "Whatever happens, you are our kin. You have a place on Valeth, if you wish. And if you need anything, either from us, or from Queen Celestia, we will ensure you receive it."

Luna and Phoebe's words touched my heart, and I knew I'd found where I belonged, be that here on Kralis or on Valeth. I had found my people. The only question that lingered in the back of my mind was whether Kalas would come with me and leave the Crown of Kralis behind if I decided I didn't want to be princess consort and instead simply wanted a quiet life on Valeth.

I tried not to dwell on that thought as Kalas and I left Luna and Phoebe's manse and made our way through the market back to the palace. I wasn't sure what I wanted, and so I decided to focus on what came next. We didn't even have the king's permission to visit Valeth yet. Before we made any more plans, we'd have to speak to Kalas's parents.

But for tonight, I had made a promise I fully intended to keep.

# Chapter Twenty-Three
# A Date For Our Wedding

I felt amazing when I woke up the following morning, and I was already wrapped in a robe and sitting up in bed when Josain knocked on the door.

"Come in," I called, and a moment later, the green-skinned woman entered with a trolley laden with food.

"Good morning, Your Highnesses," she said, curtsying in my and Kalas's direction before wheeling over the trolley to my side of the bed. "Did you both have a pleasant time yesterday?"

"We did," I replied, reaching for the glass of fresh nekka-nekka berry juice. "We visited Luna and Phoebe, the witches from Valeth."

Josain smiled. "I've never been to Valeth, though I'd love to visit sometime."

"We will be going there soon. I need to speak with Queen Celestia. We just need to gain the king's approval. But when we do go, I'll need someone there to help me with dressing and bathing and such. I'll insist you come with me." With a sly smile, I turned to Kalas and added, "You should insist Savrion join us too. I'm sure you'd appreciate having your childhood friend there when surrounded by people we don't know as well."

At my words, Josain flushed all over, and this was confirmation of the theory I'd come up with since noticing that she and Savrion wore almost identical nyxorith feather necklaces. didn't want to ask her about it in front of Kalas, though, in case she was afraid to be honest around him. I decided to stay quiet for now and ask Josain about her and Savrion later, when we were alone. Instead, I simply silently enjoyed my breakfast as I snuggled into Kalas's shoulder.

Finished with breakfast, Josain wheeled the food trolley out of the way and accompanied me to the dressing room just as Kalas's own manservant, Kaelivar appeared.

"Josain, I hope you don't mind me asking, but I couldn't help noticing your reaction whenever I mention Savrion," I said carefully as I started filling the bath with water. "Is he your secret lover?"

"No, Your Highness. I barely know him," Josain stammered, her cheeks flushing.

"It's okay. I won't tell anyone, I swear. I noticed he wears a nyxorith feather necklace with one feather missing, exactly like the single feather pendant you wear."

Josain reached for the necklace and stroked it. "Yes, we're lovers," she confirmed. "But please, you can't tell anyone. Lord Darakon doesn't approve."

"Your secret is safe with me. In fact, now we know, we can help you not only keep the secret but maybe spend some time together. You are my handmaiden, and he is Kalas's closest friend. That's why I suggested you come to Valeth with us. You can be together without having to hide so much."

Josain smiled. "Thank you, Your Highness. That would be fantastic. It's been difficult for us to sneak any time alone together. We're always so afraid Darakon will find out."

"I'll try to cover for you as best I can. I will suggest to Kalas that you're given quarters close to ours so that there's less chance of you and Savrion being seen together."

"Thank you," Josain said, settling on the stool beside the bath as I removed my clothes and climbed into the hot water. "I must admit, Your Highness, I wasn't sure what to expect when Savrion arranged for me to be your handmaiden."

I raised a brow. "Oh, so it was his suggestion?"

"Yes. He thought you might need a friend. He anticipated how Voritha and Thalyn might react towards you."

I sighed and closed my eyes the hot water feeling wonderful against my bare skin. "They were awful yesterday."

"I'm sorry you had to deal with them."

"I think Thalyn still has feelings for Kalas, and of course, Voritha wants her daughter to be queen someday. What I'm not sure about is Kalas. He says he loves me. We certainly have a good physical connection. But would he have still chosen me if Korvarith Thalun hadn't foretold it in the stars? If I asked him to leave Kralis and live with me on Valeth, would he?"

"I can't answer those questions, Your Highness, but I have seen the way he looks at you. And Savrion said he didn't stop talking about you during their hunt."

Hearing this caused butterflies to flutter in my stomach.

"The best you can do is trust your instincts," Josain went on. "But I know from experience, anything worth having is worth fighting for. Anything too easily obtained might not actually be what you need."

I thought back to my one significant romantic relationship on Earth. A man named Darin, who I met not long after my parents kicked me out of home. I thought he was everything. Turned out, he was using me for my magic. Since then, I hadn't allowed myself to believe love was something I could have. The spell I'd cast, that had bought Kalas to me, had been my one last, desperate attempt.

I stepped out of the bath and wrapped a towel around myself.

"Whatever path you and Kalas choose won't be easy," Josain said as I dried off. "But if your love is real, it will be worth it."

*If* our love was real. That was the question that continued to plague me.

I pushed the thoughts out of my mind as I dressed in deep purple robes with silver accents and accessories. The hems of the robes had celestial patterns woven into the fabric, which seemed fitting, given Kalas and I would be speaking to his parents about us visiting Valeth.

Instead of wearing my hair loose and curly, I decided to braid it and threaded the braids with strands of nyxorith, so it appeared like starlight shone in my hair.

"Your counsel is always exactly what I need to hear," I told Josain as we walked back to my chambers. "I appreciate your kindness more than you know."

Josain flushed for a moment and then took my hand. "I hope this isn't too forward of me, Your Highness, but I feel the same. As I said earlier, I wasn't sure what to expect when Savrion arranged for me to be your handmaiden. I worried you'd be some spoiled princess, but the reality is far from that."

I wrapped my arms around Josain, pulling her into a tight embrace. "I feel the same. No matter what happens in the future, I will always seek your advice and comfort. I hope someday we can become friends."

Kalas returned to the chambers just as I was releasing Josain from my embrace.

*'Everything okay, my little witch?'* he asked through our psychic bond.

*'Everything is perfect,'* I replied before saying aloud, "Josain, I won't need your services again today. I can prepare myself for bed. Please spend the day as you wish."

"Thank you, Madelyne," Josain replied. Her using my given name and not my title startled me for a moment, the implications clear. She may have been hired by the king and queen to be my handmaiden, but she was becoming more than that.

I smiled back and squeezed her hand.

As Josain left, Kalas turned to me, his amber eyes drinking in every detail of my body.

"You look exquisite, as always. I think after we've spoken to my parents and had lunch with Luna and Phoebe, we should go shopping for some clothes of your own."

I entwined my fingers with his, and we walked along the hallway to the door separating the royal quarters from the rest of the palace.

"You and Josain seem to be getting along well," he commented as we walked.

"Yes, I like her a lot. It's been difficult for me to adjust to life here on Kralis, but Josain is one of the few people I've met who I feel I can be myself around."

"That's good to know," Kalas said with a smile.

We walked the now familiar path to the parlour, and I was unsurprised to see the king and queen waiting for us.

I curtsied in front of the king, who quickly rose to his feet and pulled me into a tight embrace. "Good morning, Aelrion Vethara."

"Good morning, Aelrion Thalor," I replied, returning the Kralian greeting.

The king released me from his embrace and moved to hug Kalas, leaving me facing the queen. There was no way she'd offer me the same affection her husband had, and I moved into a curtsy.

Only, the queen stopped me, and to my utter surprise, wrapped her arms around me. Her embrace wasn't as tight and warm as the king's, and instead of kissing my cheeks, she simply kissed the air above my face. But this was huge. She was greeting me on a much more familiar level.

Was she finally coming around to the idea of Kalas and me being together?

Still shocked by what had transpired, I took a place on the couch opposite the royal couple, and Kalas joined me a moment later.

As he sat, he said through our psychic bond, *'See, I knew she'd grow to love you as I do.'*

I couldn't argue with his words, and instead added, *'I'll take it as a good omen for the day.'*

Ashryn was summoned, and we were all served nekka-nekka berry juice.

As we sipped on our refreshing drinks, the king regarded us and said, "Please, tell me everything you discussed with Ladies Luna and Phoebe."

I relayed my and Kalas's meeting with Luna and Phoebe the previous day, and that they felt certain my visions of Aster meant I was descended from the former Queen Ursula. I also discussed our theory that Korvarith Thalun and Vesper were somehow connected, and that Queen Celestia shared this belief. I told the king I wished to go to Valeth as soon as possible to discuss this with the queen and learn more about my magical ancestry.

Hearing this, the king grinned. "And so, the designs of Korvarith Thalun become clearer. We are both descendants of Queen Ursula of Valeth. Our ancestors share blood. And I agree with your assessment that there's a connection between The Twilight Crow and The Moon Mother. Queen Branwynn thought so too. I have been reading some of her old journals. I think this is why Korvarith Thalun chose you as Kalas's fated mate. They intend for the bloodlines of Queen Ursula to be united. It is also my belief that Kralis and Valeth should build on the already established relationship. If you were to go to Valeth, I would like you to take this letter I have written to Queen Celestia, in which I suggest that the children of our respective heirs be betrothed."

It took me a moment to realise that by 'the children of our respective heirs be betrothed,' the king meant he wanted to betroth his grandchildren, my and Kalas's future children, to the future children of the Princess Aurora. While this made sense and would more closely unite Kralis and Valeth, it would also defy any decree Korvarith Thalun made regarding my future child's fated mate. Could this even be done?

Even without our psychic bond, Kalas read my thoughts easily and asked my unspoken question.

"Is that even possible?" Kalas questioned his father.

"I believe so, but before anything is made official, I intend to seek High Priest Varion Drelkar's guidance. I intend to invoke Korvarith Thalun and ask for their blessing of this union. I feel it would be best for both Kralis and Valeth. The armies of Auroriathians are growing, their attacks on other planets becoming more frequent. I fear it's only a matter of time before they turn their attention to their neighbours. For both Kralis and Valeth to survive, I believe we must unite," the king said.

"So, you're giving us your blessing to visit Valeth?" I asked.

"I am," the king confirmed. "Under two conditions. The first, I have mentioned. Take my letter to Queen Celestia. If she's resistant at first, convince her this marriage arrangement benefits us both."

It felt weird thinking of the betrothal plans for a child Kalas and I hadn't even conceived yet, but I also understood that was part of royal life, and something I'd have to accept if I became Kalas's consort. What the king said about uniting Kralis and Valeth made a lot of sense.

"I'll do what I can," I agreed. "And what's your second condition?"

"I ask that when you return from Valeth, you and Kalas set an official wedding date. If we're trying to build unity and prepare for a secure future, that begins with you and my son. The people of Kralis need to know that the word of Korvarith Thalun is being followed. They need to know the royal line will continue. It's my fear that if a wedding date isn't set soon, we might face resistance from some of the nobility."

I almost blurted out, 'Darakon!' but Kalas squeezing my hand stopped me.

I'd hoped me and Kalas would have a longer engagement before setting a wedding date, but if this was one of the king's conditions for me to visit

Valeth, I knew there was little I could do to change his mind. I'd agree to get what I wanted, with the plan that when we returned from Valeth, Kalas and I could have a proper talk about our relationship. "I agree, Your Majesty. Kalas and I will visit Valeth and give your marriage proposal to Queen Celestia, and then when we return, we will announce a date for our wedding."

Beside me, I could feel waves of tension radiating from Kalas, and through our bond, he asked, *'Are you sure this is what you want, my little witch? Don't let my father pressure you into anything.'*

*'I'm not – I'm hoping we can still have a long engagement like we planned,'* I told him. *'But we can discuss it on our way to Phoebe and Luna's.'*

This seemed to reassure Kalas, and he turned his gaze to his parents. "I echo Maddie's words. We agree to your proposition, and we will set a date for our wedding as soon as we return from Valeth."

"Excellent," the king said, getting to his feet.

Following his lead, Kalas and I did the same, as did the queen. The king embraced Kalas and then me before the queen hugged me too, once more kissing the air above my cheeks.

She was as unreadable as ever, and I wasn't sure if she really had changed her mind about me, or if she was just going along with whatever her husband said. The king did have a certain way about him that made it impossible to refuse anything he asked of people.

# Chapter Twenty-Four
# Through The Moon

I tried not to dwell too much on what Kalas and I had just agreed to as we left the parlour and prepared to visit Luna and Phoebe.

The moment we stepped out of the palace, Kalas pulled me aside and asked, "Is this truly what you want, Maddie?"

I paused and stared up at him. "Which part? The alliance with Valeth, or the agreement to betroth children we haven't even had yet?"

Kalas chuckled. "Yes, it is a lot to think about. But what my father suggests makes sense."

"It does," I agreed, taking Kalas's hand as we continued walking away from the palace. "I will keep my word and broach the subject of an alliance with Queen Celestia. But I think you and I need to have a long talk when we return from Valeth."

"I agree," Kalas said.

I wanted to open up the psychic link between us, to see how he was really feeling, and so that I could share all the worries and uncertainties I felt, but the idea of doing so was too overwhelming at that moment. So instead, I closed off my mind and focused only on lunch with Luna and Phoebe.

The witches welcomed us warmly when we arrived, and as we entered the manse they were staying in, I was greeted with a variety of scents. I smelled an aroma that was very similar to seasoned roasting chicken, as well as the fresh, bright aroma of nekka-nekka berries. My mouth watered.

"Please, come in and make yourselves comfortable," Luna said, gesturing to the two sofas facing each other, with a low wooden coffee table in between them. "Lunch will be ready soon."

"Can I offer you both a drink? We have fresh nekka-nekka berry juice, or if you'd prefer, we have spiced cherry wine from Valeth."

I was torn. I loved nekka-nekka berry juice, but the spiced cherry wine from Valeth that I'd tried the day I arrived on Kralis had been exquisite. Finally, I decided it might be best to keep a clear head while Kalas and I talked with Luna and Phoebe. Though, I hoped when we visited Queen Celestia on Valeth, the cherry wine would be served.

"I'll have some juice, please," I said.

Phoebe poured out four glasses of nekka-nekka berry juice and brought them over to the coffee table before sitting down on the sofa beside Luna.

I reached for one of the glasses and took a long sip, delighting in the tart, unusual flavour I'd grown to love.

"We've had a reply from Queen Celestia," Phoebe said.

My eyes widened. "So soon?"

"Yes. We were able to speak to her via a mind connection yesterday after you left," Phoebe went on.

"You all have psychic abilities, then?"

"To varying degrees, and the bonds are closer between those who are related. I suspect when you arrive on Valeth, you and Queen Celestia will be able to share thoughts, if the queen permits," Luna said.

The idea of forming a psychic connection with anyone other than Kalas was a strange one to me. Once, long ago, before my parents had kicked me out, I would have loved to be able to telepathically communicate with those closest to me. Then, for many years, my ability to hear people's thoughts had been something I was afraid of, terrified I'd learn something I didn't want to. Since meeting Kalas, I'd grown to cherish the ability. It was a special bond only the two of us shared. I wasn't sure how I felt about that bond extending to others. Though, indirectly, Queen Celestia was my family, so perhaps it was something I'd get used to when the two of us finally met.

"What did Queen Celestia say?" I asked.

"She was unsurprised but also delighted to learn of your connection to Princess Andromeda and shares many of our theories about the origins of witches on Earth and the connection between Vesper and Korvarith Thalun. She has asked us to return to Valeth as soon as we can, and she was very insistent that you and Kalas accompany us," Luna said, pausing for a moment before asking, "How did your meeting with King Eldarion go?"

"He was pleased to learn that we share a common ancestor, and he feels as though it's in everyone's benefit if the relationship between Kralis and Valeth is strengthened."

"That means he's given you his blessing to visit Valeth?" Phoebe asked.

"Yes, but there are a few conditions. First, when Kalas and I return to Kralis, we must set a date for our marriage," I said.

"Well, that makes sense. I'm sure he wants to live to see his grandchildren, and having his heir married will only strengthen the throne," Luna said. "What was his other condition?"

"I am to present Queen Celestia with a marriage proposal, betrothing the future children of Princess Aurora with any children Kalas and I have."

Luna and Phoebe exchanged a glance, and I felt certain they were communicating with each other telepathically.

Finally, Phoebe said, "I believe this will be of great interest to Queen Celestia. Are you able to depart after we've eaten?"

"Well, Kalas and I were intending to go shopping after lunch. I didn't bring much from Earth with me."

"There are many shops on Valeth, and I'm sure Queen Celestia won't mind offering you the services of the royal tailor," Luna said.

I glanced at Kalas, opening my mind to him and psychically asking, '*Is today too soon?*'

'*If you have no problem with it, I don't. I think it would be good for you to visit Valeth and meet other witches. I also think both of us could do with a break from the royal court and a chance to be properly alone.*'

I was excited to visit Valeth and meet Queen Celestia, and Kalas's agreement was the last prompt I needed.

"We can leave today, but I will need to make some preparations first. I wish for my handmaiden, Josain, to accompany me. And Kalas will be bringing his friend. Savrion."

"That's not a problem. The queen will expect you to bring company and no doubt have the appropriate guest rooms prepared. Can Josain and Savrion make their way to Valeth? Or will they need transportation?" Phoebe asked.

"Savrion can transform, like I can," Kalas said, before turning to me. "Do you think Josain would be willing to fly with him?"

Knowing what I did about the pair, I couldn't see why not, but I erred on the side of caution. "Possibly, but another method of transportation would be useful just in case. How do you two intend to travel back to Valeth?"

At this, Phoebe smiled. "Through the moon."

My open-mouthed expression made the two witches laugh, and finally, Phoebe elaborated.

"Vesper blessed all those from Valeth with the ability to travel through moonbeams. We simply need to perform the correct incantation and then bathe in the light of the moon. The Moon Mother's magic does the rest. We will be able to bring both you and Josain with us if you do not wish to travel with the Kralians."

"That's perfect. After lunch, we will return to the palace to pack our belongings and inform Josain and Savrion of the plans," I said. "We can be ready to leave this evening, when the moon rises."

"That sounds like a good plan," Luna agreed, rising from the sofa. "Lunch is almost ready, if you'd like to join us at the dining table."

We followed her lead, leaving the comfort of the couch and moving over to a wooden dining table that had been laid out with shimmering, pearlescent plates and silver cutlery.

"You know, I think these are the first plates I've seen on Kralis that haven't been made from nyxorith," I said as I took a seat, and Kalas slipped into place beside me.

"Yes, the Kralians do love their nyxorith," Luna said with a smile as she sat down opposite me. "These are made from lunavira, which is the Valethian counterpart to nyxorith."

I studied the lunavira plates with interest. Similar to how nyxorith initially appeared black until you turned it in the light, and then hues of purple, turquoise, and magenta could be seen, lunavira had a similar quality. At first glance, the plates appeared white, but if I moved them, there was a subtle, reflective sheen to them, as though something was glowing or shimmering beneath the surface.

Phoebe didn't take her seat straight away, instead going to the oven where she pulled out a massive roast bird that looked and smelled like chicken.

She placed it in the centre of the table, and I noticed it was surrounded by many roast vegetables, some which looked familiar, and others that were completely alien.

"Is that a zelorith?" Kalas asked with interest. His fangs had increased in size, and he was practically drooling.

"It is," Phoebe said, sitting down next to Luna. "I managed to buy one especially. I had a feeling you might enjoy it, Your Highness."

"While I usually prefer hunting for my food, as you know most Kralians do, I never say no to zelorith."

"What is it? It just smells like chicken to me," I said.

"They are similar, though much more sought after, and less common than chicken is on Earth," Phoebe said, beginning to carve the meat.

I was surprised to see the flesh inside was a pale blue and wondered what colour the zelorith had been when it was alive.

"On many planets, they're considered a delicacy and are often reserved for holidays and special occasions," Luna said as Phoebe placed slices of the meat on everyone's plates and then added generous servings of the roasted vegetables.

"What are these?" I asked, picking up what looked like a small radish with my fork, although instead of the typical pink colour of Earth radishes, this roasted vegetable was a deep purple that almost looked black. The way it glistened in the light made me think of nyxorith.

"Nyxroot," Kalas said with an amused smile. "They're a root vegetable that grow near nyxorith veins. It's believed they take on some of the flavour and qualities of nyxorith."

I cut into the vegetable and gasped as the inside seemed to change colour in a similar way to nyxorith.

Intrigued, I popped half of the nyxroot into my mouth and chewed it slowly. The flavour was very tart, almost to the point of being too bitter, but there was a fragrant undertone that made it moreish. If anything, it tasted like a savoury counterpart to nekka-nekka berries.

"This is delightful," I said, cutting into a slice of meat and sampling that too.

I wasn't sure if Phoebe had added extra seasoning or if this was the zelorith's natural flavour; it had a pleasant poultry taste like the most high-quality chicken, but also a brightness that was almost zesty, as though lemon had been baked into the flesh. It complimented the flavour of the nyxroot perfectly, and when I ate the two together, my whole tongue seemed to light up as every different taste bud was activated.

"You're an amazing cook," I said.

"Thank you," Phoebe replied with a small smile. "I was lucky to get my hands on some very special ingredients."

I glanced at Kalas's plate, not surprised to see he had eaten all of his zelorith, but he hadn't even touched the nyxroot.

"Don't you like your vegetables?" I teased.

"Kralians are carnivores. We have no need for things like nyxroot in our diets," he replied, eyeing what remained of the zelorith hungrily.

"You're welcome to more," Phoebe said, placing three slices of zelorith onto Kalas's plate before he could respond.

As he neatly cut into the slice of meat with his knife and fork, I could tell it was taking all of Kalas's willpower not to lower his head and devour the zelorith straight off the plate. I wondered if he had ever had the chance to hunt the bird himself.

After we had all eaten as much as we wanted, which included a third serving of zelorith for Kalas, Phoebe cleared away the plates and then presented us with dessert.

I instantly recognized the nekka-nekka berries, along with deep, magenta fruits I thought might be cherries, all piled on top of a light, fluffy pavlova that had cracked on the outside and was oozing shimmery marshmallow goodness.

"Spiced cherries from Valeth," Phoebe said, placing down the pearlescent bowl of desert. "With nekka-nekka berries and moonbeam aelivora."

"The aelivora is a Valeth speciality, often served with native spiced cherries. We added the nekka-nekka berries as we know they're your favourite," Luna explained as Phoebe sat beside her.

Phoebe spooned generous servings of dessert into everyone's bowls, and we all tucked in.

# Chapter Twenty-Five
# Magical Ancestors

After we'd finished eating, manners drilled into me on Earth made me offer to do the washing up, even suggesting Kalas would help.

"I cannot ask the Crown Prince of Kralis and his royal consort to do the dishes," Luna said, filling up a basin with water. "Besides, Phoebe and I already have an arrangement. She cooks and I clean. It has served us well for years."

Curious, I ask, "How long have you been together?"

"We met at the royal court when we were eighteen, and we're nearing thirty now, so we've been together for more than ten years. We were officially married, with the blessings of Vesper, seven years ago."

My heart filled with warmth. "That's so romantic."

"I'm lucky to have her," Phoebe said, affectionately stroking Luna's back as she made her way over to the sofa.

"I'm the lucky one," Luna replied, turning her head to press a light kiss to Phoebe's cheek as she passed.

"Would you like another drink? Or are you eager to begin making arrangements for our journey to Valeth?" Phoebe asked as we neared the sofas.

I glanced at Kalas, whose expression told me the choice was mine. "I think I'd rather get our travel arrangements sorted out. I'm eager to get to Valeth."

Phoebe smiled. "I can understand that. I mean no offence, Your Highness. Kralis is a beautiful planet, but I can't wait to return home."

Kalas returned Phoebe's smile. "Nothing beats sleeping in your own bed."

We bid goodbye to Phoebe and Luna and hurried back to the palace, longing to prepare for our trip to Valeth.

"And you're sure it's not too soon?" I asked Kalas as we made our way to the royal quarters.

"Of course not, my little witch. As I said, I think it will do us both good to have a break from royal duties and spend some time alone together."

Once Kalas and I were settled in our room, we sent messages to Savrion and Josain, explaining that we needed to speak to them both immediately.

When they arrived, they both looked slightly dishevelled, and I tried to hide my smirk.

"Sorry to interrupt, but the king has given us permission to go to Valeth. We're leaving this evening. Phoebe and Luna said you can both come as Queen Celestia will expect us to bring some... staff." I gave an apologetic smile at the term.

Josain and Savrion's eyes widened.

"So soon?" Josain asked.

"We want to leave as soon as possible. I assumed you wouldn't have a problem with it and would appreciate not having to be so secretive."

Josain glanced at Savrion, and they both smiled.

"Well, there is that," Savrion said, standing from the bed and smoothing out his clothing. "I'd better inform my father. He will need to know that I'm accompanying the prince to Valeth."

"Of course," Kalas said, opening the door for his friend. "Will you be flying to Valeth? And are you able to take Josain with you?"

Savrion glanced back at Josain, who was already grinning.

"I've only flown with Savrion once. I won't pass up another chance," Josain replied.

"That's perfect. Maddie will be flying with me. The witches from Valeth said they know an enchantment that will enable you to breathe while on our backs," Kalas said. "We'll meet you at the flying grounds."

"Do I need to bring anything specific with me?" Savrion asked.

"No. Just clothing appropriate for a royal feast with Queen Celestia," I said, and then Savrion departed. Turning my attention to Josain, I asked, "How soon can you be packed?"

"Give me ten minutes, and I'll be ready. I don't have much with me. Certainly not something appropriate for a royal feast with Queen Celestia."

"Don't worry. We'll go shopping on Valeth, as I only have the clothes Queen Seraphina gave me," I replied as Josain rose from the bed and crossed the room.

"Thank you for inviting us along with you, Your Highness," Josain said, curtsying as she passed me and Kalas at the doorway.

Josain smiled and squeezed my hand before leaving the bedroom.

"I won't bother summoning Kaelivar," Kalas said, referring to his manservant, as the door closed. "We'll be quicker packing our own things."

"Shouldn't we tell your parents?"

"My father already gave us his blessing. I will tell him we're leaving when we head out to the flying grounds."

His mention of the flying grounds made my stomach flip. I hadn't had the chance to ride on Kalas's back when he was transformed into his wyvern-like form. In fact, I hadn't even witnessed a full transformation yet. While on Earth, Kalas had only partly transformed, taking on the appearance of a harpy-like creature.

I was not only excited to see his true bestial form, but also to ride through the stars on his back.

"Will I need a special harness or saddle to make sure I don't fall?"

Kalas's brows drew together as he contemplated my question. "I'm not sure. I have never flown with a rider before. Maybe Luna and Phoebe might know of a spell that can help."

"I can see if my telekinetic abilities are strong enough to help me remain in place," I said, lifting the bed with the power of my mind as a display of my magic.

Kalas smiled. "I am impressed, my little witch. You don't use your magic often."

"I guess I'm still used to hiding my abilities. But once we get to Valeth, I won't have to. I'll be with others like me." My voice bubbled up at the end of the sentence, as though propelled by the effervescence I felt as reality dawned on me.

I was about to fly to a planet inhabited almost solely by witches.

I could hardly believe it was happening. Back on Earth, when my abilities had first started to manifest, I hadn't dared to dream I'd find others like me, let alone a whole planet of witches. Janine had been the only magical friend

I'd had, and while she'd been good to me and offered me her home when I had nowhere else, we still had to keep a low profile and avoid the witch hunters.

Away from Earth, and about to travel to the planet my magical ancestors originated from, I finally felt free for the first time since my abilities had manifested at fourteen.

Kalas had given me that.

WASTING NO MORE TIME, we made our way from the bedroom to our dressing rooms. It was easy for me to pack my things, as the queen had only given me a handful of garments. As I folded them nearly into a trunk, I wondered what I should wear when we arrived on Valeth and I met Queen Celestia for the first time. When we'd arrived on Kralis, Josain had been sent with traditional Kralian royal formalwear for me. Would that be appropriate for meeting the ruler of another planet? I'd have to ask Luna and Phoebe for their advice.

With my magical abilities, it took no effort to move the clothing trunk from the dressing room to my and Kalas's bedroom, where I waited for him to return.

When he stepped through the door, he was carrying a trunk double the size of the one I had, along with another smaller one. I marvelled at his strength.

"Will you be able to fly with those and me?" I asked, as he laid his belongings down on the floor by the door.

"Yes. In my bestial form, I am even stronger than I am now. I could easily carry triple this amount. Though, I will send for a trolley, as getting them to the flying grounds might be difficult."

Kalas rang a small bell that rested on a table near the doorway, and a few moments later, Kaelivar arrived.

"How can I be of service, Your Highness?" Kaelivar asked with a deep bow.

"The princess consort and I are travelling to Valeth this evening. Can you please have our belongings taken to the flying grounds and the appropriate tethers arranged?"

"Of course, Your Highness." Kaelivar bowed again and then left the room.

"We should seek out my parents," Kalas said, extending his hand to me.

A small part of me worried that when we told the king and queen our intentions to leave for Valeth immediately, they'd try to stall us for some reason, or worse still, take back their blessing that we travel there at all.

I pushed the thoughts out of my mind. The king wanted to forge an alliance with Valeth, and he couldn't accomplish that without my help.

# Chapter Twenty-Six
# Wyvern-Like Creatures

We found the king and queen in the same parlour we'd met in that morning, and from the look of the empty tray of refreshments being taken away by Ashryn, they'd not long since finished hosting someone else.

When King Eldarion saw us, his eyes widened. "Is all well, my son? Did something happen during your lunch with the witches from Valeth?"

"Yes. They've asked that we accompany them to Valeth this evening. Queen Celestia wishes to speak to Maddie as soon as possible. I think she may be interested in the alliance you proposed," Kalas said.

I allowed myself a small, discreet smile, impressed with Kalas's quick thinking to ensure his father agreed to our plans.

"That's splendid," the king replied, standing. "I will get the letter I wrote to Queen Celestia. Do you have everything you need for your journey?"

"We do, thank you," I replied, dropping into a curtsy to show my appreciation to the king.

From the corner of my eye, I could feel the queen glaring at Kalas and me, although she said nothing until her husband left the room.

The moment the king had gone, she stood and crossed to Kalas and me, taking her son's hands in her own.

"Please, you don't have to leave immediately, do you? It's all happening so quickly." I was surprised by the desperation in her voice. I thought she had agreed to this alliance. Or was there some other reason for her reservations?

"Mother, please. It will all be okay. Queen Celestia is expecting us. It would not reflect well on our family if Maddie and I didn't arrive when we said we would," Kalas said, but his mother's expression remained worried. "Plus, the sooner we leave, the sooner we can return and start planning the wedding."

Queen Seraphina lifted her gaze to her son's, and for a moment, something like fear flashed in her eyes. "We were just hosting Lord Darakon," she said, seemingly changing the subject out of nowhere. "He has some concerns about your betrothed."

I balled my fists and clenched my teeth. The fucking never of that man. I reined in my anger and waited for Kalas to speak to his mother.

Kalas let go of his mother's hands, and I was surprised when he reached up to cup her face tenderly. I'd never seen such affection between the mother and son before.

"Aelrion Thalena, please don't worry. I know why you fear for me and Maddie, but this is what Korvarith Thalun wants. Not even Lord Darakon would challenge that. When we return, the wedding preparations will begin, and all Darakon's arguments will be pushed aside."

The queen sighed, raising her hands to squeeze Kalas's, which were still caressing her cheeks. "I can't help but worry about history repeating itself."

The queen's words intrigued me, and I intended to ask Kalas about them when we were alone.

After the king returned with his letter for Queen Celestia, Kalas and I bid goodbye to his parents, promising to contact them as soon as we arrived on Valeth.

From the palace, we made our way through the marketplace, and then north to where Kalas said the flying grounds were.

As we walked, our fingers entwined. I couldn't contain my curiosity anymore and asked, "What was that your mother meant about history repeating itself?"

Kalas sighed. "She's worried for us. She's scared that what happened to her will happen to me and you once we set a wedding date."

My eyes narrowed. "What do you mean?"

"My mother wasn't from this part of Kralis. She came from the south, from an area called Velithar. The customs there are different from the traditions here, and when Korvarith Thalun first chose her as Father's fated mate, it was difficult for her to settle into life at the palace. She had doubts about the marriage. Doubts other members of the court tried to use as evidence she wasn't worthy of someday becoming queen."

My mouth hung open as I absorbed Kalas's words. "Why didn't she just say that instead of being awful? I thought she hated me."

"I told you she didn't hate you," Kalas said. "I'm not sure why my mother thought it was best to act so coldly when you first arrived here. But I *knew* everything would be okay. Things worked out for my mother and father, and everything will work out for us, too."

I sighed, biting back a frustrated reply. "You didn't tell me your mother had doubts about marrying your father, or that other courtiers didn't think she was worthy of becoming queen. If you had mentioned that sooner, I might not have worried about my own position so much."

Kalas glanced at me, his brows drawn. "What is there to worry about? Korvarith Thalun declared you my fated mate for all to see. Nothing and no one challenges the word of The Twilight Crow."

This time, my annoyance bubbled over. "It's not that simple," I snapped, and Kalas's eyes widened. I had never spoken to him in such a harsh tone before.

"Maddie, my little witch, please, talk to me. Tell me what's on your mind?"

I counted slowly in my head, letting my anger subside. "We don't have time to discuss this now. We need to get to the flying grounds. But when we come back from Valeth, before we announce the wedding date, we need to have a proper talk about everything."

"As you wish," he replied blithely, and for the first time since meeting him, I felt annoyed by his nonchalance.

We arrived at a large field where various Kralians were undressing and transforming, then taking flight. Since arriving on Kralis, I had seen the wyvern-like creatures in the sky, but never this close.

My breath caught in my throat as I watched a female Kralian with short black hair transform. At first, feathers protruded from her back, like they did for Kalas, and her arms slowly morphed into wings, with her long, clawed fingers becoming talons. Her legs also changed in appearance, and she hunched over, using her talon-tipped wings as forelimbs to walk on all fours. Her face elongated into a beak filled with rows of razor-sharp teeth, and her eyes turned completely black.

The transformed Kralian started to grow in size as feathers covered her body, and a long tail grew from behind. Soon, she was the size of a horse and growing larger still. I marvelled, watching as the Kralian continued getting bigger, her neck elongating until she was about forty-foot long from snout to tail.

She opened her maw and let out a terrifying shriek akin to the sound I'd heard when Kalas and I had performed our betrothal ritual—part bird-cry, part rumbling of a crocodile—that sounded completely otherworldly.

I shuddered all over as the female Kralian flapped her wings and slowly rose into the sky.

"Wow," was all I could say.

"It's a sight, isn't it?" someone said beside me, and I turned to see Josain watching the departing Kralian with the same wonder I felt.

"I've only seen Kalas part-transformed before. I had no idea their bestial forms were so big!"

"I almost lost my mind when I first saw Savrion transform," Josain said. "Wait until you're in the air."

I felt dizzy just thinking about it and wondered if maybe it would be better if we used the witches' method of travel.

"Ah, there's Savrion," Kalas said from my other side, releasing my hand to cross the grounds to his friend.

Savrion was carrying a nyxorith trunk about the size of my own, which he laid on the ground as he neared Kalas, Josain, and me. I glanced at Josain and saw she had a simple leather satchel across her body. I made a mental note to make sure to buy my friend plenty of new outfits when we arrived on Valeth.

It wasn't long before Luna and Phoebe appeared, both smiling warmly as they greeted us.

"We have spoken to Queen Celestia, and she eagerly awaits our arrival," Luna said.

"She has been informed that you will be bringing companions, and a room will be readied for them," Phoebe added, then turned to introduce herself to Savrion and Josain.

Just as the introductions were being made, Kaelivar arrived, wheeling a trolley that held my and Kalas's trunks, as well as some thick, leather bindings.

"I have everything you requested, Your Highness," he said with a bow to Kalas.

"Perfect. The sun will be setting soon, and the moon is rising, which means you'll be ready to travel too?" Kalas asked Luna.

"Yes. Once we've cast the incantation to enable Maddie and Josain to breathe while in flight, we will return to our manse and cast the moonbeam transportation spell. We should arrive instantly and will wait for you to make your way to Valeth."

"I thought it might also be good if we cast a spell using my telekinetic abilities to ensure Josain and I don't fall from Savrion and Kalas's backs as we fly," I said, confirming both to myself and everyone else that I would by travelling with Kalas.

Despite the frustration I felt about him not telling me about his mother's experience when she'd first been chosen as King Eldarion's fated mate, I knew it was nothing we couldn't work out once we got the chance to talk properly. We'd overcome every challenge thrown at us.

"That's a good idea," Luna agreed. "How did you perform spells when on Earth?"

"Honestly, I didn't do it very often for fear someone would see and report me to the witch hunters. When I did, though, I would cast a circle, light candles, and call on the cardinal directions."

"Ah, so in much the same way as we do on Valeth," Phoebe said with a smile as she reached into the delicate pearlescent bag she was wearing. I thought perhaps it was made from lunavira.

From the bag, Phoebe pulled out five candles—one red, one yellow, one green, one blue, and the final violet—as well as what looked like a small bag of salt.

"Shall we begin?"

"Yes, please," I replied, eager to watch another witch cast a spell.

"Are we allowed to cast an incantation here, Your Highness?" Phoebe asked Kalas.

"Yes, of course. The only place incantations are not permitted are within the ritual chambers of the royal palace."

"Okay, Maddie and Josain, if you could stand beside each other, please," Phoebe instructed, handing the five candles to Luna.

Josain and I stood next to each other, our arms brushing, and Phoebe walked in a circle around us, pouring salt from the pouch as she went. She criss-crossed the circle with lines that formed a five-pointed star, with Josain and me in the central position.

Following Phoebe, Luna laid down a candle on each point of the star and then lit them in turn with a simple wave of her hand. I was amazed she conjured fire so easily and vowed to ask her to teach me.

Finally, Phoebe and Luna stood side by side at the northern point of the star, staring into the circle at Josain and me.

"If you could link hands with Josain and me, that will transfer the magic more fully," Phoebe said.

I grasped one of Josain's hands in mine, and with the other, extended my arm through the circle to take Phoebe's outstretched hand. Then, Phoebe took Luna's other hand, while Luna offered her remaining hand to Josain, completing the circuit.

Out of the corner of my eye, I saw Kalas and Savrion watching the ritual with interest. Even Josain seemed to be taking in every detail of what Phoebe and Luna were doing.

# Chapter Twenty-Seven
# The Witches From Valeth

Kalas and Savrion weren't the only Kralians watching what Luna and Phoebe were doing, and soon, a small group of onlookers had gathered.

My heart rate increased, and I looked around, worried that at any moment, someone would interrupt us, and we'd all be arrested for magic use.

But that never happened. Instead, the gathered Kralians watched with polite curiosity, the same way you might when seeing a musician for the first time. There was no hostility in anyone's gaze, only intrigue.

"Repeat the words of the spell after Luna and I speak them," Phoebe told me, and I nodded.

"We call on the Power of the North and the Element Terra to lend us its strength. We invoke the Power of the East and the Element Air to carry our voices to the cosmos. We beseech the Power of the South and the Element Fire to infuse our casting with willpower. We implore the Power of the West and the Element Water to give us conviction in our casting. In the name of the Great Moon Mother Vesper, we ask that she grant Maddie and Josain the ability to breathe in space and remain safely on their Kralian mounts as they travel to Valeth. By the power of three, we summon thee. As we desire, so shall it be."

The words were familiar, similar to the spells I'd cast on Earth, but also felt like they carried more weight, especially the combination of cardinal directions and the elements, along with the addition of the Moon Mother's name.

Around the circle, the candles flickered, their flames growing in length, and I felt the magic flowing through me. I felt connected to the universe in a way I had never experienced before, and if I had wanted to, I could have easily slipped into the minds of anyone around.

I held my telepathic abilities at bay, instead focusing on the intent of the spell, to enable Josain and me to breathe in space and keep us safe as we rode on Kalas and Savrion in their bestial forms.

As I gazed up at the sky, the magenta sun of the Throvani Ethrionth Star System sank into the horizon, and the pale purple moon rose in the enveloping indigo. As I watched the moon, it almost seemed as though it had a face—the most kindly, feminine face I'd ever seen. The perfect example of a loving and doting mother.

The moon smiled down on us, and I knew we had the Moon Mother Vesper's blessing.

"The spell is cast," Phoebe said, stepping back, and then bending to extinguish the candles in front of her while Luna cleared away the salt. I turned to Josain.

"Do you feel any different?" I asked.

Josain's brows drew together, and she chewed on her bottom lip. "I think so. But I can't really explain how. I guess we'll know for sure once we're in the air."

"What if the spell hasn't worked?" Kalas asked, coming to stand beside me and taking my hand.

"It has," I insisted. "I'm certain of it."

I glanced at Phoebe and Luna, who both nodded.

"Well, I guess the only way to know for sure is for us to transform and take flight," Savrion said.

Without warning, Kalas and Savrion began pulling off their clothing. I should have anticipated this, given the female Kralian I had watched transform when we'd first arrived had been naked too. But somehow, that hadn't registered in my mind until now.

Most of the Kralians who had gathered to watch Luna and Phoebe cast the spell were now departing, and none seemed surprised to see their crown prince half-naked. In fact, aside from me, no one even batted an eyelid. Perhaps the attitude to nudeness was different on Kralis, which made sense for a race who could shapeshift.

Still, it felt wrong seeing anyone other than Kalas naked, so I kept my focus solely on him, even if I was slightly curious to see how Savrion compared.

Josain had no such problems, openly staring at Kalas's naked body, and then giving me an approving wink.

Her blatantness put me at ease, and I relaxed as Kalas began to transform.

Even though I'd not long ago seen a female Kralian transform, I still watched with interest as feathers pierced Kalas's skin and his limbs elongated. Once his transformation was complete, he was even bigger than the female had been; I guessed about fifty-foot long. To his left stood Savrion in his bestial form, only slightly smaller than Kalas, and with lilac-streaked white feathers that matched his hair instead of the dark feathers Kalas had.

Kalas rearranged a few of his feathers with his beak and then stared at me pointedly. Though his eyes were completely black, they still held the same intelligence I was used to.

"You're gorgeous," I said, stepping forward and running my hands through the feathers on his head.

Kalas nipped at my hand affectionately, and then lowered his back, bending his wing so I could easily climb on. There was a natural niche between his wings where I slotted easily, and I grabbed a handful of feathers to keep myself steady. Beside me, Josain was mounting Savrion in a similar way.

Once we were settled, Kaelivar spread the leather straps over Kalas's back just behind me and then attached them to our trunks, which were already bound together to form one large unit.

Kalas opened his wings, and I let out a gasp. His wingspan was easily double the length of his body. He flapped his wings, causing the air to swirl around us and dust to fly up from the ground. Before I knew it, we were in the air.

For a moment, I screwed my eyes up tightly, afraid to look at the ground below, but I could hear Josain hollering with joy and knew this wasn't something I wanted to miss.

Slowly, I prised open my eyes and dared to look down. We weren't that far above the top of the trees yet, and I could still make out the details of the people below, including Luna and Phoebe, who were waving up at us.

From the leather straps, the trunks hung below Kalas's legs, though they didn't seem to obstruct his movements, and as far as I could tell, the extra weight was no issue for him. I forced myself to keep my eyes open as we flew higher. Soon, Phoebe, Luna, and Kaelivar were just tiny dots on the ground below us.

Josain seemed in her element on Savrion's back, and I was shocked to see she wasn't even holding onto his feathers. Instead, her hands were raised to the sky, as though she was trying to capture the stars.

I wasn't quite there yet, but I could feel an invisible tether keeping me securely on Kalas's back, and even as Kralis grew smaller below us, my ability to breathe remained unaffected.

Air rushed around me as we left Kralis's atmosphere, and we were out, flying in the expanse of space. Below me, Kralis looked like a giant orb of nyxorith. The moon was a pale purple disc that remained steadfast in the inky sky, and to the west was another orb, this one a pearlescent white that shimmered like the lunavira plates and cutlery had.

Valeth.

Around us, stars twinkled, and as Valeth drew closer and became larger, so Kralis diminished in size until it was just a black speck in the sky.

Oddly, I wasn't cold, despite only wearing a thin robe the queen had given me, and I assumed this too was to do with the spell Luna and Phoebe had cast.

Feeling a little braver, I unclutched Kalas's feathers and extended my hands to the skies. I could still feel the magical tethers keeping me rooted to Kalas's back, and I knew I wouldn't fall.

From nearby, I heard an excited cry and turned to see Josain astride Savrion's back. She was reaching up so far that her legs were barely clamped around his body, but still, the spell Luna, Phoebe, and I had cast held her firmly in place. The grin on her face stretched from ear-to-ear, and her eyes sparkled with unabashed elation.

I opened my mouth, letting a cry of exhilaration escape me in a jumble of incoherent words.

Valeth drew closer, appearing as a giant orb of lunavira in the sky, the exact same size as Kralis, its perfect twin except for their opposite colouring.

Suddenly, Kalas dove down, and I clutched onto his feathers tightly. Rapidly, the streets and towns of Valeth came into view, and we approached a massive crystalline palace. It was taller than the obsidian palace of Kralis, with twice as many turrets and spires. One tower was tallest of all, reaching into the clouds and tipped with a shimmering silver sigil—a large, full moon that glowed with magical adularescence.

In front of the crystalline palace was a large, open courtyard, where I could see many people gathered. To my delight, almost all of them had the same coppery hair as Luna, Phoebe, and I; a mark of the witches from Valeth.

In the middle of the gathering stood a trio in resplendent silver and white gowns, all wearing jewel encrusted diadems. From a distance, they looked almost indistinguishable from each other, all three women appearing to be around their mid-twenties. I assumed from the extra grandeur of her clothing and crown that the woman in the middle was Queen Celestia.

Staring at these women, my grip of Kalas's feathers grew slick, and I felt nervousness akin to when we'd arrived on Kralis. Not only were these women the monarchy and princesses of Valeth, but also my kin, all of us having descended from Queen Ursula.

As we neared the ground, I couldn't take my eyes off the royal trio. Now we were closer, I saw the subtle signs of age on Queen Celestia's face, the soft lines around her eyes and mouth, but it was still hard to believe she was much older than thirty.

Looking at her and her two daughters was like looking at the family I'd always dreamed of. I could see shades of not only myself but my mother and grandmother in all of them. Though, Queen Celestia and the princesses held more love in their gazes than my mother had for me.

Kalas's taloned feet touched down on the courtyard floor, and I quickly dismounted, giving his head an affectionate stroke before rushing forward to greet Queen Celestia.

I hesitated for a moment, wondering if I should curtsy as I did to Queen Seraphina, but then Queen Celestia strode forward confidently and opened her arms to me.

She pulled me into a tight embrace, pressing a kiss to each of my cheeks as she whispered into my ear, "Welcome home, daughter of Vesper."

A hundred emotions surged through my body. Relief, excitement, love. Tears rolled down my cheeks. Queen Celestia gently wiped them away with her thumbs and then linked her arm through mine.

"Come, let me introduce you to my daughters, Princesses Aurora and Nima."

Out of the corner of my eye, I was vaguely aware that Kalas and Savrion had transformed back into their humanoid forms, and someone had presented them with simple silver robes to cover themselves.

They stood with the gathered Valethians, and I noticed that Luna and Phoebe had arrived, although when and where from I wasn't entirely sure.

# Chapter Twenty-Eight
# Moon Mother, Vesper

I was surprised with the familiarity and lack of formality Queen Celestia showed me as she led me to Aurora and Nima. She treated me like an equal, as though I was already part of her family.

Princesses Aurora and Nima were as beautiful as their mother, with hair like molten copper and emerald green eyes. I guessed Aurora was the slightly older of the two, and I estimated her to be about the same age as I was, while Nima looked to be in her early twenties. Both were dressed in white gowns decorated with silver embroidery that depicted the moon, stars, and cosmos. On their heads, they wore crowns only slightly more modest than their mother's, both topped with lunavira full moons in the centre.

"Welcome home," Princess Aurora said, embracing me with the same warmth her mother had.

Princess Nima also greeted me like a long-lost family member, and soon, I was huddled with the three women as we stood in the centre of the courtyard, the nobility of Valeth gathered around.

I scanned the area for Kalas and noticed him talking to a handsome man with golden blonde hair and beautiful blue eyes. I wondered for a moment if he were the king, Queen Celestia's husband, but he looked too young.

The man with the blond hair ushered Kalas and Savrion over to us and then folded into a polite bow.

"Your Majesty, I am at your service," he said to Queen Celestia before turning to me and adding, "And I welcome you, Princess Consort Madelyne."

"Thank you, sir."

"Forgive me. I am Lord Orpheus, betrothed to Princess Aurora," he said, extending his hand to me.

I took it, and he gripped my hand tightly, shaking it firmly. I stared into his eyes, dazzled by how beautiful they were, and for a moment, I felt a little giddy.

It wasn't until Lord Orpheus released my hand and Kalas appeared at my side that I felt like myself again.

"It's a pleasure to meet you," I said, hastily adding, "And may I introduce my betrothed and Crown Prince of Kralis, Kalas."

Kalas stepped forward, extending his hand to Queen Celestia first before greeting each of the princesses, and then Lord Orpheus. Finally, he beckoned Savrion and Josain forward and introduced them too.

We were quickly joined by Phoebe and Luna, who also greeted the queen and princesses warmly.

"I imagine you would all like a moment to rest and refresh yourselves before we meet in my solarium, and so I will have Lord Orpheus show you to the guest quarters. I will have someone bring your belongings," Queen Celestia said.

"Thank you, Your Majesty," I said, this time dropping into a curtsy, as I was aware of the watchful eyes on me. While Queen Celestia had initially greeted me with familiarity, I'd already learned enough about royal etiquette on Kralis that I knew it was best to err on the side of caution.

"Please, follow me," Lord Orpheus said, stepping forward.

As Kalas, Savrion, Josain, and I followed Lord Orpheus across the courtyard and into the crystalline palace, I just caught a glimpse of Queen Celestia talking in hushed whispers to Luna and Phoebe.

Inside the crystalline palace was just as stunning as the outside. It was equally as extravagant as the Palace of Kralis, but due to the different materials used in its construction, it felt light and airy. Everywhere I looked, there were columns and pillars made from lunavira, along with other architectural or decorative pieces made from what I assumed were opals, moonstone, and quartz.

I could feel the magic humming through the palace, its tendrils tickling the edge of my mind, and I knew if I allowed myself, I could easily call on my telepathic or telekinetic abilities. Yet, at the same time, I felt more in control of my powers than ever, and I knew I wouldn't accidentally read someone's mind or cause an object to levitate.

Kalas held my hand as we continued along the corridor and up a grand staircase. He too looked around the palace with interest, and behind us, I could hear Savrion and Josain whispering to each other.

As we reached the second floor, Lord Orpheus pointed out portraits of past monarchs, and I paused, interested to look at them.

I quickly found the familiar face of Aster, accompanied by their sisters, Alsephina and Andromeda, as well as a portrait of Queen Ursula.

My eyes landed on a portrait of a woman who looked so much like my own mother that it made me gasp.

"Who is this?" I asked Lord Orpheus

"That is the late Queen Cressida, mother of Queen Celestia and daughter of Queen Alsephina."

I stared at the portrait of Queen Cressida for a moment, stunned to see such warmth and happiness on my mother's face. I wondered, was this what she could have been like if we'd lived on Valeth?

Pushing the thought out of my head, I allowed my gaze to travel to the portraits of the queen and princesses and saw a picture of a handsome man with long silver hair similar to Savrion's. He had a neatly trimmed white beard and bright blue eyes.

"And who is this?"

"The late King Sterling, husband and consort of Queen Celestia. He sadly passed away a few years ago." Lord Orpheus's voice told me how much respect and reverence he had for the late king consort, and I bowed my head.

"I'm sorry for your loss," I said.

"The whole realm felt his passing. He was a great man, and a dedicated king consort. I wish to be even half as distinguished as he was when I marry Princess Aurora and she eventually ascends the throne."

I felt a sudden kinship with Lord Orpheus. I didn't know his background, or if he'd grown up as part of the nobility, but regardless, we were both in a similar situation, betrothed to a realm's heir, with all the weight of the future hanging on our shoulders.

I gave him a small, soft smile. "I'm sure you will be."

Beside me, Kalas tensed a little, and I couldn't help wondering if he was jealous.

We turned away from the portraits, and Lord Orpheus led us to a hallway with two doorways facing each other.

"These are the guest quarters. The room to the left is for yourself and the crown prince, and the room to your right is for your attendants. I hope you find them to your liking," he said, bowing politely. "I will leave you to settle in and return later to escort you to the queen's solarium."

The doors he indicated were huge, taking up most of the wall and made from what appeared to be solid lunavira. I pushed on the door to the left, expecting it to be heavy, but it opened with surprising ease.

At the opposite doorway, I saw it took the efforts of both Savrion and Josain to enter their chamber. It took me a moment to realise the door had opened so easily for me because I'd used my telekinetic abilities. It felt nice that, for once, I was the one with the extraordinary power, and I wasn't having to rely on Kalas.

The room was almost as large as my and Kalas's quarters at the Obsidian Palace, with a small sitting area and a massive bed. Two doors led off from the room, which I assumed were the bathroom and dressing room.

Even though these were guest quarters, I instantly felt at home and more relaxed than I did at the Obsidian Palace, where it still largely felt like Kalas's home, not mine.

I lay down on the bed, delighted by not only the softness of the sheets, but the thick plushness of the mattress. It felt like sinking into a marshmallow, and I knew if I allowed myself, I could easily have drifted off to sleep.

I felt Kalas's weight join me on the bed, and I turned to him.

"I wish you would have told me sooner about your mother and father's history. Knowing that she struggled with some of the same feelings I am would have helped me," I said, bringing up the earlier argument we'd had before leaving Kralis.

"I'm sorry, my little witch. Sometimes I forget that you're not familiar with all the customs and history of Kralis. When we return, I will speak to mother about how she treated you when you first arrived."

This set my mind at ease, and I closed the distance and pressed my lips to his.

"You know, you don't have to be jealous of Lord Orpheus. He's handsome, but no one will ever compare to you. I was only thinking how similar our situations are, both of us being betrothed to the heir to a realm."

Kalas didn't blush often, but a pink flush covered his alabaster cheeks, and he gazed away guiltily. "You felt that?"

I chuckled, cupping his face in my hands and turning his gaze back to me. "I did, and I want you to know you have nothing to worry about. I love you, and only you."

"I'm sorry. I'm not usually so possessive, but something in the way Lord Orpheus looked at you brought out my animal instinct."

"It's probably just strange for him, meeting a witch who isn't from Valeth. Plus, there's the family resemblance. While I share some features with Luna and Phoebe, it's clear we're not related, whereas looking at Queen Celestia and the princesses is like looking at my cousins or something. You know, my mother looks exactly like Queen Cressida. It startled me when I first saw her portrait. It makes me wonder about what could have been."

Kalas pressed his lips to mine, then said, "It must be difficult for you, invarali taleni."

I shrugged. "Part of me can't help but wonder what my life would have been like if I were born on Valeth, or if Earth was more tolerant of witches. But at the same time, I'm glad to be here. It feels like home."

After checking on Josain and Savrion, it wasn't long before Lord Orpheus returned to escort us all to Queen Celestia's solarium. We were led up another flight of stairs, and I realized we were going to the tallest tower I had noticed on our arrival.

"The royal family has always had their quarters in this area of the palace, as it's closest to the moon, and therefore our Moon Mother, Vesper," Lord Orpheus explained as we ascended.

We entered a circular room that was, once again, made from a mixture of lunavira, opals, moonstone, and quartz. Instead of windows were rounded archways covered by sheer curtains, but all open to the night sky. The sun had set, and the sky was a deep indigo, dotted with bright, twinkling stars. The moon was prominent in the inky darkness, and its presence in the sky felt comforting.

Queen Celestia and the princesses were gathered around a circular quartz coffee table, where refreshments were already laid out.

"Please, make yourselves comfortable," Queen Celestia said, gesturing to the unoccupied chaise lounges opposite where she and the princesses were seated.

Lord Orpheus settled himself beside Aurora, while Kalas and I sat on one of the empty chaise lounges.

"Please, help yourselves to refreshments. There is spiced cherry wine, along with crackers and lunithar."

Lunithar turned out to be a smooth, velvety rich cream cheese that paired perfectly with not only the salty crackers but the spiced tartness of the cherry wine.

As we enjoyed the refreshments provided, Queen Celestia spoke openly about the research she had been doing, and her conclusion that Vesper and Korvarith Thalun were lovers; two sides of the same coin.

"Yes, I wondered the same," I agreed. "And it seems King Eldarion has similar thoughts too, or at the very least, he wishes to strengthen the alliance between Valeth and Kralis."

I told Celestia about King Eldarion's alliance proposal, and she smiled. "Vesper came to me in a dream recently and told me that King Eldarion would make such an offer. She said it was for the benefit of the entire Throvani Ethrionth Star System that I accept. I know you and Prince Kalas are still to be married, as are Aurora and Lord Orpheus, but I agree that when children of these unions are born, they should be betrothed. I propose an exchange of my second grandchild for your second child, so that the bloodlines of Queen Ursula will once again be united and sit on the thrones of Valeth and Kralis respectively."

It was exactly as King Eldarion wanted, and though it was strange for me to think about betrothing a child I hadn't even conceived yet, I wasn't completely opposed to the idea. If I had to send one of my future children to live on another planet, there was no better home than Valeth. And if Aurora and I oversaw the betrothals, we could ensure our future children grew up knowing each other.

I just had one condition. "I'd be open to betrothing any children Kalas and I have to any children Aurora and Lord Orpheus have as long as they're free to end the betrothal if they don't love their intended. Would you agree to this?"

Celestia smiled. "I would. The intentions of Vesper and Korvarith Thalun are clear to me. This is why you are Kalas's fated mate. You were meant to return to your true home and unite the separate bloodlines of Ursula."

Celestia's words warmed my heart. I now had no doubts that no matter what happened between Kalas and me, I'd have a home here on Valeth. I also knew it was the designs of two benevolent deities that had bought Kalas and me together. Uniting the bloodlines of Ursula and strengthening the alliance between Kralis and Valeth was a *huge* honour. An honour the deities had bestowed on me.

My and Kalas's love really *was* bound in starlight.

# Chapter Twenty-Nine
# Exhilarating

Leaving Valeth and returning to Kralis was bittersweet.

The few days we spent on Valeth, getting to know Celestia, Aurora, and Nima, learning more about the history of the planet and its royal family, visiting the markets of Valeth and getting new clothes for Josain and me, and attending the Temple of Vesper to have my magical gifts expanded were the happiest of my life.

I had found where I belonged. I was a child of Vesper, and a descendant of Queen Ursula. No matter what happened in the future, Valeth was my home and the royal family were *my* family.

It didn't take long for Aurora and Nima to become like sisters to me, and plans were made for us to attend the marriage of Aurora and Orpheus. Celestia became the mother I'd longed for; warm, loving, and full of advice about anything and everything.

I confided in her how Lord Darakon had treated me since my arrival on Kralis, and Celestia assured me that if anyone objected to my and Kalas's marriage, she and the might of Valeth would support me against them.

It was also wonderful to see Josain and Savrion freely enjoying each other's company and the love they shared without fear of his father finding out or anyone remarking on their class differences.

The bond I'd already formed with Luna and Phoebe grew, and I made more friends within the nobility and courtiers.

While Kralis was welcoming on the surface, there was an undercurrent there I could no longer ignore. Lord Darakon, Lady Voritha, and others like them who believed the bloodline of Kralis should remain 'pure' were hard to turn a blind eye to. Their feelings about outsiders, especially those from the planets farthest from Kralis, was all too similar to how the people of Earth treated anyone different, especially witches.

While witches were tolerated on Kralis due to their connection to Valeth, I knew if I hadn't been descended from the Valethian royal family, there would be more pushback against my and Kalas's impending marriage.

An Earth human, witch or not, just wasn't worthy of the crown prince in their eyes.

It was strange, thinking about how leaving Earth with Kalas and accompanying him to Kralis had traded one set of prejudices for another. I was no longer feared for my magical abilities, but in many ways, I was still an outsider.

Part of me longed to stay on Valeth forever. I knew we could be happy there. We could even have Josain and Savrion join us. I could continue expanding my magical abilities, and Kalas could still live in the luxury he was accustomed to, only without any of the responsibilities of being heir.

Despite my preference to stay on Valeth, I made the decision not to let the prejudices of people like Darakon and Voritha come between me and me fated mate. I was now utterly convinced that both Vesper and Korvarith Thalun meant for Kalas and I to be together, and I wasn't going let a group of narrow-minded bigots ruin that.

As we said our goodbyes to Celestia, Aurora, and Nima and made plans to visit again soon, it was with a renewed determination that I climbed on Kalas's back and prepared for the journey back to Kralis.

The flight back to Kralis was exhilarating. Confident that my magic would keep both Josain and me safe, we reached up from our respective mounts, chasing stars as our lovers carried us home. Our jubilant cheers filled the air, and by the time we landed back on Kralis, our faces were flushed. My eyes were watering from the cosmic wind, and my face ached from smiling so much.

I pulled Josain to my side, wrapping one arm around her shoulder as Kalas and Savrion transformed from their bestial forms. Kaelivar had been informed of our pending return and was waiting with a change of clothing for the two Kralians as we landed in the field used for transformations.

"I'm going to have a special chamber allocated to you as close to my and Kalas's quarters as possible. I'll ensure only you and I have access to it, so that you and Savrion can use it whenever you need some time alone," I told her in a whisper.

"Thank you, Maddie," Josain replied, squeezing my hand. "It's been amazing just being with him without watching over our shoulders these past few days."

"The joy that radiates from the pair of you is unmistakable."

Josain's green eyes widened to comical proportions. "Thank you, Your Highness," she said.

"I'll have none of that. I'm your friend, not your master."

Josain smiled. "Thank you for everything, Maddie."

"Thank you for being the first true friend I made when I came here," I replied, pressing a kiss to her cheek.

I was thankful we weren't summoned to speak with the king and queen as soon as we returned. In fact, I was pleasantly surprised to find a note waiting for us in our quarters inviting us to meet with Kalas's parents the following morning, meaning Kalas and I would have the remainder of the day alone in our chambers.

While on Valeth, along with the clothing I'd bought, I'd purchased many books, trinkets, and other items to make the room feel more 'mine'. I had portraits of Celestia, Aurora, and Nima, as well as pictures of Ursula, Alsephina, Andromeda, and Aster, and a massive tapestry of the royal family tree of Valeth. I'd also bought an enchanted looking-glass that would enable me to speak with my loved-ones on Valeth whenever I wished.

I dismissed Josain for the rest of the day, insisting she spend some quality time with Savrion, and that I was perfectly capable of readying myself for bed. I took a long, hot bath, and then with no plans for the rest of the day, I changed into a lightweight nightgown I'd bought on Valeth. While the clothing Queen Seraphina had given to me was gorgeous, it wasn't my style, as Kalas's mother favoured lighter colours than I preferred. My nightgown was black satin, fringed with lace, and I knew the tantalizing glimpse of my cleavage it revealed would drive Kalas wild.

ALL TOO SOON, MY NIGHT of undisturbed bliss with Kalas was brought to an end by a gentle knock on the door.

A glance out of the window showed the magenta sun rising in the sky, and I knew it was morning.

"Please come in," I called, reaching for my discarded satin robe.

Josain entered, looking like she'd had an equally blissful evening of her own, wheeling in the customary trolley containing breakfast. I quickly covered myself and sat up in bed, offering her a warm smile.

"Good morning., Thanks for bringing breakfast," I said, reaching for the glass of nekka-nekka berry juice. "Did you sleep well?"

"I did, thank you," Josain replied, a faint blush tinting her cheeks that made me assume Savrion might have kept her up late into the night, just like Kalas had with me.

"How are your new quarters?" I asked, reaching for a piece of light bread that I spread with nekka-nekka berry jam.

"They're wonderful, thank you," Josain said.

"I'll need your help dressing for my and Kalas's meeting with the king and queen, but after that, you're welcome to spend the day as you please. Kalas and I will probably head out to the market for lunch, and I can get ready for bed myself."

Josain grinned. "Thank you. And if you *do* need anything, don't worry about disturbing me. I'm at your service."

After breakfast, and with the help of Josain, I bathed and dressed for the day. Much of the clothing I had bought on Valeth favoured the style of the planet, and while light, moon colours were popular with the queen and princesses, a variety of hues could be found in the merchant stores and tailors. While the fashion of Kralis was reminiscent of ancient civilizations from Earth, like Egypt, Greece, and Mayan, the clothing on Valeth was more akin to Earth's mediaeval fashion, with corset bodices and long, dagger-tipped sleeves. I blended the styles of Valeth and Kralis together, adding my own Earth-flair, into a style that was uniquely mine.

Once I was ready, I returned to my and Kalas's chambers and found him sitting on our bed, dressed in one of the outfits I'd bought for him on Valeth.

He looked amazing in the leather tailcoat that cinched in his waist and fastened with laces up the back in a similar way to my own corset. The front featured contrasting panels of purple damask and faux moonstone buttons that glittered in the torchlight. The tails of the coat flared out and ended in points around his tight black trousers and sturdy boots. Usually, Kralian regalia was quite revealing, so something about the almost suited look made my heart race. I saw Kalas naked so often that seeing him in finely tailored clothing, shaped to his lean, lithe body was a rare treat.

"You look gorgeous," I said, crossing the room to him and offering my hand.

"As do you, my little witch," he replied, taking my hand and kissing my knuckles before he got to his feet. "I wasn't sure about the Valethian fashion to begin with, but I have to admit, we make quite the pair like this."

I smiled, lacing my fingers with his. "We do, don't we?"

I wanted to talk to Kalas before we spoke with his parents, as I knew the king and queen would be eager for us to set a wedding date now that we'd returned from Valeth. But we didn't have time to discuss anything before Ashryn arrived at our chambers saying Kalas's parents wanted to see us both immediately.

Hand-in-hand, we made our way to the royal parlour, where the king and queen awaited us. The royal couple's eyes widened when they saw our new clothing, but then Queen Seraphina smiled and beckoned us to her.

"I always did love the fashions of Valeth," she said as we greeted her and the king in turn. "And those dark colours really suit you, Maddie."

I was taken aback by the warmth in her voice. Was the queen finally growing to accept me?

We sat and were served juice, while Kalas and I filled the king and queen in on our time on Valeth. I told them Queen Celestia had accepted not only the alliance between the two planets but the marriage pact between Aurora's future children, and the children Kalas and I would someday have. I also revealed the connection between Korvarith Thalun and Vesper, and that the pair were a couple bound in starlight, just as Kalas and I would be.

The king grinned broadly. "Korvarith Thalun's blessing to us all. And it seems, just as I have the love of a beautiful and dedicated queen, so The Twilight Crow has their Moon Mother."

There was a small lapse in conversation before Kalas said, "I hope you don't mind, Mother, but I told Maddie about how you originally came from

Velithar and had trouble settling in when you first moved here. I also told her about how other members of the royal court tried to use this as evidence you weren't worthy of someday becoming queen. Maddie has been having similar doubts herself, so I thought hearing what you went through would ease her mind. I also wanted to ask if that's why you were cold towards Maddie when she first arrived here. I understand you feared history repeating itself, but that's no reason for you to have made her feel so unwelcome."

Silence filled the parlour, and for a moment, I feared Kalas had said too much. The king and queen stared at us steadily, hardly blinking, and the air in the room felt thick.

My heart rate increased as Seraphina rose from her seat beside Eldarion and crossed the room to stand in front of me. I feared she was about to strike me and then banish me from Kralis.

Instead, Kalas's mother offered me her hands, staring down into my eyes with genuine affection.

"Forgive me, please, Madelyne, for I judged you too quickly. I feared you wouldn't be able to rise to the challenges of being betrothed to the crown prince. I feared the nobility would tear you apart like they tried to do with me, and that my only son would be left heartbroken. I now see you have strength I didn't have at your age."

My breath left me in a whoosh, and I smiled up at Seraphina, tears filling my eyes. "If I am to forgive you, then you are to forgive me. When we first met, I accidentally read your thoughts and heard something you never intended to say aloud. I based my perception of you on a handful of comments instead of getting to know you."

Seraphina knelt in front of me, her own eyes brimming with tears. "Aelrion Vethara," she said, and I realised she had called me 'cherished daughter.' "Let us start anew, please?"

I squeezed her hand tighter. "I would like that very much, Aelrion Thalena."

# Chapter Thirty
# They Will Do Everything
# They Can To Tear You Apart

Queen Seraphina stood, pressed kisses to my and Kalas's cheeks, and then returned to her place beside the king.

The royal pair entwined fingers, and then Seraphina continued speaking.

"Eldarion, I love you deeply, but both you and Kalas underestimate the threat Lord Darakon poses. While you visited Valeth, I was approached by someone named Zarathian, who had once trained to be a priest of Korvarith Thalun. He told me that Darakon believes that only he knows the true intentions of The Twilight Crow and that Madelyne being chosen as Kalas's fated mate was a mistake.

"From what Zarathian told me, Darakon is building a rebellion against us, and we must act swiftly but carefully if we are to have peace in Kralis. While I have no objections to the plans of unity between Kralis and Valeth, I think it is best that we speak of them as little as possible until *after* the wedding. For now, we must keep those who wish to rise against us on our side."

Feeling more comfortable in my relationship with Queen Seraphina, I asked, "But why? If you believe mine and Kalas's marriage is the will of Korvarith Thalun, and that The Twilight Crow punishes all who defy Them, why is Darakon even a threat? Can't we just let him get on with his schemes, and then Korvarith Thalun will punish him accordingly?"

Queen Seraphina sighed. "I wish it were that simple. But if Darakon believes that what he does is in fact in the name of Korvarith Thalun, then he does not fear The Twilight Crow's punishment. This makes him unpredictable, and dangerous. He may find some way to *force* you and Kalas to end your relationship Madelyne. Or worse, he may attempt to harm you. We can't let that happen."

"Zarathian told me that Darakon has enlisted Voritha and Thalyn in his schemes. As wedding preparations begin, their attempts make Thalyn Kalas's bride will only increase. Voritha is a vain and ambitious woman who will stop at nothing to get what she wants. On her own, Thalyn would probably be harmless, but her mother has twisted the once genuine love Thalyn and Kalas shared, shaping it to fit her machinations. They will do everything they can to tear you and Kalas apart. My advice is to do as I do and keep a close eye on them."

"Thank you for your advice, Your Majesty. I will keep it all in mind," I said, genuinely grateful for the queen's warning.

Kalas's mother smiled. "Please, when we are in private, feel free to call me Seraphina."

"In light of all that Seraphina has told us about Darakon, you must announce the date of your marriage immediately," King Eldarion said, picking up where his wife had left off. "We will arrange for a ball to be held as soon as possible and during the celebrations, you are to announce the date of your marriage one moon's turn from now."

A moon's turn. That was only four weeks away. I shouldn't have been surprised, given all that the king and queen had already said, but it still seemed fast.

While, on the surface, things with Kalas and me were good, I still felt a shadow of distance between the two of us. We still hadn't had a proper chance to talk everything through yet.

I'd promised the king we'd set a wedding date when we returned from Valeth, but I hadn't expected for it to be so soon.

I glanced at Kalas helplessly, our minds connecting in an instant.

*'Four weeks is still too soon,'* I said telepathically. *'There are things you and I need to discuss before I can agree to marry you. Do you think your father would be willing to give us more time?'*

*'I will certainly ask him, my little witch.'*

I watched nervously as Kalas's focus shifted to his father. "Actually, we were hoping to have a longer engagement, if possible, please. Maddie and I are still getting to know each other."

King Eldarion sighed. "I wish I could allow that, but if Darakon plots against the royal family, I believe the best way to foil his schemes is for the two of you to marry as soon as possible. Once you're married, there's nothing he can do to tear you apart."

While Eldarion made a good point, my mind lingered on what else Seraphina had said – that Darakon might attempt to harm me.

"Will I be safe? What if Darkon attacks me?"

"I won't let anyone hurt you," Kalas said, squeezing my hand tightly. "If I can't be with you, I will ensure someone we trust is."

"Don't worry, we will protect you, Madelyne," Eldarion said.

"WE will make sure Darakon is stopped," Seraphina said. "Zarathian has in his possession an ancient book that might reveal the key to proving Darakon's untrustworthiness. Once he's finished translating it, we can move against Darakon."

The king and queen's words reassured me, but it was Kalas's strong and steady presence beside me that eased my worries the most.

THE NEXT FEW DAYS PASSED in a blur as preparations for the ball were made.

Despite the looming threat Darakon posed, Kalas was in good spirits. He was excited about our forthcoming marriage, and constantly told me how happy he was that I was to officially become his consort.

I was happy too, mostly. It was easy, when I was with Kalas, and we were alone in our chambers, to forget everything and everyone else. The way he looked deeply into my eyes and the things he made my body feel as his fingertips and tongue gently caressed my every curve chased away the dark, lingering doubts.

Even when we weren't together, and I was in the company of Seraphina as we were fitted for outfits for the ball, it was easy to imagine a happy future together with my newfound family.

Kalas had promised once we were married, we'd take an extended honeymoon, visiting both Valeth and Valoriani Ealuna, and anywhere else I wanted to go. He even suggested returning to Earth if I wanted, and seeing some of the beauty and wonder there.

Likewise, King Eldarion was making plans. He told us that once we were married and had taken our honeymoon, steps would be made to ensure the crown's complete control.

Apparently

The queen continued to caution me to keep Voritha and Thalyn close and give them no reasons to doubt my conviction to marry Kalas. That was easy enough, as I'd had limited contact with my romantic rival and her mother since we'd returned from Valeth. I knew that peacefulness wouldn't last for long, however. Once my and Kalas's wedding day was announced, no doubt Voritha would increase her schemes, and of course, they'd be expected to be involved in the wedding preparations. Not including them would be a massive political faux pas that could turn the nobility against me.

Finally, the day of the ball arrived, and much of the morning was spent in the company of Seraphina and her handmaiden, Taena, along with Josain as we got ready for the celebrations.

I was trying to strike a balance between having Josain with me whenever appropriate, so that no one asked any awkward questions about her whereabouts and allowing her time to herself.

I was especially excited for the ball, as my loved ones from Valeth would be attending, including Celestia herself, who hadn't visited Kralis since before her husband's passing. Another small step we were taking to prepare the people of Kralis for the strengthened alliance between the two planets.

I knew having Celestia, Aurora, and Nima here with me would help me withstand whatever obstacles Darakon, Voritha, and Thalyn tried to throw in my and Kalas's path to happiness.

To my surprise, Darakon was conspicuously absent from the ball, and Voritha and Thalyn were on their best behaviour, even complimenting the Valethian gown I had chosen to wear. Though, I didn't miss their sneers in my direction when they thought I wasn't looking.

But hand in hand with Kalas, while his parents looked on approvingly and I was surrounded by my loved ones from Valeth, I didn't give my rival and her mother a second thought.

# Chapter Thirty-One
# Surrounded By People Who
# Truly Cared About Me

The good mood I was in thanks to being surrounded by people who truly cared about me quickly evaporated when I walked into the tailor's shop to meet with Seraphina to begin planning what I'd wear for the wedding. Although Kalas and I hadn't confirmed a date at the recent ball, we'd all agreed to continue planning the wedding as if we had, so that none of the courtiers grew suspicious of us delaying further.

Standing on either side of the queen were Voritha and Thalyn, sickly sweet smiles on their faces.

Seraphina caught my gaze and offered me a small, subtle, and sympathetic smile.

Before I could even get out a greeting, Voritha rushed forward, linking her arm through mine.

"When we heard you and Her Majesty were discussing outfits for the wedding, we simply *had* to be here. As your most loyal courtiers, it's our duty to ensure you uphold Kralian traditions on such an important occasion," Voritha said, steering me away from Seraphina. "While those robes you're wearing may be the height of fashion on Valeth, they're hardly appropriate for a Kralian wedding."

I looked around hopelessly, wanting someone to come to my rescue, but unfortunately, Thalyn had already taken Seraphina to another area of the shop.

Their intentions were clear, but I wouldn't allow myself to fall into their trap.

Smiling back just as sweetly, I said, "I welcome your expert advice, Lady Voritha."

Matching me beat for beat, Voritha said, "Nothing can be done about that *distinct* red hair of yours, but at least we can make sure your outfit and makeup are perfect. I suggest favouring the colours of Kralis and sticking to magenta and turquoise."

I was lucky in many ways that Kralis's darker colour palette suited me much more than the light moon colours common on Valeth. Still, magenta clashed with my hair and turquoise washed me out.

Purple was the colour that made me feel confident and most like myself.

Voritha held up a sheer turquoise toga that would leave me very exposed. "Of course, we'd have to find some way to straighten your hair. I was thinking you could wear eyeshadow to match, and then a nice, bold magenta lipstick. With the correct nyxorith accessories, you will look fit to be queen."

I tried to hide the grimace as I said, "Your suggestion is lovely, Lady Voritha, but I'd like to see what Queen Seraphina thinks too."

Voritha tried to grab my arm again, but I slipped out of her reach and scurried away as quickly as possible, calling out, "Your Majesty, I'd like your advice on what I should wear, please."

Seraphina appeared from behind a row of gowns, leaving a scowling Thalyn behind her.

"Of course, Madelyne," she said, coming to my side. "Were you thinking of something traditionally Kralian or something more in the Valethian style?"

Out of the corner of my eye, I saw Voritha frown, but she wouldn't dare challenge the queen directly.

"I definitely want to uphold Kralian traditions," I said, knowing I couldn't make too many overt declarations right then. "But I would also like to represent my Valethian heritage."

Seraphina gave me an understanding smile. "I did something similar when I married Eldarion, incorporating styles from my home in Velithar."

"And what a sight you looked," Voritha muttered under her breath, though loud enough for me and the queen to hear.

Seraphina fixed Voritha with a hard stare, but her voice was still soft as she asked "Is there something you wish to say to me, Lady Voritha? You're one of my most trusted companions, after all."

"Incorporating traditions from Velithar was one thing, but Valeth is not Kralis, and we'd all do well to remember that," Voritha said stiffly.

"But they're still our neighbours, and Madelyne *is* descended from their royal family," Seraphina replied.

I wasn't sure if the king or queen had made public the knowledge that I was descended from the Valethian royal family, and judging by the wide-eyed expression from both Voritha and Thalyn, I guessed that they hadn't.

"But you're from Earth," Thalyn blurted.

"I am, but it was discovered that the witches on Earth all descend from Andromeda, one of the late Queen Ursula's children. Given that Queen Branwynn married another of Queen Ursula's children, it also means that Kalas and I share a common ancestor," I said, unable to keep the smirk from my face as I revealed this information.

"Even more reason to uphold tradition, then," Voritha said. Her expression revealed less than Thayln's, but it was still clear from her tone that she was rattled by my revelation.

"I am certain whatever Madelyne chooses to wear, she will look beautiful on her wedding day to my son," Seraphina said, smiling at me warmly.

The queen's words seemed to put a stop to whatever else Voritha and Thalyn had planned, and they remained silent as Seraphina and I continued to look at clothing options.

We viewed countless gowns and robes that I might wear for the wedding, but I didn't make a final selection, hoping I could return to the tailors at another date with Celestia, Aurora, and Nima.

The queen found something she was happy with, and while she took it to the tailor to pay, Voritha linked her arm through mine again and pulled me aside.

Thalyn blocked the path back to Seraphina, and all I could do was stand helplessly as Voritha launched another tirade at me. This time, she did not keep her words saccharinely sweet.

"You may have won the favour of Her Majesty, but you're still an out-sider," she hissed. "And despite your connection to the Valethian royal family, you will *never* be worthy of the Crown Prince of Kralis."

"It doesn't matter what you or anyone else thinks. Korvarith Thalun chose *me* as Kalas's mate," I bit back, holding my head high.

"Be that as it may, he doesn't really *love* you, does he? He is only agreeing to marry you because it is the will of Korvarith Thalun. We all know his heart belongs to Thalyn."

Voritha had pierced the heart of my biggest insecurity, and despite how much I wanted to argue to the contrary, I couldn't. Even though Kalas had told me he no longer loved Thalyn, he *still* hadn't eased my worries that he was only marrying me because of the will of Korvarith Thalun.

My silence told Voritha everything she needed to know, and she smiled triumphantly. "My daughter will become queen one day. I will make sure of it. Why don't you make this easy for everyone and just leave now? You can make a home on Valeth with *your people*, and Kalas can be happy with his true love."

I opened my mouth to argue, but no words came out. I glanced around, hoping desperately that Seraphina had finished paying for her gown, but to my dismay, the tailor was causing a fuss about something and taking up all the queen's attention.

Thalyn joined her mother, smiling smugly. "You don't just stop loving someone overnight. Kalas will be mine."

I wanted to scream that I'd never let that happen, but instead, all I could think about was my mother rejecting me all those years ago, and how it would feel if Kalas did the same; if he chose Thalyn over me.

I turned and ran from the shop before anyone could stop me, tears streaming down my cheeks. My chest and legs hurt as I made my way back to the palace, and I locked myself in my and Kalas's quarters.

The room was completely empty and silent, and the lack of sound was overbearingly oppressive. The vacant air left plenty of room for the voices of my mother, Voritha, Thalyn, and everyone else who'd ever doubted me to fill the void.

*"You don't just stop loving someone overnight."*

*"You're no daughter of mine."*

*"Kalas can be happy with his true love."*

*"If I ever see you again, I will report you to the witch hunters."*

*"Kalas will be mine."*

*"The royal bloodline of Kralis must remain pure."*

My chest tightened, my heart pounding so painfully I thought it was going to burst from my rib cage.

I don't know how long I lay on the bed, sobbing as the various voices of my detractors tormented me.

Eventually, I had no tears left to cry, and exhausted, I slipped into a dreamless sleep.

# Chapter Thirty-Two
# All I Ever Wanted

I was startled awake by the gentle weight of someone sitting next to me on the bed, and I opened my eyes to see Kalas staring down at me, his dark brows knitted together.

"Mother said you left the tailors without a word. Are you okay, my little witch?"

His soft voice and gentle touch to my arm soothed me, and I started to wake up fully.

Once I'd regained my senses, I sat up and wrapped my arms around Kalas, inhaling his scent deeply.

Finally, I found the courage to ask the question that had been plaguing me for days. "Do you still love Thalyn?"

"Of course not," Kalas insisted, taking my hands in his.

I felt a little of the heaviness lift from my chest. There was just one more question I needed an answer to.

"And would you still want to marry me if it wasn't the will of Korvarith Thalun?"

"Of course I would, invarali taleni." Kalas paused, and I held my breath.

Everything rested on what Kalas said to me next. If it was more of the same, that it was Korvarith Thalun's will that we were together, I wasn't sure we could get through this. Even if he didn't love Thalyn, I needed more than just his deity's pronouncement. I needed to know that Kalas's feeling for me were genuine.

Kalas let go of my hands, but before I could panic about him moving away, he raised them up to cup my cheeks. He stared directly into my eyes as he said, "Madelyne, I would want to be with you even if Korvarith Thalun forbade it. You are my fated mate because my heart chose you, not because The Twilight Crow chose you."

Glimmering, oil-slick tears trickled down Kalas's alabaster cheeks, causing the damn on my own emotions to break, and I too started to cry.

"I am so, so sorry for ever making you doubt my feelings for you. If you give me the chance, I will spend my life making it up to you. I will devote my whole body, mind, and soul to you. If you don't want to be queen someday, we can leave Kralis and go to live on Valeth. Whatever you want, I will give it to you. I will give you the universe if that's what you ask for."

My whole body trembled as I leaned forwards, pressing my forehead against his. "I don't need the whole universe. All I ever needed was for you to love me, Kalas."

"And I do love you." He moved his head, capturing my lips with his, and pulling me into a deep kiss. When we broke apart to catch our breath, he added, "I will do whatever it takes to make things work between us. Our future together is more important to me than one day becoming king. The choice is yours."

The weight that had slowly been dragging me deeper into despair finally fully lifted and I felt like I was floating on air.

Kalas loved me. He really, truly loved me, and not just because it was the will of Korvarith Thalun. And now he was giving me the choice of what our future would be. We could move to Valeth, away from all the drama of the court of Kralis if we wanted. We could travel the universe. Anything. All I had to do was say.

It was all I'd ever wanted and more. I had a man who would turn the universe upside down for me, and a family that loved me unconditionally. Despite the best efforts of Darakon, Voritha, and Thalyn trying to tear us apart, Kalas and I were stronger than ever.

I knew where I belonged.

A slow smile crept over my face. "We're going to get married. We can't let Darakon win now."

"Darakon *hasn't* won," Kalas said. "We're together, and nothing will tear us apart again. What we do next is up to you."

My heart felt lighter than ever. He really was giving me the final choice. If I wanted, we could start anew on Valeth, or anywhere else in the universe we wanted.

But what *did* I want? All I'd ever wanted was for Kalas to love me completely, and now I knew he did. It didn't matter where we lived. Nothing would change the way we felt about each other.

But as his consort, as the future queen of Kralis, I could do so much good. I could strengthen the alliance with Valeth. Kalas was already talking about changing some of the old Kralian traditions. Together, as the future king and queen, we could shape the destiny of Kralis.

It was what Vesper and Korvarith Thalun wanted for us. But more importantly, it was what *I* wanted for us. I'd spent too much of my life being powerless despite my magic and hunted because of it. I couldn't change the attitude toward witches on Earth, but as Kalas's wife, I could hopefully get him to pass laws preventing the persecution of others.

I could make the future better for everyone.

I could make Kralis my home.

"What if I want to be your consort? What if I want us to shape the future of Kralis together? What if I want our children to marry the children Aurora eventually has with Lord Orpheus?"

The grin Kalas gave me took my breath away. "Then I will give it to you, my precious one. My little witch, my consort, my future queen." Kalas stood and reached for my hands, helping me to my feet. He then gripped me by the waist and twirled me around. "My love. My fated mate. My Madelyne."

# Chapter Thirty-Three
# In The Name Of Korvarith Thalun,
# I Challenge You

Before Kalas and I could even get comfortable in our bed, there was a frantic knock at the door.

Kalas rose to answer it, and I lingered behind him, curious to see who was seeking us out with such urgency.

Ashryn, the royal messenger, stood on the other side of the door, glancing around nervously.

"Is there a problem?" Kalas asked.

"Perhaps you should see for yourself," Ashryn said, still unable to make eye contact with either of us. "Your parents are in the ritual chamber with Lord Darakon."

Kalas entwined his fingers with mine, and together, we left the royal quarters and made our way along the corridor. As we got closer to the ritual chamber, his grip on my hand tightened.

We stepped into the circular room, and the first thing I noticed was the presence of Thalyn and Voritha. Thalyn was wearing the semi-transparent turquoise gown her mother had suggested I wear for my wedding to Kalas. She was always beautiful, but she was currently made up as though about to get married.

The sight of her made my blood freeze in my veins, and I took a step back, letting Kalas take the lead.

"Ah, Kalas, you're here at last. We've been waiting for you," Darakon said.

"Whatever you're plotting, Darakon, it won't work," Kalas said in a firm voice that left no room for argument. "Madelyne and I are to be married as Korvarith Thalun intends."

I stepped from behind Kalas, taking his hand as I stood by his side, and the looks on Darakon, Thalyn, and Voritha's faces were priceless.

Voritha went as pale as snow, which was saying a lot given Kralians already had fair complexions, but she lost the iridescent sparkle and instead looked like a corpse.

Thalyn pouted, jutting her bottom lip out like a toddler who'd been told 'no' for the first time, her eyes brimming with tears.

It was Darakon's expression that intrigued me most, though. It was equal parts fury, disappointment, and disturbingly, resignation.

"Ah, yes. I anticipated this would happen. But I came prepared," he said calmly.

Darakon stepped aside to reveal the king and queen bound to their seats, their mouths covered with gags.

"Set aside the sapien and agree to marry Thalyn, or I'll kill them both," Darakon said, one long claw extending like a blade as he stepped closer to Kalas's parents.

We were on the other side of the room, with Thalyn and Voritha blocking our path. We wouldn't get to Eldarion and Seraphina before Darakon slashed their throats.

I glanced at Kalas, whose skin and eyes were turning black, and laid a gentle hand on his wrist.

"I love you, but I won't make you choose between me and your parents' lives," I said, bowing my head. Despite Kalas's reassurance to the contrary, Darakon had indeed won. "I'll leave."

"Maddie, no. I can't live without you," Kalas said, reaching for my hand before I could walk away.

"And I couldn't live with myself if your parents died because of me."

"See, even now, the human knows she's lost," Darakon said smugly.

"I forbid it," a voice bellowed, and everyone's attention was drawn to Eldarion, who had chewed through the leather gag that previously prevented him from speaking. "Kalas, your and Maddie's happiness is more important than mine and your mother's lives."

Darakon rolled his eyes. "Oh, don't be so dramatic. No one has to die. Give me what I want and we can continue peacefully. Banish the sapien from

Kralis, make Thalyn the prince's consort and appoint both myself and Lady Voritha to a new ruling council."

"I'd rather die than force my son to marry someone he doesn't love," Eldarion said, straining at the bindings holding him. "In the name of Korvarith Thalun, I challenge you to a fight to submission in our bestial forms."

I'd never seen Darakon lose his composure before, but for one instant, he looked genuinely terrified, and I thought maybe Eldarion's challenge would be enough. We could still get out of this with our lives.

But then all of Darakon's talons extended, and feathers pierced through the skin on his back as his nose and mouth elongated into a beak-like snout full of razor-sharp teeth.

At the same time, Eldarion broke free of his restraints and started to transform too. Soon, both Kralians had lost their humanoid appearance and were like Kalas had been when he'd hunted the boar in the forest on Earth. They looked almost like dinosaurs, standing on their hind legs, their arms having transformed into wings and their bodies covered in feathers.

By some sort of magic I wasn't aware of, the ceiling of the ritual chamber faded, leaving it open to the night sky.

Darakon and Eldarion grew larger still, both growing long, feathered tails that they whipped at each other. Before they got too big to fit in the ritual chamber, they flapped their wings and took flight.

With Darakon and Eldarion in the air, Kalas and I rushed forward to release his mother, who had chewed through the leather gag in her mouth like her husband had.

"Kalas, help your father," she cried.

"He invoked the name of The Twilight Crow. To intervene in the fight now would mean he forfeits," Kalas said, his gaze moving between his mother and the fight going on above.

"We can still stop this," Voritha said, rushing forward. "If you agree to marry Thalyn."

"I will not marry her," Kalas ground out. "My heart belongs to Maddie."

Thalyn joined her mother, looking at Kalas with pleading, tear-filled eyes. "Didn't the time we spent together mean anything to you?"

I could not believe, even in the midst of a battle between Darakon and Eldarion, that Thalyn and Voritha were still scheming. I'd had enough. I might not have been able to stop the wyvern fight above, but I could at least do *something*.

"I think I've heard enough from both of you," I said, conjuring new binding from the rope Darakon had previously used.

With a wave of my hand, Thalyn and Voritha were magically forced into the seats that the king and queen had previously occupied, and the ropes tied themselves around the Kralian women. With one final flick of my wrists, I made sure they couldn't speak either.

"We'll deal with you after we've stopped Darakon," I said.

"Maddie, can *you* do something to stop the fight?" Seraphina asked desperately.

I glanced at Kalas. I thought there might be some way to stop Darakon, even in his bestial form, but I needed to know my actions wouldn't endanger Eldarion first.

Kalas shook his head. "We can't risk it. We don't even know if your magic would be enough to hurt Darakon when he's transformed."

I wanted to argue that we couldn't just let Darakon and Eldarion fight to submission. What if Darakon won? But a screech from above drew everyone's attention.

We all gazed at the sky, where the two Kralians were fighting. They were almost equally matched in bulk and size. The key difference was that Eldarion was jet-black, streaked with shimmering turquoise, magenta, and violet hues, whereas Darakon was a pearly white, gleaming with iridescence.

If it wasn't for the fact they were fighting to submission, the contrasting 'Yin-Yang' they made would have been beautiful.

he flashing of razor-sharp talons and teeth worried me. From my vantage point on the ground, it didn't seem like either had the advantage. One minute, Darakon was clawing at Eldarion, only for them to somersault in the sky as the king's teeth tore at his enemy.

Without warning, Darakon lunged, his talons raking through the air. Eldarion reared back just in time, but not fast enough to avoid the sharp claws that scraped along his flank. With a snarl, the king retaliated, swinging his massive tail toward his enemy's head.

Darakon darted to the side, narrowly avoiding the bone-crushing blow. He moved quickly, darting and weaving like smoke, aiming for weak points on Eldarion's body. His jaws snapped dangerously close to the king's neck but missed by a breath's width.

Eldarion bellowed in frustration and lunged forward, using his bulk to drive Darakon back to the ground. His talons clamped down on Darakon's left wing, pinning it to the floor of the ritual chamber.

With a ferocious snarl, Eldarion opened his jaws wide, aiming to crush his opponent's throat.

My heart surged. This was it, Eldarion was about to win the fight and end this madness.

But to my dismay, Darakon wasn't finished yet. He twisted violently, using the momentum to rip his pinned wing free. Feathers tore and blood spattered across the ground, but Darakon didn't falter. Instead, he lashed out with his hind legs, claws sinking deep into Eldarion's underbelly.

Eldarion roared in pain, staggering back and loosening his grip. Darakon seized the opportunity and surged forward, jaws snapping around Eldarion's throat. Eldarion thrashed, but Darakon clamped down harder, refusing to let go. Blood poured from Eldarion's neck as he fought desperately to break free, his strength ebbing with every second.

With a final, vicious twist of his neck, Darakon ripped his opponent's throat out in a spray of oil-slick blood. Eldarion collapsed to the chamber floor, his body twitching once before falling still. The echoes of the battle faded, leaving only the sound of the wind howling through the open ritual chamber.

Breathing heavily, Darakon raised his head, blood dripping from his jaws. He let out a triumphant roar that reverberated through the chamber.

There was silence for a moment, before Seraphina's heartbroken shriek filled the air and her legs collapsed from under her.

My body shook all over as I processed what had just happened.

King Eldarion was dead.

# Chapter Thirty-Four
# The Laws of
# Korvarith Thalun

"This defies the laws of Korvarith Thalun," Kalas cried, almost all of his skin turning black. "Kralians are supposed to fight to submission, not death. The fact Darakon killed my father shows how he is without honour."

"Screw honour! That psychopath is a murderer. He's going to pay for this," I said, striding forwards.

Around me, the air rippled and the debris on the ground began to levitate.

I didn't care what it took, I would make Darakon pay with his life.

As I approached the massive white wyvern, Darakon transformed back into his humanoid form, though his mouth was still streaked with Eldarion's blood.

"Stand down, human," he snarled. "The king is dead, and as I was the one to kill him, I declare myself King of Kralis."

Disregarding my magic, Darakon pushed me aside as though I was an insignificant twig and strode straight for Seraphina. He grabbed Seraphina by the arm, pulling her to her feet, and glared at Kalas, who was now standing beside me, radiating waves of hatred.

"And your mother will be my queen. We will start a new dynasty." He spat at Kalas's feet. "As a mark of respect, I will let you and your *human* live, but you are banished to Earth. If you return, I will kill you both."

Seraphina yanked herself out of Darakon's grip. "I'd rather die than marry you!"

"That can be arranged," Darakon drawled, pushing the queen aside.

On her hands and knees, Seraphina scrambled over to Eldarion's body, which in death, had turned back into his humanoid form. She cradled her lost lover in her arms, her whole body shaking as she sobbed onto his naked chest.

"So, what will it be, Kalas? Will you leave Kralis with your precious human, or will you too perish like your father?" Darakon said, glaring at Kalas.

Kalas ignored Darakon and stared directly into my eyes. Our minds connected. *'Madelyne, invarali taleni, I love you, and if there was any other choice, I wouldn't do this, but my father must be avenged.'*

I wanted to argue with Kalas. What if Darakon killed him too? But then I thought of Eldarion and how welcoming he'd been to me since the very beginning.

*'My love, avenge our Aelrion Thalor.'*

Kalas nodded once to let me know he understood my words and then zeroed in on Darakon. Even as he started to speak, his feathers pierced through his skin.

"Darakon, in the name of Korvarith Thalun, I challenge you to a fight to submission in our bestial forms," he said.

Darakon smirked and turned back into his bestial form, once again growing larger. Kalas transformed too, and the Kralians took to the skies.

Seraphina scrambled to her feet and rushed into my arms, wrapping her own around me. We turned our attention to the sky as we watched the fight between Kalas and Darakon.

Kalas was slightly smaller than Darakon, but Darakon was bloody and worn from his fight with Eldarion. Still, I didn't want to think about the outcome of the fight.

Kalas *had* to win. This had to be over.

It was clear from the way he was flying that Darakon's wing was injured, and I was pleased to see Kalas making that the focus of his attention.

Flying swiftly, Kalas hurtled towards Darakon, his jaws closing around the already mangled wing. Without hesitation, Kalas tore Darakon's wing from his body.

With only one wing, Darakon struggled to stay in the air, but as he fell, he hooked his hind legs around Kalas, dragging him down with him. The two wyverns crashed to the floor of the ritual chamber, and in an instant, their jaws were snapping as their teeth clashed.

Kalas was incensed, out for blood, but Darakon used this to his advantage. Even with one wing and having already fought one battle, he wasn't about to surrender.

My heart was in my throat as I watched Darakon's talons claw at Kalas's underbelly. I desperately wanted to intervene, but I dared not do anything to make the situation worse. Even in his humanoid form, Darakon had shaken off my magic as if it were nothing, and I wouldn't ignore Kalas's claim that interfering in a challenge invoked in the name Korvarith Thalun would doom us all. All I could do was prey to the deities that Kalas won and Darakon was defeated.

I closed my eyes and opened my mind to the universe. *'Korvarith Thalun, Vesper, please, hear my pleas. Kalas is innocent. Darakon murdered Eldarion. Please, don't take my love from me and leave only this monster.'*

Above me, thunder rumbled, and I opened my eyes to the battle once more.

Kalas and Darakon were still tangled on the ground, talons and teeth flashing as they tore feathers and strips of flesh from each other.

If Darakon hadn't already fought Eldarion, I was certain he would have beaten Kalas already, but now he was at a disadvantage. Plus, losing his father made Kalas fight with a ferocity I'd never seen before.

He aimed for Darakon's remaining wing, clamping his jaws around it even as Darakon's lower legs continued to tear slashes in Kalas's flank and legs.

I knew Kralians could heal, but how much could they regenerate? Could Darakon do permanent damage to Kalas?

In my arms, Seraphina was still quivering. I didn't know how she was even able to watch the battle. I was barely holding myself together, and she'd already lost her husband. She couldn't lose her son too.

"Isn't there anything we can do?" I asked desperately.

Seraphina shook her head. "Kalas is right. To interfere would doom us all. These type sof fights are meant to end when one of the combatants surrenders. You're never supposed to kill. Darakon broke the laws of Korvarith Thalun."

"Trying to stop Kalas and me from marrying was breaking the laws of Korvarith Thalun too. Has the Twilight Crow ever intervened in such a situation?"

"Nothing like this has ever happened in the history of Kralis before," Seraphina said.

Our attention turned back to the fight as there was a pained, bird-like screech as Kalas tore Darakon's second wing from his body.

I couldn't see a way Darakon could beat Kalas now, but I still held my breath. Even if Kalas didn't surrender first, he could still be grievously wounded.

I felt sick as Darakon tore into Kalas's lower body, shedding a mass of black feathers and pulling apart the skin so that blood spilled out onto the ground of the ritual chamber.

At the same time, Kalas snapped at Darakon, his jaws trying to close around the other beast's throat.

Darakon kicked full force with his legs, sending Kalas sprawling backward before he could get his bite locked in properly.

The blood spewing from Kalas's lower region coated the floor and pooled out in all directions, reaching so far it almost made it to my and Seraphina's feet.

On the other side of the chamber, Darakon was struggling to stand. Without his forelimbs, it was impossible for him to lift his neck properly. It would only be a matter of time before Kalas was on him again.

Kalas licked at his wound and it started to close up, and then he flapped his gigantic wings. With Darakon grounded, Kalas was able to take to the skies. He flew higher; so high he was almost invisible.

I clutched at Seraphina. A cry of fury filled the air and made my whole body turn cold. A flash of lightning illuminated the dark sky, and the form of Kalas came darting back down, aiming directly for Darakon.

Instead of moving out of the way, Darakon raised his hind legs, I assumed in an attempt to re-injure Kalas as he attacked. But Darakon's plan failed. Kalas was expecting the attack and had curled his own legs up to protect his lower body.

He lunged straight for Darakon, aiming for his throat, and this time, Kalas's bite didn't miss. His jaws locked around the neck of the beast that had killed his father.

Part of me desperately wanted Kalas to tear Darakon's throat out and end this now, but I knew that wasn't the will of Korvarith Thalun. Justice had to be served properly.

With his wings torn off and blood now spewing from his neck, Darakon was desperately fading as Kalas bore down upon him. I was certain if he didn't surrender soon, Kalas would begin attacking his lower body too.

But before that happened, Darakon transformed back into his humanoid form. I wasn't sure if this was an intentional ploy or simply that he no longer had the power to hold his bestial form.

Darakon's arms were missing from the shoulders where Kalas had torn off his wings, and his neck was still leaking blood.

"I surrender," he stammered helplessly.

For one moment, I thought Kalas was going to ignore Darakon's pleas and kill him, but then he too transformed back into his humanoid form.

I was disturbed to see the large lacerations on Kalas's stomach, leading down to his groin area. The wounds were no longer bleeding, but they were still bright red and swollen. He'd need medical attention as soon as possible. Additionally, as Kalas straightened, I noticed that he was favouring one leg and walking with a limp.

"Bind him," Kalas commanded, staring at me.

I felt the magic within me surge. From my palms flowed chains made from a mixture of nyxorith and lunavira, which snaked along the ground and wound around Darakon's body.

With our enemy defeated and in chains, Seraphina and I rushed to Kalas, throwing our arms around him as we both started to cry.

"It's over. Darakon has been beaten. My father has been avenged," Kalas murmured wearily.

# Chapter Thirty-Five
# One of Both Bloodlines

The doors to the ritual chamber flew open, and Savrion and Josain stormed in, accompanied by an older Kralian man with long black hair, wearing robes similar to what the clergy wore.

"What happened here?" the one I assumed was Zarathian demanded.

We filled them in on what had happened from the moment we'd entered the ritual chamber, from Darakon having captured the king and queen, to him trying to blackmail Kalas into marrying Thalyn, right through to the two wyvern fights, the first of which had resulted in the death of King Eldarion.

"Where is Varion Drelkar?" Zarathian asked.

That was a good question. The high priest hadn't been here when we'd arrived, but surely, Darakon would have needed him to officiate Kalas and Thayln's marriage, if Kalas had agreed.

"He has a bedroom adjacent to the ritual chamber. He should be in there," Seraphina said, slipping out of Kalas's arms.

She returned to Eldarion's body, once more cradling him in her arms. I felt Kalas pull away, and I let go of his hand so he could be with his mother and father, while I turned to the others.

"What happens now?" I asked.

"We must find Varion Drelkar, and I must speak to him about what I have uncovered in this book," Zarathian said.

"Which is?" I tried not to let my frustration show, but Eldarion was dead, Kalas was injured, and Darakon was in chains, while Zarathian seemed almost oblivious to the chaos around him.

"I will explain everything once I have located Varion Drelkar," Zarathian said, and then strode out of the ritual chamber, I assumed to look for the clergy.

Close by, Josain and Savrion were whispering as they embraced each other.

The chamber doors opened again, and Celestia entered with Aurora and Nima. They rushed towards me, pulling me into their arms.

"We were told there was a fight. Are you okay?" Celestia asked, smoothing out my hair.

I leaned into her embrace, appreciating the motherly comfort. "No, but I will be. I'm more concerned about Kalas and Seraphina."

We all glanced at the two Kralians, who were both seated on the floor, Eldarion's motionless body resting between them.

"Go to him. Comfort him," Celestia said.

I hesitated. "I feel like I'm intruding on their moment."

"You are Kalas's fated mate. You will soon be his consort and queen."

In everything that had happened, I hadn't even considered the implication of Eldarion's death. Did that mean Kalas was automatically King of Kralis now? What about Seraphina? Did Kralians even have roles such as a 'King Mother'?

I shook the thoughts from my head. That didn't matter. What mattered was being there for them both.

I left Celestia's comforting embrace and crossed the chamber to sit with Kalas and Seraphina, taking one of their hands in each of mine.

I stared down at Eldarion's body. Someone had covered his modesty, and the fatal wound in his neck was sealed. If I didn't know better, I would have just thought the king was sleeping.

Tears rolled down my cheeks, and then Kalas and Seraphina began to sing in Kralian, their bird-like sounds filling the air. I instantly recognized the melody. It was the same Kralian love song Kalas had sung to me on Earth when we'd first met. A song he said his father used to sing to his mother.

"*Stellavarien ethrionth, lunaviel solemna*," the lyrics went, and I added my voice to theirs, mourning the fallen king. "Stars weave, moon's embrace."

The music filled the chamber, drawing Celestia and the princesses closer, along with Josain and Savrion. They gathered around Kalas, Seraphina, and me as we all paid our respects to Eldarion.

"He was a fantastic king," Celestia said eventually. "I am sorry for your loss. I lost my own mate only a few years ago, and some hurts never heal."

Seraphina glanced up at Celestia and a look of understanding passed between the two queens.

With the song ended, the chamber fell silent until Zarathian returned with a rather dishevelled looking Varion Drelkar.

"Your Majesty." Varion Drelkar dropped into a low bow at Seraphina's feet. "May The Twilight Crow's wings carry King Eldarion's spirit to the stars and beyond."

"Thank you," Seraphina said, wiping the tears from her eyes. As she helped Varion Drelkar to his feet, her expression changed. She put a wall up to shield her grief and went into 'ruler' mode as she addressed everyone gathered in the chamber.

"Zarathian, tell us what has been uncovered. What does this book of yours say? I am eager to move onto the trials of Darakon and his consorts."

"That's what the book is about, Your Majesty. I was able to translate it fully, and I discovered it was written in an ancient language that predates Kralian, from a time when Kralis and Valeth were one."

"What do you mean, when Kralis and Valeth were one?" Celestia asked.

"Long ago, when Korvarith Thalun created all we know, They did not do it alone. They were assisted by their partner, their consort, their fated-mate, Vesper, the Moon Mother. Together, they made a beautiful, harmonious planet known as Kralethia, which was inhabited by both witches and those with the ability to transform into great feathered, winged beasts.

"But the people of Auroriath were jealous of all that the people of Kralethia had. For legend says that Vesper had once been the consort of their deity, Ar'Vaalok, and that The Twilight Crow had stolen her away. And so, in the name of Ar'Vaalok, the people of Auroriath tore Kralethia apart. Over time, the origins of Kralethia were forgotten, the union between Vesper and Korvarith Thalun thought of as legend and folklore, but nothing more. Kralis and Valeth became two separate planets instead of one, like Korvarith Thalun and Vesper had intended."

All I could do was stare at Zarathian in shock. While the revelation about Kralethia was fascinating and had implications that would need to be discussed at length, I didn't quite understand how it pertained to the fates of Darakon, Voritha, and Thalyn.

It was obvious Seraphina felt the same as she heaved out a breath and asked, "Your point is?"

"My point is that I read in the ancient language of Kralethia a spell that would summon Korvarith Thalun and Vesper to the mortal plane for them to pass judgement on those who'd broken the laws of their land. However, the spell can only be performed by one of both bloodlines."

# Chapter Thirty-Six
# A Blessing From
# Korvarith Thalun

"Someone of both bloodlines?" I questioned. "Do you mean like Kalas and me? We both descend from the former Queen of Valeth, Queen Ursula, through her children, Aster and Andromeda."

Zarathian smiled. "You do, and therefore the babe that grows within your womb is the true combination of both bloodlines. The heir of Kralethia."

I felt dizzy. This was all too much to process. The first words that escaped my mouth were, "I'm pregnant? But how do you know when I don't?"

"Korvarith Thalun and Vesper came to me in a dream and revealed this miracle to me," Zarathian said. "For your babe is the chosen one of the Throvani Ethrionth Star System, who the deities have selected to restore Kralethia and defeat Auroriath."

Zarathian's revelation did nothing to stop the spinning in my head and instead made me feel dizzier still. My legs wobbled beneath me, and only the support of Kalas's strong arms around me stopped me from collapsing to the floor.

"Korvarith Thalun and Vesper also told me that there are further challenges you will all face before the final confrontation with Auroriath. The plot of Darakon was just the beginning, though the deities were unable to show me what threat comes next," Zarathian said, pausing for a moment so we could all absorb his words. "However, for now, there will be peace. And during this time of peace, the rituals must be followed. First, you and Kalas, using the power of your growing child, must summon Korvarith Thalun and

Vesper to the mortal plane for them to pass judgement on Darakon, Voritha, and Thalyn."

I could barely keep up. Only that morning had I been wedding dress shopping with Seraphina. And now, there we were, with King Eldarion dead and me pregnant with Kalas's child. Not to mention that said child was meant to unite the bloodlines of Kralis and Valeth and stand against the might of Auroriath.

Part of me thought Zarathian was insane. What he was saying certainly was. Yes, the ancient Kralethian book proved that once, Kralis and Valeth had been one planet. But everything else was too bizarre to even comprehend.

And yet, I knew at least some of what Zarathian said was true. I hadn't noticed it before, perhaps because I'd been too wrapped up in everything else that had been happening, but there were certain changes within my body. My breasts felt fuller, my stomach more rounded, and I hadn't had a period since before I'd left Earth.

Even without a test or medical exam, I knew I was pregnant. The thought filled me with a mixture of emotions that warred within my body, and another wave of dizziness and nausea washed over me.

Kalas gently guided me over to the front row of seats that looked down into the ritual chamber, his hand reaching out to stroke my stomach. "Invarali taleni, do you really carry my child?"

I laid my hand over his, squeezing his fingers. "I do. Don't ask me how I know for certain, but I'm sure of it."

The smile Kalas gave me in return was the most breathtaking I had ever seen, more dazzling than the time we'd first met, filled with more devotion than when told me he'd love me even if Korvarith Thalun forbade it.

Tears rolled down my cheeks, and despite everything that had happened, despite the fact we weren't even married yet and everything was happening so quickly, I felt a blissful joy I had never experienced before. I was going to be a mother.

Seraphina came to sit beside us, and though she was still sniffling, she too smiled. "A blessing from Korvarith Thalun."

"A blessing from Korvarith Thalun and Vesper," Celestia added, joining us. "We will honour the agreement made with King Eldarion. The babe Maddie carries will be wed to the first of my grandchildren, and the second will be wed to Aurora's next child. The bloodlines of Kralethia will be united as the deities intended, and together, we will defeat Auroriath."

Seraphina reached out and took Celestia's hand. "I agree, but first, justice must be sought for the murder of my husband. Darakon, Voritha, and Thalyn must be tried by the deities for their plots against the crown."

Knowing only Kalas and I had the power to summon Korvarith Thalun and Vesper, I called Zarathian over to us.

Zarathian approached and handed me the ancient book, which I laid on the bench between Kalas and me, so we could both read it. Before we began, we were joined by Aurora and Nima, as well as Savrion and Josain. We all sat together, staring at the still bound bodies of Darakon, Voritha, and Thalyn.

"In the name of the Moon Mother, Vesper," I began.

"And her consort, the Twilight Crow, Korvarith Thalun, we summon thee," Kalas said, his voice joining mine.

In unison, we continued, "We are the parents of the heir to Kralethia, the child that will unite and bring peace to the Throvani Ethrionth Star System. In the names of Korvarith Thalun and Vesper, appear to us now and pass your judgement on those who schemed against us."

Suddenly, the night sky turned a bright, blinding white. I heard the shriek of a bird that reverberated through my very soul, but instead of being afraid, I felt comfort; like I was being embraced by a loving parent.

And when the brightness faded, there was Korvarith Thalun in Their full glory. Bigger than even King Eldarion had been in his bestial form, with magnificent feathers of black, pearly white, turquoise, magenta, and lilac all blending together. One of Korvarith Thalun's eyes was amber like Kalas's, the other amethyst. And on Korvarith Thalun's back rode the most beautiful woman I had ever seen. Her skin shone with the lustre of lunavira, and Her eyes were like emeralds. Her hair whipped around Her like tongues of flame; Vesper, the Moon Mother.

"Be at peace, our children," Korvarith Thalun and Vesper said in unison, their voices merging so they sounded neither male nor female.

Without warning, the bindings that confined Darakon, Voritha, and Thalyn vanished, leaving the three schemers standing before the deities.

"Oh, great Twilight Crow, please have mercy on us," Darakon said, scrambling forward as best he could without arms. "I only ever acted in the best interests of Kralis. I never meant it to end like this. I never meant to kill King Eldarion. Please forgive me, and I will be your devoted servant."

Korvarith Thalun opened Their shiny black beak, revealing rows and rows of razor-sharp teeth, and said, "I see into the hearts of all my children, and you lie still, Lord Darakon. You've only ever acted out of ambition and a lust for power. Even now, deep inside your black and twisted soul, you would dispose of my appointed rulers if you could and claim the throne of Kralis for yourself. It is my decree that you must die."

"Please, no. I beg for mercy," Darakon cried desperately, but his pleas fell on deaf ears as Korvarith Thalun opened Their great maw and inclined Their head, swallowing Darakon whole.

I was stunned. Had Korvarith Thalun really just devoured Darakon? Not that he hadn't deserved it. He'd killed Eldarion and tried to tear Kalas and me apart. If death by the mouth of his deity was Darakon's fate, well, he truly deserved it.

With Darakon disposed of, Korvarith Thalun turned their attention to Voritha and Thalyn.

"And what of your hearts and souls?" the Twilight Crow asked. "Voritha and Thalyn, you both acted out of love, even if your versions of love were twisted. Lady Voritha, I see that you loved Darakon since you were children and only acted out of love for him. If Darakon had been a true child of Kralis, he would not have abused your love and led you astray. What do you have to say for yourself?"

Lady Voritha bowed in front of Korvarith Thalun. "What you say is correct. I acted out of misguided devotion to Darakon. Everything I did was to gain his affection. But upon seeing Darakon's true nature, that he could kill King Eldarion, I regret that I helped him. I am willing to accept any punishment you inflict on me."

"Lady Voritha, I thank you for your honesty. I see in your heart the words you speak are true, and that you have no ambitions to plot against the true rulers of Kralis. However, your actions must still be punished. Therefore, I banish you into exilement from Kralis, and if you ever return, your life will be forfeit," Korvarith Thalun said.

"I accept your judgement, great Twilight Crow, and hope that through my actions, I can someday be redeemed."

Korvarith Thalun said nothing else to Voritha and instead focused Their mismatched eyes on Thalyn. "And what is the truth of your heart and soul?"

Voice trembling, Thalyn answered her deity. "I still love Kalas, and that's why I went along with my mother's and Darakon's plot. I never wanted to hurt the princess consort, though, and I definitely didn't want King Eldarion to be killed. I can see now that the royal couple's love is stronger than anything I may have shared with the prince, and I only wish them the best. I seek your forgiveness, great Twilight Crow, and if you will allow it, I wish to leave Kralis, so that I may truly find out who I am away from my childish love for Kalas or the influence of my mother."

"Your heart and soul speak the truth," Korvarith Thalun said. "You only acted out of love for Prince Kalas, no matter how your mother twisted and misguided that love for her own schemes. But again, this would not have been possible without the machinations of Darakon, who has paid for his crime. It is therefore my judgement that you be given a second chance to do as you intend and find your true self. It is my hope, that in time, you will walk the path I have chosen for you."

"Thank you," Thalyn said, bowing to Korvarith Thalun as tears rolled down her cheeks.

Their judgement proclaimed, Korvarith Thalun turned Their attention back to me and Kalas.

"Everything Zarathian told you is true. You carry the heir to Kralethia, who will someday reunite Kralis and Valeth, so that the two halves are whole again, as my consort and I intended. When Kralethia is one again, then you will have the power to defeat Auroriath and bring peace to the Throvani Ethrionth Star System."

"However, that time is not yet," Vesper said, taking over from Korvarith Thalun. "Yet more challenges await you all."

"Can you tell us about these challenges?" I asked desperately.

Both Korvarith Thalun and Vesper shook their heads sadly. "Even as deities, we do not have that power," Vesper said simply, offering no further explanation.

Part of me wanted to argue. Not only was it unfair after everything Kalas and I had been through that we'd still face more challenges, but that the deities couldn't even give us a hint of what was to come. But then I remembered Korvarith Thalun swallowing Darakon whole and thought it best not to argue.

"Keep the faith and remain strong and united," Korvarith Thalun said.

"Beware the dark side of the moon," Vesper added, and then blinding white light once again filled the chamber.

The cry of Korvarith Thalun reverberated through the nyxorith walls, and into my heart and soul, and then the light returned to normal, and the two deities were gone.

# Chapter Thirty-Seven
# Funerals and Celebrations

Queen Seraphina faced the people of Kralis with as much composure as she could when she told them their king had been murdered and his killer executed. Only those who'd been in the ritual chamber at the time knew the full story.

After the announcement of King Eldarion's passing, Kralis spent almost a week in mourning. All businesses were closed, and a massive nyxorith statue of the king was erected so that people could pay their respects.

No announcement about Kalas ascending the throne or our marriage was made at the time. Instead, everyone respected the privacy of Seraphina and her son and allowed them space to mourn.

Kalas's mood fluctuated between sobbing endlessly for his father and being filled with joy at the prospect of becoming a parent. He told me how there was more he wished he and his father had had chance to talk about, especially now he was about to become a father himself. Kalas's biggest regret was that Eldarion would never know his grandchild.

"I know he is with Korvarith Thalun and Vesper now, in the great beyond, and there, time doesn't work the same way as it does in the mortal realm. I'm sure, somehow, his spirit knows the spirit of our baby."

I agreed with him and knew that Korvarith Thalun and Vesper would use all the power they had to ensure Eldarion knew what his sacrifice had achieved.

Kalas and I agreed that if the baby I was carrying was male, we'd name him Eldarion in his father's honour. We were yet to decide on a name for if the baby was female, but both Ursula and Branwynn were top choices, to honour our ancestors.

I was still trying to grasp that I was going to be a mother. Nothing about my relationship with Kalas had been conventional, and we'd had to fight to get where we were, so why would our first child be any different?

I also worried about the prophecy that one day in the future, our child would unite Kralis and Valeth and fight against the Auroriaths to bring peace to the Throvani Ethrionth Star System. That was a lot of pressure for one person alone, especially someone who hadn't even been born yet, and I wanted my child to have the happiest, most peaceful life they could.

Then there was the question of the physiology of having a child with Kalas. Would they inherit his shapeshifting abilities? And if so, was our child likely to transform into a wyvern while I still carried them? And what about magical abilities?

Based on the precedent of Queen Branwynn's child with their consort, Aster, it was likely my and Kalas's baby would inherit Kalas's Kralian abilities, but no one knew for certain.

All I could do was trust in the will of Korvarith Thalun and Vesper and believe they wanted the best for the baby growing inside me.

Back on Earth, I had never been overly religious. Yes, witches had worshipped the Moon Mother, but no one had really been sure who or what that was, but now, I had seen Korvarith Thalun and Vesper with my own eyes. It was impossible to doubt the will of the deities when they'd spoken directly to you.

Still, I tried not to live my life thinking everything was pre-determined for me. I knew Kalas loved me for who I was, and not just because Korvarith Thalun had chosen me as his fated mate. I also knew our lives would be whatever we made of them, and not just the path Korvarith Thalun and Vesper intended for us.

One thing that none of us could ignore, however, was Vesper's final warning to 'beware the dark side of the moon.'

After talking at length with Celestia, Aurora, and Nima, as well as Seraphina, Zarathian, and Varion Drelkar, we all agreed the threat the deities spoke of likely pertained to the throne of Valeth. Celestia had agents in place searching for any information they could find. If someone, or something, was plotting against Celestia and the princesses, they would be discovered.

AFTER A WEEK'S MOURNING period, King Eldarion's funeral was held in the ritual chamber at the Obsidian Palace. All Kralian nobility were invited, as well as honoured guests from other planets, such as Celestia and her daughters.

I stood between Kalas and Seraphina, all of us dressed in traditional Kralian regalia, only with the addition of semi-transparent mourning veils covering our face, at the front of the ritual chamber.

Varion Drelkar conducted the ceremony, while Zarathian assisted him. Since Darakon's defeat, Zarathian had been invited back to court by Seraphina and served as part of a council that would advise Kalas and me once we were officially coronated.

Varion Drelkar spoke at length about King Eldarion's wisdom and integrity, and how until only very recently, Kralis had been at peace under Eldarion's rule. Though Darakon's plot wasn't mentioned in detail, Varion Drelkar made it clear that Eldarion had given his life in the ultimate sacrifice to ensure Darakon would be brought to justice and Kalas would ascend the throne unchallenged.

After the service in the ritual chamber, the nobility and other guests gathered in the great hall for a feast in King Eldarion's honour. This gathering was livelier than the funeral had been, and more closely resembled the other Kralian banquets I'd attended. Many, including Kalas and Seraphina, talked about how much Eldarion meant to them, and their fondest memories of the king.

There was just one day's intermission between King Eldarion's funeral and my and Kalas's marriage ceremony, which was combined with our coronation. During that day's recess, Kalas and I oversaw the appointment of a new advisory council.

As Kalas was still young by Kralian standards, and he hadn't expected to ascend to the throne so soon, it was decided that instead of the two of us ruling alone, as had been common for the monarchy of Kralis in the past, instead, there'd be a ruling council, the members of which were chosen by Kalas and me. Of course, the first person we appointed to the council was Seraphina. Other members included Varion Drelkar, Zarathian, and others of the nobility. We would also take advice from Queen Celestia, though she and the princesses planned to return to Valeth soon after the wedding, eager to arrange Aurora's marriage.

Under Kalas's direction, Savrion now stood in a position of power just below the royal family, as he had been appointed lord of his late father's estate and made a member of the ruling council. I released Josain from my service and made her a Lady of Kralis in her own right, giving her Voritha's lands and title that had been forfeited after her banishment. Josain wasn't part of the ruling council, but I intended to give her a position as soon as I could.

ON THE MORNING OF MY wedding to Kalas, I sat in my dressing chamber with Celestia, Aurora, Nima, and Josain. I had insisted I no longer needed a handmaiden, but I *did* want my closest family and friends with me. The only reason Seraphina wasn't there too was because she was with Kalas, who was also accompanied by Savrion and Zarathian.

For the wedding, Kalas and I had agreed to a mixture of Kralian, Valethian, and Earth traditions, including exchanging vows we'd written ourselves. I wore a gown that was a hybrid of Kralian and Valethian styles, with lots of nyxorith and lunavira accents. The bodice was almost entirely sheer, as was the custom on Kralis, but my modesty was preserved by a necklace similar to the one Seraphina wore for official occasions and was made up of rows of gemstones. The skirt flared out in the Valethian style, which was made up of ruffles and many layers. The prominent colour was a deep indigo reminiscent of the night sky, and it was decorated with lunavira beads that looked like twinkling stars.

Traditionally, the royal crowns of Kralis were passed down from monarch to monarch. However, as Seraphina still lived, it was decided she should keep her crown. Eldarion's was also in Seraphina's possession, who kept it locked in a safe place. Instead, the royal jewel smith had crafted new, custom crowns for Kalas and me.

Kalas's crown was made mostly from nyxorith, with lunavira accents, and mine was its counterpart, made mostly from lunavira with nyxorith accents. The new crowns were intended to usher in a new era on Kralis, one in which we were more closely allied with Valeth and working towards unification in the future.

As well as exchanging rings and vows, Kalas and I planned to place the other's crown on our head during our coronations.

"Are you nervous?" Celestia asked as she braided my hair and threaded it with lunavira, nyxorith, and gemstones.

"No," I said with a grin. After everything Kalas and I had been through, it was impossible to be nervous now. We'd faced the worst and were still together. In many ways, our wedding was a formality. In my heart and mind, he was my husband.

Celestia smiled knowingly. "Yes, by the time my and Sterling's wedding arrived, we'd already been through so much that all the nerves had faded away."

"I hope the same is true for me. I feel like I barely know Lord Orpheus, despite the fact he's been courting me for years," Aurora said. The princess didn't often speak of her betrothed, and when she did, it was with a certain amount of detachment.

Once I was fully ready, I picked up the ring and crown I had commissioned for Kalas and waited for Ashryn to arrive, telling us the ritual chamber was ready.

When Ashryn knocked on my chamber door, the nerves finally came. I wanted nothing more than to officially be Kalas's wife, but a small part of me still worried my happiness was about to be snatched away from me at the last moment.

With lots of hugs, kisses, and best wishes, Aurora, Nima, and Josain left the chamber and followed Ashryn through the palace to the ritual chamber. Only Celestia and I remained in my room. As Celestia was the closest thing to a loving mother I had, I asked her to give me away as was tradition for the bride's father or parents on Earth.

Celestia took my hands in hers and smiled fondly at me, tears rimming her eyes. "You looked beautiful, Madelyne," she said. "I remember when I first met you, I thought what a striking queen you'd someday become, and now look at you. I know your coronations are happening much more quickly than either you or Kalas anticipated, but I am certain you will be wonderful rulers. Not just that, though, I know you'll be a perfect team and have a life-time of happiness together."

Even though much about the future was still uncertain, that was one thing I no longer had any doubts about. I knew Kalas loved me wholly and not just because it was the will of Korvarith Thalun.

# Chapter Thirty-Eight
# I Am In Control Now

Ashryn returned to my chamber with a bow. "Everyone is ready and waiting for you, Your Majesty."

Smiling, I replied, "Let's not keep them waiting, then."

Celestia linked her arm through mine, and together, we followed Ashryn through the palace and to the ritual chamber.

I held my breath for a moment as we approached the curtained archway and then let it out slowly in a calming stream.

"Are you ready?" Ashryn asked.

"I'm ready," I replied.

Ashryn slipped into the chamber, and a moment later, the herald announced my arrival.

"Accompanied by Queen Celestia of Valeth, Madelyne, betrothed and beloved of Kalas, and soon to be his queen."

I didn't care for the Earth wedding march, and instead, light music popular on Valeth played as Celestia and I entered the chamber. All eyes turned in my direction, but unlike in the past when people had stared at me with judgement and even hatred, all I saw on the faces of the gathered crowd was respect.

I waved and smiled at guests, including Luna and Phoebe, as Celestia escorted me to the front of the ritual chamber, where Kalas stood with his mother and Varion Drelkar in front of the sacred pool.

As Kalas turned to face me and our eyes met, everything else faded away. I was barely even aware of the words Varion Drelkar spoke as I gazed into the eyes of my beloved.

When it came time for our vows, Kalas spoke first. "My Madelyne, my precious one. While Korvarith Thalun chose you as my fated mate, my heart chose you as my universe. I promise to spend our lives together showing you exactly how much I cherish you. In the name of Korvarith Thalun and Vesper, I pledge myself to you as your devoted husband, from now until the end of time."

I grinned at Kalas as tears rolled down my cheeks and squeezed his hand. "Kalas, *invarion na,* my beloved, I prayed to the Moon Mother to take me to where I belonged. In answer to my spell, she brought you to me, and through your love, I found my true home at your side. I promise to spend our lives together supporting and loving you in any and every way you need, just as you support and love me. In the name of Korvarith Thalun and Vesper, I pledge myself to you as your faithful wife, from now until the end of time."

Varion Drelkar continued the ritual, "In the name of Korvarith Thalun and Their fated mate, the Moon Mother Vesper, and in the eyes of all of Kralis, I now pronounce you husband and wife."

Kalas cupped my cheeks in both hands, bringing his lips to meet mine in a kiss that eclipsed any other kiss we'd shared; our first as man and wife. Around us, those in the ritual chamber clapped and cheered.

Once everyone had calmed down, Varion Drelkar officially proclaimed Kalas the new king of Kralis and me as his wife, the new queen. We took turns placing our new crowns on each other's heads and then exchanged matching nyxorith and lunavira rings.

Finally, Varion Drelkar instructed us to approach the sacred pool. He handed the ritual nyxorith blade to Kalas, who pricked his finger and allowed a few drops of blood to fall into the water. I did the same, and then we both crushed a handful of nyxorith and lunavira nuggets, sprinkling the dust on top of our intermingling blood.

This time, I was ready and waiting when the chamber filled with a bright, white light, and a raven's shriek filled the air.

Korvarith Thalun, once again in Their gigantic wyvern form, and Vesper riding on Her mate's back appeared before us, both of them smiling.

"Blessings to the new King and Queen of Kralis," Korvarith Thalun said.

"Blessing to the parents of the one who will make Kralethia whole again," Vesper added.

"Praise be to the Twilight Crow and the Moon Mother," Kalas and I said in unison.

I WAS EXHAUSTED BY the time the joint wedding and coronation ball ended, and Kalas and I returned to our chambers, but never too exhausted for my new husband.

Wearing only a satin slip, this time in a shade of deep amethyst, I pulled Kalas into bed, my mouth claiming his even as my hands tore off his sleeping clothes.

We'd been so busy recently that we'd barely gotten a moment to ourselves, and I knew that was only going to get worse as we took up the duties of ruling Kralis.

But tonight, I intended to remind Kalas exactly what we meant to each other, and the future that awaited us as husband and wife.

I kissed him slowly, drinking him in as my hands explored the hard, smooth planes of his chest.

I knew he longed to take control, but I didn't let him, instead setting the pace.

"Lean back," I whispered in his ear, pushing him back against the pillows with a light shove to his chest.

Kalas's eyes widened in surprise for a moment, and then he smirked, his sharp incisors growing in length.

"And what does my new bride have planned?" he asked, and beneath me, I could feel his cock hardening.

"All will be revealed," I replied mysteriously, calling on my magical abilities.

In the lead-up to the wedding, Celestia, Aurora, Nima, and I had chatted about many things, including how our witchy gifts could be put to good use in the bedroom. Despite the initial awkwardness of hearing Celestia talk about the early years of her marriage to Starling before the princesses were born, something she'd said put a wicked thought in my head.

I'd never fully explored my telekinetic abilities until recently when I'd conjured chains of magical energy. I'd been fascinated to discover that with enough practice, witches could create magical constructs made from the aether. Those constructs could be shaped into anything—weapons, armour, or even constraints to hold a shape-shifting king.

With a flick of my wrists, I sent out tendrils of magic that wrapped around Kalas's forearms, the opposite ends attaching to the posts of our bed and holding him firmly in place.

"Oh, what new trick have you learned, my little witch?" Kalas asked, grinning lasciviously, his eyes darkening to almost black.

"I remember once, while we were still on Earth, you telling me that you were in control, and that if I wanted to be your bride and consort, I'd need to learn patience. I think I've more than proven what a good girl I can be for my king. But are you worthy of me?"

"I worship at the altar that is your body. Let me show you my dedication," Kalas said, pulling against the magical constraints.

"Oh no, my King. I am in control now."

I slid down his body, pulling off the thin material that covered his hard cock as I went, until he was lying naked and supine in front of me.

Sitting up a little, I wrapped both of my hands around the shaft of his dick, and then slowly lowered my head. I flicked out my tongue, gently caressing his tip before straightening back up.

Kalas's hips jerked, and the skin from his clawed fingertips all the way to his shoulders had turned black as he continued to fight against the magical energy holding him in place.

"Patience," I said, giving his cock a squeeze.

Kalas growled, and I moved my body back up, pushing my pussy down on his erection as I went and leaving it slick with the evidence of my desire.

Now sitting on Kalas's chest, I squeezed my breasts together and pushed them into his face, practically smothering him. He responded exactly as I'd hoped he would, his tongue lashing out to work my nipples into hard buds before his fangs pierced the sensitive skin, and a thrill of delicious pain shot through my body.

I replaced my breasts with my mouth, capturing his bottom lip between my teeth.

"Let me taste you, my love," I whispered, and bit down a little harder.

Kalas's blood filled my mouth, and he growled again, forcing his tongue down my throat and biting my own lip, so that our blood mingled together. His hips continued to jerk as he fought for more control, and he pulled again at the restraints.

Knowing I had all the power in the situation emboldened me, and even though I didn't want to break away from the dizzying kiss, I also wanted to continue teasing Kalas.

I pulled back and shuffled away, pressing my hands against his chest to force him to lie flat against the pillow.

"Now I want you to taste me," I said as I carefully repositioned myself. "And maybe if you do a good job, I might loosen control of my magic."

I'd never done anything like this before, but I felt like a goddess as I lowered my mound down on Kalas's mouth and began to rotate my hips so my clit brushed against his lips.

Usually, when Kalas used his mouth to pleasure me, he was in control and set the pace, but now it was my turn. I braced my hands on the wall above the bed and continued gently moving backwards and forwards as Kalas licked, kissed, and sucked my core.

My legs started to tremble as I reached my peak, and then, just as I was about to climax, I lost control of the magic holding Kalas to the bed.

That one moment was all he needed, his hands moved at lightning speed to grip my thighs, and he flipped me over, his mouth still pressed against my clit.

My body shuddered around him as Kalas continued lapping at my juices, my hips jerking as the orgasm crashed over me in delicious waves. He didn't stop until I was writhing beneath him, a second and then a third orgasm quickly following the first.

I cried out, an incoherent string of words and gasped to catch my breath, but Kalas only gave me a moment to recover before his lips moved from my lower regions and instead claimed my mouth. I could taste myself on him, but the thought was quickly lost as he plunged inside me and another orgasm started to build.

I floated on the air, my whole body vibrating as I rode the high of the carnal release, and magic reverberated between Kalas and me. My mind filled with visions of the sprawling cosmos, and the beautiful sights were soon accompanied by Kalas's soft, ethereal singing.

"*Invarali taleni, Stellavarien ethrionth, lunaviel solemna.*"

-The End-

# Acknowledgements

No book is ever easy to write, but this one was particularly difficult for me, as it came after an almost five-year writing hiatus while I dealt with some real-life issues, including being diagnosed with both autism and ADHD.

To say the last five years have been hard would be an understatement, but there have been many bright spots along the way, including completing this book.

Completing The Starlight Prince wouldn't have been possible without the following people;

Hubby, I hope you never get tired of hearing me ramble about my insane stories. Your unwavering love and support through all of life's challenges means the world to me. I love you.

Kiddos, you inspire me every day just by being the awesome people you are. Extra thanks to Youngest, who introduced me to the anime Jojo's Bizarre Adventure, without which, this book might never have been created.

On that note, special thanks to Hirohiko Araki for creating the manga Jojo's Bizarre Adventure, and thus the character Kars, who 'awakened' something in me. *Ayayayayayayayayayaya!*

The Write Here, Write Now Community, for being the most supportive, caring, encouraging group of people imaginable. Special thanks to Karen Sanders, for not only creating the group, but being an awesome editor, and putting up with all my insanity. Clare Bentley, for your unwavering encouragement and support, and our shared love of Aaron Taylor-Johnson. N.S. Armstrong, for your fantastic artistic talent bringing Maddie and Kalas to life.

Suzy Jackson of the Technicolour Project, for coming into my life at the moment I needed you most, and for helping me re-frame my brain so that I finally accepted I'm not lazy or broken, I just have ADHD.

Mom, for always believing in me, even when I was a little pain in the butt, and for leading me back to God's path, without whom I wouldn't be here today.

Finally, everyone in the wider writing community on social media and other places online for being an uplifting, encouraging community I'm very proud to be a part of. From the cover designers to the character artists. From the cheerleaders to the reviewers. Each and every one of you weave together to make a tapestry of stars that shine bright every day.

# Also by Clare Dugmore

The **Pact of Protection - The Moonlit Crossroads Saga Book One - Coming August 26, 2025.**

Fleeing her ruined home and apothecary, witch Evelyn Blackthorn finds unexpected refuge with the Leythorpe Pack—a fearsome gang of wolf-shifters led by the brooding and magnetic Lukas Voss. His emerald gaze and fierce devotion ignite a passion Evelyn never expected, even as she resists being drawn in—romance has no place in her fight for survival.

But Lukas has his own demons. His unstable shifting abilities threaten to tear him apart, even as he fights off the deadly supernatural hunters targeting his pack—and those within it who covet the alpha's throne.

As danger tightens its grip, Evelyn and Lukas must decide if their growing bond is strong enough to face the deadly Purity Enforcers—or if their love will be torn apart before it can truly begin. Passion, peril, and power collide in this sizzling paranormal romance.

**To be the first to know all the latest news about Clare Dugmore's forthcoming stories, please subscribe to their mailing list at:** https://claredugmore.com/free-book

# About Clare Dugmore

As a child, Clare believed faeries lived at the bottom of the garden, sparking a lifelong fascination with the strange and magical. That early wonder evolved into a passion for all things weird—whether it's faeries, vampires, witches, aliens, or any other non-human beings.

For Clare, storytelling has always been a form of escape. Now, as an author, they strive to offer readers that same thrilling getaway through stories packed with spice, adventure, and seductive supernatural characters.

Clare lives in the West Midlands, UK, with their spouse and two children. When not crafting new worlds or devouring books, you'll find them binge-watching series with their partner, gaming, or indulging in creative hobbies like crafting.

Beyond writing, Clare is driven by a desire to build a vibrant, supportive community of creatives—one that champions individuality, shared passions, and meaningful causes.

Thus, Clare's Kindred Book Club was born.[1]

---

1.      https://claredugmore.com/kindred-bookclub?hsLang=en

# Other Books You Might Enjoy

S on Of The First (Lord Of Shadows Book 1), by N.S Armstrong (Author) Format: Kindle Edition

Hell Hath No Fury Like a Man Finding Himself... in Hell

Alyx Archer never planned to go to Hell—he was more of a "fashion degree and fabulous dresses" kind of guy.

All Alyx wanted was to ace his classes and design outfits with his best friend, Brie. Instead, his life is upturned by a demon attack on campus, and by Brie effortlessly ripping said demon to shreds. Turns out, Brie isn't your average BFF, she's the Queen of the Hounds of Hell.

To top it all off, the woman who raised him isn't his real mum. His actual mother? The legendary Lilith. Cue identity crisis.

Now, instead of worrying about grades and fabric swatches, Alyx is getting dragged down to Hell (literally) by someone Lilith would rather smite than see on her doorstep.

**Learn More Here:** https://www.goodreads.com/book/show/221189318-son-of-the-first

**SHELTER ME FROM DARKNESS (Shelter Me Trilogy Book 1) by Katie L. Smith**

**To break her curse, she must face her past.**

Piper Hart never planned to return to her hometown, Stonehill. However, with a death curse slowly killing her, she's out of other options.

But Stonehill—a border town that crosses to the Otherworld—is not how she remembers it. A darkness is creeping across the area and werewolves are turning up dead.

In exchange for answers to break the curse threatening her life, Piper agrees to work for Stonehill's founder to solve the mystery of the dwindling wolf population. But there's one catch.

She has to work alongside the man who broke her heart and caused her to leave town in the first place—Dean Lewis, heir to the werewolf pack, vice president of the Iron Wolves MC, and most importantly, her fated mate.

Can Piper learn to trust her magic, solve the town's problems, and break her curse all while avoiding old feelings and the heat that still simmers between her and Dean?

**With her life and Stonehill's fate on the line, will Piper rise to the challenge or fall to the curse?**

**Learn    More    Here:**    https://www.goodreads.com/book/show/219183273-shelter-me-from-darkness

**A DAGGER IN THE IVY: A Spicy Fae Romantasy (Blade Bound Book 1) by Dorothy Dreyer**

**"A binge-worthy story with strong characters, slow burn romance, and incredible world building. Get ready to be swept away." Mary Ting, International bestselling, award-winning author**

In a world plagued by darkness and deceit, half-fae Celeste Westergaard is torn between her duty as the Commander of the Royal Regiment and her station as the next in line for the throne. On the rise are attacks from supernatural creatures, the carnivorous beasts sent by the Shadow Tsar to claim the lives of third-born fae throughout the realm of Terre Ferique. But as Celeste's homeland of Delasurvia faces turmoil and unrest, she is thrust into an arranged marriage to the Prince of Hedera, the Land of Ivy.

While the destiny of her kingdom rests on Celeste's shoulders, she must also face the threat of madness, a fate which could befall her if her fae powers do not manifest. And to make things worse, the prince's brooding half-brother carries a hatred for her she can't understand.

As Celeste unravels the mysteries hidden within Hedera, she must navigate a treacherous path to protect her kingdom and uncover the truth hidden within her own bloodline.

A Dagger in the Ivy is a gripping tale of intrigue, danger, deception, and unexpected alliances.

**Learn    More    Here:**    https://www.goodreads.com/book/show/ 214141188-a-dagger-in-the-ivy

# Thank You For Reading

Thank you for reading The Starlight Prince, I hope you enjoyed the story. If you did, please consider leaving a review on Goodreads, social media, and whichever retailer you brought this book from. Reviews help other potential readers find new stories they might love!

www.ingramcontent.com/pod-product-compliance
Lightning Source LLC
Chambersburg PA
CBHW072212170626
46813CB00003B/902